It is said that the loyal, became betrayer, as darkness in the form of greed and corruption consumed the soul. This dark Lord soon learned that the promises made to him were never to be honored, so he waited for the right time to seek his revenge. When the time came to be, the enslaved became the hunter, and the trophy he sought was the soul of his former master.

Sytaine,
Chief Priest to Queen
Mother Bonna Min

AuthorHouse™
1663 Liberty Drive
Bloomington, IN 47403
www.authorhouse.com
Phone: 1-800-839-8640

Published by AuthorHouse 3/14/2013

ISBN: 978-1-4817-2079-3 (sc)
ISBN: 978-1-4817-2080-9 (e)

Library of Congress Control Number: 2013903605

Any people depicted in stock imagery provided by Thinkstock are models,
and such images are being used for illustrative purposes only.
Certain stock imagery © Thinkstock.

This book is printed on acid-free paper.

Because of the dynamic nature of the Internet, any web addresses or
links contained in this book may have changed since publication and
may no longer be valid. The views expressed in this work are solely those
of the author and do not necessarily reflect the views of the publisher,
and the publisher hereby disclaims any responsibility for them.

Billy opens his eyes to find that he has awakened in a dark and dreary place.

"Am I dreaming?"

It's hard for him to see into the void that has enveloped him, but his hearing is working fine, and he doesn't like what he hears. All around him are the sounds of suffering, but he can't determine the origin or distance away out their in the inky blackness.

"Maybe I'm dead."

A touch of fear settles in over William Raymond McBride, as he wanders about.

"Suppose I didn't survive that explosion, and this is the entrance to hell?" He laughs to himself as a thought comes to mind. "The lighting sucks if this is the lobby."

Is it really possible that he is dead? Has everything he's done, earned him this supposedly miserable afterlife? These questions bring out a little anxiety and paranoia in Billy, causing him to sit up. For a man who cared less a few hours ago, about living and dying, he has suddenly developed a strong desire to find proof that he is still alive. There's no sense in giving up all hope just yet.

Then as if on cue, the blackness in front of him begins to move, as if someone or something is moving through the darkness towards him, from far off in the distance. Just as fast, the black void in front of him stirs, swirls, and then parts like the Red Sea to reveal Jezana's presence. "Warrior McBride," she addresses him, "You have risked your life how many times now to save the ones you love?" Jezana reaches out and runs her long fingernails across his cheek as she slowly starts to walk around him. Is she some sort of dark temptress working her ways of seduction, or some sort of predator sizing up her next kill? Since Billy must be dreaming, he decides to hold judgment until he knows where this is going. "How has that worked out so far?" She asks, in a condescending tone. "What if I told you that with one word from my lips those still alive would be spared the dark times soon to come?"

For whatever reason, Billy recognizes Jezana as the image he spotted in the cloudy bathroom mirror, days ago, even though he never got a clear image of anything or anyone in the first place. He doesn't know why, but he is sure that it was her. That alone is enough to trouble Billy to no end, and he states his refusal, very clear, and very loud, "NO!!!" He doesn't know why, but he's sure that it was the right thing to do.

Horrible images of everyone he loves, being tortured and tormented by terrible creatures of darkness, race through his mind chaotically, until it forces Billy to open his eyes. Unable to move, for whatever reason, he looks around to recognize his surroundings. "I'm home," he mumbles, barely able to breathe. Then, it's off again. You know what they say, "A body at rest heals the best."

North & South: Mysery Loves Company

Stacy Wright

authorHOUSE®

Chapter I

Ten hours ago, JD, Billy, and the others arrived at the ranch in Alabama, via Commander Ryker's shuttle. Isaiah told JD and Saphyre a little later that it looked like some kind of close encounter movie scene. Home, or as close to it as JD knows for now, he's glad to be away from New York and all of the insanity that was there. To most, their "mission" would seem like a success, with acceptable losses. Some would even be surprised that any of the hostages, Billy, Taylor, or JD, made it out alive. But to JD, his efforts ended in failure when Billy's mother, and the others, lost their lives. It's not like anyone holds JD accountable for anything. In fact, there is no reason for anyone to be pointing fingers at anybody at all. Still, he feels guilt over the outcome. With even one hostage lost, JD feels that he has dishonored his teacher, because Nick believed JD was capable of doing far more than that. Nick; somehow there are events that took place in New York that are connected to Nick's destiny. That is one thing that JD is sure of. If he is ever going to have a moment's peace again, JD will have to figure out what the connections are, and better yet, why they exist.

After helping Ryker's medical officer with the supplies up to Billy's room, JD said his good nights and began his

STACY WRIGHT

term of seclusion. It wasn't much really, the medical supplies, mostly monitoring equipment that Ryker's medic instructed Taylor on how to check Billy's status. JD was hoping to block out the thoughts of the night's experiences by keeping himself busy. He did take notice to the tension that seemed to exist between the medic and Kaitlyn, but dismissed it just as quick having his thoughts occupied by Nick's destiny. His battle with Shalimar, and the goons earlier at the loading docks, was all part of something much bigger than an old man wanting revenge against Billy. What bothers JD the most about it, is the only man that he could ask about this is nowhere to be found. For the first time, he finds himself cursing Nick for dragging him into this. He knows that it isn't Nick's fault, and if Nick was around, JD wouldn't be so quick to condemn his closest friend. But unfortunately, rash times tend to bring out rash behavior.

Destiny, how much of that can be real? Is there really some all knowing being that drew out the histories of everyone alive, at the beginning of time? It would be a good question to ask his father, but JD wonders if there is more to this than simple religion. How does he find these answers, when there is no one to ask?

After lying in his bed for an hour trying to figure this all out, JD finally fell asleep, brought on by the waning adrenaline flow in his system, coupled with his extreme fatigue. He has yet to suffer any sort of headache from using his force field the way he did, which is a welcome relief to him, because his mind has been way too active to deal with that sort of pain. Still this added advantage of clear thought has not helped him to decipher the clues associated with his new friends and his present life. Frustrated, JD finally fell asleep as the moon made its presence known from behind the clouds. To him, this was a glimmer of hope that life could also return to some measure of normality. His outlook about that is about to change.

"Jefferson David Johnston," a voice calls out; deep and booming, echoing through the thick blackness that surrounds JD. "Awaken, student of the Guardian. You must hear what I have to say."

JD opens his eyes with a start. He quickly recognizes the fact that the room is completely devoid of any light. Immediately, he returns to his previous train of thought, questioning the possibility of more intrusions of darkness. "Who's there? Show yourself to me immediately and declare your intent!" JD jumps to his feet and takes a strong defensive stance. Part of him doesn't want to wake the others, but right now, he would be more than happy to have a little assistance with this matter. Either way, he can't let this intruder proceed any further into the house.

Slowly, methodically, he begins to spin in a circle, straining his eyes to see into the pitch black around him. Where's the door? JD was sleeping on a bed. Where did it go? Okay, there is a logical explanation for this. Remember the room, JD. Walking in the room, there was a desk along the wall. Across the room, over by the window was a cushioned bench. To his right, was the queen size bed that took up half the room. The question now is where is his location in the room as opposed to the furniture he envisions? "Answer the question," he demands while continuing his defensive spin, "Who are you?"

My name was once Hyldegaarn," the voice states sounding as if it is coming from behind JD. Whipping around to face the intruder, JD sees only the same blackness in front of him as before. Judging by the sound of the voice, he expected to see a gargantuan creature standing there, and yet there is nothing to be seen. "I represent the Council, who you are familiar with through your alliance with the Guardian, and his Master, Masamoto. I have come to you delivering a warning."

Again, JD spins around trying to follow the sound of this Hyldegaarn's voice. "If what you say is true, then why haven't you shown yourself to declare your true intentions?"

"Alas, young warrior of light, it is not permitted at this time," the voice replies echoing all around JD. "Student of Landry, you are about to embark on a new journey that is fraught with even more peril than the last. You must embrace your destiny and stay the course. What is about to happen can not be prevented. But above all else, the unlikely ally must not fall. Awake, young warrior, and embrace your role for the end of times."

JD suddenly opens his eyes and sits up in his bed. He notices right away the moonlight cascading into his room from the window. His heart is racing, and his breathing is shallow and rapid. Anxiety over the brief encounter is racing through him, but he isn't quite sure why. For whatever reason, an image of a majestic bull's head is all that remains and it's just as much a mystery as the rest.

Running through the house screaming like a hysterical kid who had a bad dream seems like a little much, but JD feels the strong desire to do something, none the less. The clock on his nightstand shows the time being four forty five. After everything he's been through, after everything that has happened, all JD wanted was just a few hours of silent rest. After this disturbing image, or dream, or whatever it was, he knows that sleep is the last thing that will happen for him. Turning on his bedside light, he rifles through his bag and retrieves Nick's journal. Nick left it unfinished, so JD decides to write down what happened to him on this little expedition to New York. Certainly, the strange occurrences he witnessed there, and in Atlanta, warrant mention in his teacher's journal of strange happenings. The thing is that after a few minutes, JD is oblivious to what he is writing, but he continues to fill page after page right up to sunrise.

Chapter II

Taylor awakens to the smell of fresh coffee brewing in the kitchen. She rolls over and sees Billy lying there beside her, barely holding onto life. After condemning herself for falling asleep, she resumes her duties of last night. She has kept her vigil at his side, since Ryker and his team left, believing that it was her duty to do so. She kisses the scar on the back of his right hand and brushes his hair away from his face. "Good morning, Billy Ray." So much has happened to them all, but especially Taylor. The torture she endured is bound to leave some kind of emotional scars. But, at the moment, she is able to block all of that out by focusing on her man's condition and needs.

A rap at the door catches Taylor's attention. She looks up to see Saphyre standing there holding a steaming cup of fresh coffee. "Good morning, Taylor," Saphyre says softly. "Would you like a cup of coffee? My grandpa made it fresh just a little while ago."

"That sounds wonderful, Saphyre, thank you." Taylor motions for the young woman to walk around the bed, so they didn't risk dripping any of the hot beverage while reaching over Billy. Both have endured terrible acts against them with Taylor's being worst of the two. And yet, as the savvy veteran of "Billy antics", Taylor dismisses her pain long enough to admire Saphyre's ability to deal with the PTSD. "You have no idea how good this smells," Taylor declares, taking the hot cup from Saphyre.

"Do ya want any cream or sugar? I could run and get some for you."

Appreciating the gesture, Taylor waves Saphyre off, preferring her coffee just the way it is. "No, no, this is perfect. I've had Isaiah's coffee, and he knows how to get it exactly right, every time." She takes a sip of the coffee, burning her lip as usual, and then asks, "How are you doing Saphyre? You sorta got pulled into a big smelly cow patty, didn't ya?"

"Can I be honest with you, Taylor?" Saphyre sits down on the side of the bed before looking around, as if she was about to reveal a great secret. "Even as terrifying as that was, it was the most exciting event of my life. I still can't believe we made it out of there alive. And yet, I feel really bad about Billy's mother." Looking over at Billy, Saphyre asks Taylor, "How is he doing? After all that he and JD did to save us, it seems pretty shitty if he isn't able to pull through to see the result."

"That is an understatement, to say the least," Taylor agrees, having everything she's got riding on Billy pulling out of this. The only thing that kept her going was the sound of Sarah's voice telling her that Billy was coming for them. Taylor believed it, knowing that deep down inside, Billy loves her as much as she loves him. "But, you have to understand that deep down inside of Billy; he lives by a code that demands he give himself for the safety and welfare of others. It's one of the reasons that I love him so much."

"So, how are you doing, Taylor?" Saphyre lays her hand over the top of Taylor's, and adds, "I know you don't know me from squat, but I'm a good listener if you want to talk about it. I guess, I don't know, I thought that it might be easier for you since we were there together and all. It's kinda like, you know, we shared some common ground together."

She understands Saphyre's attempt to connect, but at the moment, Taylor doesn't want to discuss what happened with herself, much less anyone else. "Thanks Saphyre, but not right now. I guess stuff like that takes time before you start to open up about it." In all honesty, Taylor would prefer to forget all of the horrible madness that took place to her in New York. She doesn't want to talk about what happened. She doesn't want to recall any of it for the sake of conversation. All she wants now is for Billy to recover so that they can move on with their lives and put all of this behind them. Antonio Callistone is gone, dead, and can never hurt Billy again.

"I understand," Saphyre replies. "But, you'll let me know if there is anything I can do for you, right? You really should try to get some sleep though. You don't want your man to wake up to see you looking like the underside of a hog pen, do ya?"

Taylor laughs at the remark, knowing that her appearance must look pretty rough. "Sure, maybe I will try, and you'll be the first asked when I need someone to talk to, okay? Obviously, you don't pull your punches. I like that. Ya know, speaking of opening up and good will gestures, have you seen our latest member of the household?" Taylor leans back against the headboard and begins to nurse her coffee.

"No, not since we got up this morning. When I went by our bedroom while ago, the door was open but she had already bailed out of the house. I'm sure she is around here somewhere. I know it's sad to say, but where else does she have to go?"

The rains have stopped for the time being, giving Kaitlyn the first chance to get out of her room and out of the house. The first few hours at the ranch, she slept due to sheer exhaustion. After waking up to a horrible feeling of dread, she laid there in the bed crying, while watching the rain drops splatter against the panes of the bedroom window. Each crack of thunder, and flash of lightning, reminded her of how her father would comfort her during the storms of her childhood. It also served as a constant reminder that Jonathan was no longer with her, which perpetuated her crying. Bad weather really does bring on the blues.

As for now, she is wandering through the stables of the McBride ranch, trying to come to terms with what has happened. Never in her wildest dreams did she think that she would be missing her father the way she does right now. Everything and everyone, Jonathan, Toby, and even Henry and Amanda are gone, destroyed or killed, leaving Kaitlyn feeling all alone.

The horses welcome her though, nodding and snorting for her attention as she stumbles along. If she seems aimless, it's because Kaitlyn has no direction at the moment. How could she, after all that has happened? What is a seventeen year old girl suppose to do when her life has been erased. Jonathan taught her well on how to take care of herself. Although, he did wonder from time to time about how much was sinking into her thick head. She may have acted like she wasn't paying attention, or just didn't care, but she always took everything he said to heart. Kaitlyn just never thought she would have to be using the information so soon in her life.

Now she's stuck in a completely different world, with no one to turn to for guidance. Sure, there's Billy and the others, but honestly, they're all strangers. Well, she and Billy met like a lifetime ago, when she was little, but no one even knows if he is going to pull through or not. Not knowing which way to turn, Kaitlyn just continues on her meandering way, wandering the farm with no determined destination. Sooner or later, she will have to face the others and return to the house. At the moment, she decides that it should be later.

"I miss you, daddy." A ray of sunshine breaks through the gloomy skies to spotlight the ground around her. This brings a slight smile to her face as she looks up to the warmth of the sun, hoping that somehow it was Jonathan responding.

Everyone on the farm is doing their best, in their own way, to recover from the New York episode. JD is diligently searching for something to do, or at least something to occupy his mind. His current activity is hunting down the ranch manager who seems to be avoiding him, or at least that's what JD thinks. "There you are, Isaiah," JD declares, finding the old man sitting in a stall, eating a sandwich. "Have you got anything else for me to do?"

The old man wraps his sandwich back up and shoves it into the bib pocket of his overalls. "As a matter of fact, JD, I do." I want to replace that bottom rail of this here stall gate." After unclipping his tape measure from his pants, he hands it to JD and says, "Get me a measurement for length, will ya?"

Happily, JD takes the tape and stretches it out the length of the board. "I'm reading, five foot, eleven and a half inches." Then to be thorough, he measures the top rail to find it the same length. Turning to face Isaiah again, he reports, "Next time, you can save yourself the trouble of getting down on the ground, by just measuring the top rail. They're both the same length."

Isaiah shakes his head. "I know that."

"Then why didn't you say something before I squatted down to measure the board?"

Isaiah lowers his head a little and looks at JD over the tops of his glasses. "To prove my point that sometimes you have to do things, even if you think you know the answer." The old man stares at the confused expression on JD's face and then shakes his head. "Boy, why don't you just sit down right there and cool your heels a little. Before we get any deeper in the mud, I want you to tell me what is troubling you."

This catches JD completely off guard. "Wh-what makes you think something's bothering me?" He looks around welcoming the opportunity for Saphyre to come checking up on him again. "Right now, I think we're all pretty happy and grateful to be alive. Sure, we all faced certain doom, and some of us never made it back, but other than that, what makes you think that something is bothering me?"

"Well, for one thing, if I'm not mistaken, you suffered the least out of the group, and you seem to be taking it the hardest." Isaiah pauses to give JD a chance to disagree, but the young man doesn't bother. Obviously, JD is more readable than he thought. Continuing with his point, Isaiah states, "You don't have to open up to me, JD, but you do need to open up to somebody, before whatever it is eats you up inside."

The old man picks himself up off the straw strewn floor of the stall. He has said his piece for now, and gives JD a confident and reassuring smile. To his surprise, Isaiah is caught off guard by JD throwing out the question, "But what if what you have to say could destroy the friendship involved?"

Finally, a break through shows itself. "If the truth hurts, it's supposed to," Isaiah replies, "If this person is your friend, he will listen to what you have to say." Isaiah looks out through the stable doors to see Saphyre exiting the house. Watch out, Romeo, my granddaughter is on the prowl again."

Without knowing whether or not Isaiah was serious, JD suddenly becomes real nervous and makes a hasty exit saying, "I'm not ready to talk to her yet."

Chapter III

Back in New York, the air is cold and crisp as the sun shines down on the Manhattan skyline. In one such building, Margaret sits at her father's seat at the Cornerstone Corporation's boardroom table. Seventeen hours ago, her father was brutally murdered seventeen floors above them in the tower's penthouse, by a masked vigilante, or so it was reported in the New York Times. This morning was spent with the police, presenting everything she knew, just as it was rehearsed. Now she sits in his chair, as she has since her brother's unfortunate demise, only this time is different. Today represents the first day of her occupying the chair permanently, as detailed in her grand scheme. To do so, she must go through the proper channels making sure her lawyers do their job as her takeover begins, without anyone being the wiser, at least until it is too late to matter.

As the board members file in to take their seats, Margaret retrieves a stack of papers from her briefcase for Carlton to pass out around the table. This is the chore he can't wait to lose. After serving faithfully as Antonio's right hand man, his position as Margaret's lap dog is unnerving. The sex is good, but it doesn't make a fair balance for being treated like a second rate servant. Perhaps this is the punishment he must suffer, for his betrayal to Antonio.

With the Vice President finally entering to take her seat, Margaret clears her throat and takes on the professional personality that suits her. "Ladies and gentlemen, as you may already know, approximately seventeen hours ago, my father was taken from us in a gruesome, murderous act. I have called this meeting on such short notice, during this painful time, to address this matter with you." Margaret motions for Carlton to hand out the literature that she has prepared. "I plan to remain in this seat, until all legal matters can be resolved, and a new President can be named. I want to assure you that your financial investments in this company will remain intact, and the Cornerstone Corporation will continue to strive forward towards a prosperous future."

One man stands up to declare his distaste for the situation. A wiry tall man, in a suit that looks to be wearing him, the middle aged executive adjusts his wire framed glasses. Staring out the wall of glass of the conference room, he watches a news chopper fly by before stating, "I'm sorry, Ms. Stanford, but I'm having a hard time understanding all of this. If you would, I'd appreciate a more clear explanation about how this all came about in the first place. I mean, I'm no authority on the Callistone family affairs, but from what I understand, you and your father were estranged until just a short time ago. The fact that you deny the family name would suggest that you and Antonio were not close. I still don't understand how a man would name his daughter as his successor, when he doesn't even know if she is capable of doing the job."

Margaret stares at the executive for a few moments, while she contemplates how a Callistone would handle this man. Instead, she simply replies, "No, Mr. Jenkins, you are not an authority on the Callistone family, but none the less, you are right. My father and I were estranged, until the death of my brother gave him reason to reach out to me. None the less, he didn't despise me, or I him," she lies through her teeth. "All fences can be mended with time, Mr. Jenkins. As for me taking my mother's maiden name, I wanted to achieve my merits on my own, instead of my father's influence. I would say that I have done well with that, wouldn't you agree? After all, my yearly net worth is more than this board's combined annual salaries. I'm sure I've done alright with Stanford."

The distinguished woman sitting at the other end of the board room table motions for Jenkins to take his seat. The time has come for her to make her play in this poker game. "With that said, Ms. Stanford, I feel that I must ask, are you planning some kind of merger, or takeover? We, representing the Cornerstone Corporation, deserve to know."

Margaret smiles before the lies begin to slide between her teeth. "Madam Vice President Bonwell, I assure you that I have no plans like that whatsoever. Once the new President and CEO are elected, I will hand over the authority given to me as Proxy, and remain on this board as a silent partner to facilitate the progression of what my father started with this company."

Jenkins slides his narrow framed glasses to the end of his pointed nose and remarks, "I heard that Caesar said the same thing about Rome once."

A sneer crosses Margaret's face for Jenkins' remark. At the moment, she is teetering back and forth between reality and the illusion of her grand scheme. Unfortunately, Jenkins' remark pushes her a little too far one way. "Mr. Jenkins', I will soon be the most powerful woman in the world! What would I want with anything you might have?" Immediately, she realizes that she crossed the boundaries by overstating her position. She looks around at the faces of the board members to see that most were confused by her statement, but show some measure of compassion and condolence for her apparent emotional state. Still, she is pressed to correct herself in front of the Board, if for nothing else but to save face. "I apologize for that outburst, Mr. Jenkins. Obviously, all of this is weighing heavily on me right now, with the continuing losses of my family." Playing the role, Margaret pretends to wipe away a tear from her cheek, and then motions to her lap dog. "Carlton will handle the legal specifics. I believe you will find everything in order." Margaret gathers her dark sunglasses and returns them to her face. "We can proceed with this matter next week when I return."

"Next week," Gloria Bonwell, Vice President and once Antonio's right hand person when it came to the Corporation's business dealings, sits up straight to state her distaste for the change of plans. "Next week will not do, Ms. Stanford. We have contracts and schedules to keep, with the success or failure riding on your shoulders now. I am afraid that the Cornerstone Corporation cannot be paused while you go off to lead your life."

"And it won't have to, Gloria," Margaret motions for her lap dog to walk over to her, and then hands Carlton the necessary forms so that he could deliver them to Gloria. "We all know what the by-laws state about bereavement. That's how I was voted in by this Board, to serve as my father's voice while mourning the loss of my brother. According to those same by-laws, those standards apply now to me as well. However, it is written that should I not choose representation; the duties of said officer can be taken over by the next officer in line. That would be you, wouldn't it, Gloria." Margaret gathers the rest of her papers and shuffles them back into her briefcase, while Gloria looks over the writ. "Besides, you're a smart cookie, Gloria. That's why my father offered you the job when he bought out that bar you were running thirty years ago. I'm sure dear old daddy would approve of you sitting in his chair for a week." With a wave of her hand, Margaret signals to Carlton that it was time to leave, and then exits the Boardroom, leaving the occupants confused about the whole ordeal.

"Where are we going next, Margaret?" Carlton hurries to catch up to Margaret. His tone expresses his dislike for the treatment he received in front of the executives. As Antonio's executive assistant, even the board members gave him more respect than Margaret did, ordering him around like some kind of slave servant.

Margaret asks as she pushes the call button for the elevator, "Have our people in New Orleans made contact yet?" Her question comes across as if she dismisses his.

When the doors open, Carlton pushes Margaret inside, welcoming the opportunity to confront her about this part of her plan. Shoving her up against the back wall of the elevator, Carlton looks into her eyes as if trying to figure out her scheming mind. "It's time to come clean, Margaret, and for you to explain the rest of this madness that you are pursuing, because none of this is making any sense to me, whatsoever."

Surprising him, Margaret leans in close to him and kisses Carlton hard on his lips. "You know I love it when you get forceful, don't you?"

Carlton pulls away from her to turn around and face the elevator doors. "Don't play games with me, Margaret. I want to know why we are going through with this. It is so unnecessary, and you know it as well as I do! You've got what you need to put this guy away from us for the rest of his life, no matter how long that is. Why do you need to go to this extreme?"

"Because, Carlton, this person possesses something I need. Surely you can see how in this day and age, you need more than just a hired gunman to get the job done. McBride will take out our friend in New Orleans, and I will get what I want. Once McBride has served his purpose, we can hand over the information to the police to get him off our backs."

"And what if by chance, your friend in New Orleans happens to accomplish his job?"

"By then, what I want will already be in my possession, and nothing else will matter." The doors open giving Margaret reason to turn and face Carlton. "All I need from you, lover, is to facilitate the meeting and the arrangements. I don't need or want your approval." She exits the elevator giving her the quick exit out of the conversation. In all honesty, she's not sure if she has an answer to Carlton's question any way. The euphoric feeling of the power promised to her is reason enough, blinding her to the realities of what she's doing. Carlton will keep, as long as she feeds him enough to satisfy his curiosity.

Chapter IV

Taylor sleeps on Billy's bed beside him, maintaining her vigil at his side, as she has for most of the day. According to Saphyre, earlier, JD has found every little chore he could do to avoid everyone, especially Taylor. Of course, Taylor found this to be odd, but he did check in on her a few hours ago, but she didn't think anything about it until Saphyre brought it up. She knows that they all mean well and are worried about Billy, as much as their personal futures. Still, the questions are the same every time, no matter who is doing the asking. "How's Billy doing? Is Taylor okay? Do they need anything? Taylor went through a lot during her torturous episodes in captivity, capable of leaving a lifetime of psychological scars, but all she needs for now, is the man lying in bed beside her. Well, to have him wake up and take her in his arms forever would be nice too.

Her quest to find Billy started with that team of newcomers who showed up just as Taylor was beginning her chase after Billy. At that specific moment in time, she had no idea who they were, or what they wanted. Not to mention, why they had arrived in New York at that very spot, at that specific moment. The fact that the leader of the team seemed surprised to see Taylor, gave her an opening to break up his team and escape without conflict. How was she supposed to know that they were there to help apprehend Crossfire and his men?

The way her rampage through New York ended was another thing, when she leaped into the Cornerstone Building from the rooftop next door. From point A to point B, there was nothing safe about her pursuit, or the way she caught up to Billy, sending pedestrians and cars swerving to avoid her rampaging pursuit. Needless to say, when she entered the building through its glass exterior caused quite a stir with the cleaning crews, who were working the late shift to take care of the vacated offices. What can she say? Extreme times require extreme measures. Within minutes, alarms were sounding with security guards, and the janitorial staff, running into each other.

Somehow, amidst all of the chaos, Taylor got herself turned around while searching for the stairs, and trying to dodge security. Winding up on the gymnasium floor was not what she wanted. She could see the glass roof of the lower tower from the ground and knew that Billy was heading for the rooftop penthouse of the building's taller tower. No matter where she wanted to go, the security team finally had her pinned down, with the DSC agents closing in. That is, until the explosion goes off in the penthouse above. Taylor just stood there as the guards ran right by her, abandoning their chase of her, to see to the catastrophic event that required their attention, more than she did.

Standing beside the pool, she watched as the flames lashed out at Billy, sending him over the railing above her. Steadfast with fear, there was nothing she could do as his body fell towards the glass roof. Even when he released his energy, she withstood the abusive rain of glass to continue to watch his descent. Later on, Commander Ryker pointed out that it was a good thing Billy played that card when he did, because the pitch of the glass would have sent him off the building to the street below.

Even when he broke the surface of the water, she continued to stare up at the penthouse as debris followed Billy to the pool. Diving into the water, Taylor grabbed him and pulled Billy over to the pool steps just in time, before a section of the balcony from above hits the water. Once free from the water's embrace, Billy gasped for air which gave her some measure of relief. For the moment he was still alive, but she still had one problem. Somehow, she had to find a way to get him out of the building.

While everyone ran to the front of the building to be pulled to safety by the emergency crews, Taylor took Billy out the back, using blankets from the pool cabana to hide their identities. The streets were quickly filling up with emergency vehicles, only adding to her dilemma. When all seemed hopeless, Commander Ryker and his team moved in to assist Taylor's needs. Fortunately, Ryker's medical officer was able to have better luck with Billy, than she did with Sarah.

Since that terrible night, plans to lay Billy's mother to rest beside her husband, Walter, have already been made and carried out. Taylor insisted that she be the one to tell him about his mother's passing, if he ever wakes up. While she was at it, she would also explain Commander Ryker's contribution to their escape. The problem with her plan is that Billy hasn't moved a muscle, since their return from New York. Everything possible has been done to aid him with his recovery. Now, the rest is up to him. How long that will take is any man's guess. But when she feels his fingers tighten around hers, Taylor receives her first glimpse of hope that he is going to pull through. This allows her to finally fall asleep to get some much needed rest.

Immediately, she slips into a dark, ominous setting of a terrible nightmare. The rest of her friends and loved ones are lined up beside her, as they stare into the black hole forming in the cloud filled skies. A being steps forth from the blackness, and Taylor knows that the end is near. Dressed in black armor trimmed with gold, this being looks at them with his red eyes, and points his finger at each one, as if condemning their existence. Taylor is horrified to witness her friends being reduced to ashes right in front of her. When the being reaches Billy standing beside her, Taylor reaches for her lover, only to watch him turn to dust and blow away in the wind. All she can do is scream, which breaks her from the nightmare.

She awakes immediately, and searches him over for any more signs of movement. She had a reason to be optimistic, even though he remains still, but the nightmare she just had kinda put a damper on her optimism. Surely, a dreadful dream like that must have some sort of meaning. Figuring out what that meaning is isn't as important as the fact that Billy moved his fingers. A tear rolls down her cheek as she watches his chest heave and relax with each breath of life giving air. She can see that he is getting stronger. If he really is a miracle man like Ryker said, Billy will continue to improve, and will be back with them real soon. Until then, she plans on staying right where she is, at Billy's side.

"Isaiah," JD pops up behind the elderly ranch manager, startling him, and causing him to spill some of the chicken feed he was carrying to the hen house. "Would you like me to finish that up for you?" Then it dawns on JD what Isaiah had in the small pail, and where he was going. "By the way, I've been meaning to ask you. Why do you have chickens on a horse ranch?"

Isaiah looks at JD for a second and then states, "Boy, if I didn't know any better, I'd say that you were doing everything you can to fill your time with something, with the sole purpose of avoiding what you need to do."

JD suddenly stiffens, and then looks around wondering if his efforts were that transparent. "Uh, no, I uh, I just want to do my part to earn my keep around here, that's all."

Isaiah nods in a patronizing manner. "If that's the case, then you need to take a break for a while, because you earned your keep the first three hours this morning." Isaiah heads for the henhouse sensing that JD was right on his heels. "To answer your question about the chickens; the first two started out as an Easter present for Billy's grandmother, Clarice, from his grandfather. She became so infatuated with the little chicks that raising them became a hobby of hers. Cyrus, Billy's grandfather, had me build this henhouse for her chickens nearly forty years ago. In fact, Billy and Saphyre's daddies were there to help me, way back when. Keep in mind that both of them were barely in grade school, and weren't much help for me at all, come to think about it."

As he walks into the chicken coop, Isaiah begins to fill the feed dishes stationed along the center of the floor, as he finishes his story. "Any how, Miss Clarice seemed to have a green thumb so to speak when it came to these chickens, and before you knew it, we were selling chickens and eggs to everyone around. When Miss Clarice passed on, Mr. Cyrus kept the chickens in memory of her. I guess I do the same now for both of them."

JD watches in awe as the chickens come running to greet the old man. However, he isn't made to feel as welcome, by the way they keep attacking his ankles with fierce aggression. He tolerates the pecking as long as he can, but the first chance he has that Isaiah wasn't looking, JD deploys his force field to shoe the birds away. Turning around to see the chickens scurrying away, Isaiah asks with a suspicious expression, "Why are you here, JD?"

"To offer my assistance to you," he replies. "I thought I made that clear while ago."

"No son, why are you here at the ranch?"

The young man stares at Isaiah for a few seconds and then simply shrugs his shoulders. "To be honest, I'm not sure if I know the answer to that. I mean, I think I know, but I'm having a hard time understanding it, much less believing it."

"The old man laughs and replies, "Well one thing is for certain; if you don't believe it, nobody else will. What you should be asking yourself is, what do you believe, Jefferson? Once you determine that, based on you and no one else, then run with it and stick to it no matter what. If you believe it to be true, then spread the word and others will follow your beliefs."

"I think I understand what you're trying to say, but it still sounds easier to say, than it is to do," JD mumbles as he makes a quiet exit from the extravagant chicken coop.

"I don't think you give yourself enough credit," Isaiah counters, stopping JD at the door. "I remember a young man who took off to New York to rescue a bunch of people he didn't even know. It'll happen when the time is right, but frettin' over it ain't gonna make it any easier."

Instead of trying to argue the point, JD simply concedes with his exit and walks off towards the pasture. Isaiah stops what he is doing and walks over to watch JD make his way down to the pond. He can't help but wonder what is really on the young man's mind. Seeing his granddaughter walking into the barn, Isaiah can only assume that she was looking for JD again. With the bad weather starting to clear out, he hopes that the sunshine will help to brighten everyone's mood. All of these kids have been through a lot, with each one of them taking their own time to come to terms with what happened.

Heading for the barn, he watches the clouds race across the sky as they begin to break up. The warmth of the sun feels good to him, but the chill riding in the shade of the moving clouds quickens his step as each one passes over. Once inside the barn, Isaiah sees Saphyre entering one of the horse stalls a few feet away. "Child, are you alright?" He asks, propping himself up against the barn door, as he watches Saphyre tend to the newborn foal. "Have you talked to your grandma yet?"

"Yes, Grandpa, I'm alright and yes, I called her a couple of hours ago. She asked me how my trip to New York was. I had to tell her that we just got in and that I would fill her in later after I got some sleep." Saphyre sets the empty nursing bottle down and watches the beautiful creature walk away on its wobbly, spindly, legs. She then turns around and looks at Isaiah for a second, before throwing herself into his arms. "I was so scared, Grandpa. I kept remembering the stories that dad told me about how the hostages rarely escaped with their lives. But the last thing you said to me was that Billy would come for me, and bring me home." Pulling away from Isaiah, she looks up into her grandfather's loving eyes as a single tear of joy rolls down her cheek. "You were right, Grandpa. I believed you, and you were right."

Isaiah pulls her close and hugs her long and tight. "You're gonna be alright, child. You're gonna be alright."

Stepping back again, Saphyre dries her eyes and gives Isaiah a big smile. "Listen, I was wanting to go check in on my new friends, but I don't want to be a pain to Taylor. So, I was thinking that if you went with me, she wouldn't mind so much."

The batting of her big soulful puppy dog eyes won't work on him this time. "No, you go ahead and give her my best while you're at it." For whatever reason, Isaiah doesn't want to see how bad Billy really is. There's a feeling that's come over him lately, and Isaiah believes in his heart that Billy will survive this. Perhaps he believes that by staying away and not seeing the truth, Isaiah can have faith in his ignorance that Billy will pull through. The young man has to, for all of these kids. Isaiah steps up and gives Saphyre a kiss to her forehead, before turning away to see to his chores. "Ya know, there's another young lady that is wandering around here that could use a friend right about now. I expect you to reach out to her, ya hear?"

"After all she's been through, how do I do that?" It's not that Saphyre abhors the idea of trying. It's that she honestly doesn't know where to start.

He stops at the barn door and turns to give her a mischievous smile. "Find a common ground. You need to know about New York so you have something to tell your grandmother. I'd say the girl is your best bet for big apple information." Isaiah starts to mention the fact that Saphyre knows what it's like to lose her father, as well, but decides to keep that one to himself.

"What about JD?"

Isaiah quickly drops his smile and replies with a sarcastic tone, "He's not from New York."

"No, I mean, have you seen him since this morning?"

"That boy is too old for you, Saphyre."

Immediately, her hands hit her hips, and then she takes a firm stand against her grandfather, stomping her feet. "He's only a few months older than me, Grandpa!"

Isaiah can't help but laugh at her antics and replies, "I think he was headed down to the pond." Then he takes a more serious tone, "Be careful Saphyre. That boy is mixed up with some crazy stuff right now and he needs time to sort it out." With his warning given, Isaiah exits the barn to resume his duties and finish off the day.

Chapter V

own by the pond, JD has resorted to the only means he knows to work out his problems. Involved in an extreme martial arts workout regiment, JD is going through each exercise that Nick taught him. It is a customized combination of moves that JD has choreographed together, taken from all forms of martial arts. Each move, gesture, and attack, has been memorized, by this student of the Guardian. Each exercise flows into the next creating a loop of sorts. In its entirety, the loop consists of the sum of JD's knowledge of the arts. His execution is flawless stating that Nick has taught JD well. With it memorized and practiced daily, most of the time, JD can put his body on auto pilot; and let his mind work through his problems.

At the moment, his biggest problem is trying to figure out how to tell Billy the truth. Coupled to that is the anxiety of trying to convince his friend that it's all real, and that JD hasn't lost his mind. Spinning around, he suddenly stops his exercise with his outstretched hand halted at Saphyre's raised arm. "Oh damn, I am so sorry." He straightens his shirt while trying to hide his embarrassment for the near wounding experience.

"No worries, sugar, I had ya blocked." She smiles at him like a bashful little girl and asks the obvious, "What are you doing?"

Realizing that this was his opening, JD puts his worries aside for the moment to focus on the young woman in front of him. Rule number one; impress the lady. "Well, to be honest, while I was living in Miami, I had the opportunity to study Martial Arts under one of the greatest instructors alive. Not to boast or anything, but I was the only student under his tutelage to learn his highest forms.

"Really, do ya wanna spar a little?" Saphyre sees this as her opening to get to know JD better as well, and what better way to do it than on his level? Before JD has a chance to object, she pulls off her coat and raises her fists.

He's impressed by her offer, but his inflated ego causes him to laugh, stating, "Darling, what I know is way beyond any kind of self defense class at some community college. My knowledge and expertise is on a much higher level.

Then, before he realizes what is happening, Saphyre drops down and sweeps his legs out from under him, and then rolls over to sit on JD's chest. Smiling at her accomplishment, she replies, "Don't worry about hurtin' me, tough guy. My daddy was an Army ranger, who wanted to make sure that nobody ever messed with his little girl," she pauses, and then adds with a devious grin, "Unless I let you." She gives him a wink and hops up to take a defensive stance while waiting for JD to do the same.

Whether or not he would admit it, JD is open to the idea of spending a little one on one time with her. Not to mention the fact that he needs to redeem himself for falling prey to her little sneak attack. Granted, it's not a nice quiet dinner for two, or an uneventful walk along the river, but with this is the challenge. Not for Saphyre, but for JD. He has to find a way to impress her with his skills without inflicting any harm. This is where he comes up with a great idea. "I'll tell ya what. Why don't I let you set the pace, and then we'll take it from there."

"Fair enough," Saphyre replies, and then offers two quick jabs and a kick to get JD on his toes. Then, to warm up a little, she steps back a couple of feet and begins her own regiment of Tae Kwon Do exercises to warm up.

In his defensive stance, JD watches each move that she makes, and becomes caught up in the poetry of her body in motion. He watches as her hips and shoulders raise and drop with each turn and thrust. He marvels at how her long legs and arms cut through the air around her as she leaps and spins towards him. Helpless, he can only watch as she wraps her legs around him to pull him to the ground for another takedown. Embarrassed by his lack of concentration, he jumps up to his feet laughing, mostly at himself, and then points to Saphyre signaling that round one belonged to her.

"No, that's two." She knows that he is playing right into her trap. "Come on, tough guy, you're not going to let a girl whip ya like that, now are ya?" The smile crossing his face tells Saphyre that her trap is now set and she is just waiting for the perfect moment to spring it on him.

Her challenge tells JD what he wanted to know as well. Saphyre's overconfidence is about to become her downfall. Charging at her, they begin a regiment of offensive attacks, with JD setting the pace. He never offers more than she can handle, but he frustrates her even more by denying her victory time and again. Each time he backs away, he chuckles, or giggles, almost mocking her abilities. The time had come for her to bring him down a notch or two. Taking the offensive, she moves in again, only to stop and pucker her lips up seductively to blow him a kiss.

This was obviously a first for JD. Never have any of his opponents ever blown him kisses, much less look as sexy as Saphyre did blowing said kiss. Dumbfounded, he is left open to her attack again. Moving on in, throwing everything she has at him, she succeeds in sending him completely off balance and finally stumbling to the ground. With a tree branch serving as her ally, JD trips over the fallen branch and finds himself heading back to the ground again, as Saphyre lands right on his chest again, to score the third and final takedown and finish their session. "You cheated," he declares, slightly enjoying being her captive audience.

Looking down and breathing heavy from their workout, Saphyre smiles and replies, "you were holding back." Stepping her play up a notch, she leans in real close as if she was going to kiss him, but says, "Never hold back, okay?" Then, to trip him up a little, she rolls over to lie down on the ground beside him. "So, tell me something, Jefferson David Johnston, how long have you known Billy and Taylor? Are the three of you like the modern day Mod Squad, or something?"

JD laughs at her comparison and replies, "No, we're just three people who are mixed up in something we don't understand." Careful, JD, you don't want to get too close to that topic with her. "As far as any alliance or something like that, I would say that we are more friends than anything else." Rolling over on his side, JD smiles at her and says, "To tell ya a funny story, though, when we were heading up to New York to get you, he told me about how Taylor fronted up a cop and declared to him that they were the Confederate Soldiers, and that Billy was their leader. But from what I have put together, Billy was ready to give up his vigilante ways, until you got involved," he adds to toy with her a little.

"So, what's your story, tall, dark, and handsome?" Staring up at the tree limbs above them, she wonders if she is pushing too much. It's not her fault, really. Saphyre has never felt this way about someone, so she doesn't have any kind of reference point to work from. "This teacher that you studied under, he was pretty special to you, right? I mean, I can hear it in your voice, the way you talk so proudly about him. It's almost like it's an honor for you to know him." Rolling her head to the side to look at JD, who was already looking at her, she adds, "There's something there, kinda' like you know something secretive about the guy." Propping herself up on her elbow, JD can see a slight gleam in Saphyre's eyes, as if she is truly intrigued by who Nick is. "You know what I mean, right? Like he's someone so special that he outranks the Pope, or something."

JD rolls his head to look up at the naked branches of the large oaks swaying above them wondering how he should answer this. There is obviously a connection being attempted, and the last thing he needs is to be worried about scaring someone else off with what he knows. "Let's just say that Nick saved my life, and not to throw you off, but probably saved the world at the same time. So, yeah, I'd say that he is someone that is pretty special, at least to me."

"Wow," She replies, not expecting an answer like that. Lying back down she assumes the same position that JD is in, to watch the white clouds blowing over them. "I don't suppose you'd want to share that tale one night over hot chocolate and a campfire, would you?"

I don't see why not, but let's wait until everything settles back down around here." He looks over to see her smiling because of his answer, feeling the same way about the response she is giving to him.

While lying on her back, Saphyre rolls her weight up onto her shoulders, and then kicks her feet out to propel her into a standing position. This is all to impress JD, which it does rightfully so. "Come on and go with me to see Billy and Taylor."

He wants to oblige, but the mere mention of Billy returns his concerns to the forefront of his thoughts. The one thing he hasn't accomplished yet is figuring out how to approach Billy about what he's seen, and knows. "Ya know what? Why don't you go ahead and I'll meet you up there in a little bit. I can't let your grandfather find this mess down here," he explains, pointing to the fence post targets and makeshift sparring dummies he had set up for his workout.

"Okay," she replies, letting her disappointment be heard. "I guess I'll see you up at the house later on then." She gives him a smile to let him know that there are no hard feelings, and that his rejection hasn't lessened his chances with her. With her coat in hand, she takes off up the hill towards the pasture, feeling confident that she has made her infatuation known about JD, without being too forward.

All JD can do is watch as she walks away, and marvels at her grace and fluid motion as she reaches the top of the hill. "Be careful JD," he warns himself, "that is a good distraction that you can't have right now."

Now all she has to do is watch for JD to make his move. Not the type to just sit around and wait, she sees another distraction that could occupy some of her time while she is waiting on JD. Deciding to take her grandfather's suggestion to heart, Saphyre calls out, "Hey Kaitlyn, wait up." She takes off running across the pasture, to try and catch up with the displaced teen. "Wow, you've really been on the move most of the day, haven't you?"

With her hands shoved deep into her coat pockets, Kaitlyn doesn't offer a response as she makes her way around the side of the house. Her coat, yeah right. Kaitlyn no longer owns a coat, any more. She's lucky that Saphyre had this extra hoodie, or Kaitlyn would be walking around freezing to death. Then, as they reach the front yard, she turns to face Saphyre and asks, "Here's a roll of mints you left in the pocket. Out of nowhere, Kaitlyn blurts out a comment to start a conversation. "Have you ever woke up in the morning and feel like you haven't got a clue about how to start the day, or where to start at? Well, that feeling has been with me all day, and I don't see any relief in sight."

Always the one to seize the day, Saphyre replies, "Girl, what you need is purpose." It's not like Saphyre is trying to sidestep Kaitlyn's grief. To be honest, she is really just following her grandfather's suggestion. "For instance, have you ever told your parents that you were going one place, only to sneak away to go somewhere else? Then, after the fact, you have to come up with a good alibi about where you were supposed to be, right?"

"Sure," Kaitlyn responds, showing a small spark of life. Sometimes, common ground is all that it takes to bring two people together. This was Saphyre's rule of thought, and it seems to be working. "I had to do that to keep my dad off my back all the time." Oops, now she is recalling one of those things that she wished she could take back, if she could. This doesn't mean that Saphyre's inquiry didn't wake up the mischievous teen inside Kaitlyn though. "But, if you don't mind me asking, what does that have to do with giving me purpose?"

Saphyre walks up onto the front porch and motions for Kaitlyn to take a seat on the swing with her. "Well, ya see, my grandfather played the game with my grandmother, when I was taken away to New York. He knew that he couldn't tell her the truth, because of Billy's activities, so he told her that I went with Billy and Taylor to go sight seeing. Needless to say, I didn't see much while I was there, so I was wondering, would you could give me some specifics to help keep my grandfather out of the doghouse?"

This is something that is right up Kaitlyn's alley, and in all honesty would happily take her mind off her feelings of despair. Letting a smile cross her face, Kaitlyn replies, "Saphyre, you truly have come to the right person." Finally, she found a way to take Kaitlyn's mind off her new lifestyle. Feeling like her old self, a little, she points out, "I'll have you an alibi that is guaranteed to pass any bullshit detectors. Now, how many days were you supposed to be gone?"

"I'm not sure, but grandma is one for the specifics. You know, like where, and what, I would see. Oh, and give me some out of the ordinary shit that you wouldn't see as a common tourist. I'd say we should figure on three days worth of seeing the sights. The rest of the time can be scratched off for shopping or just plain down time."

Saphyre is sure that this has to be the perfect thing to take Kaitlyn's mind off her troubles, and is happy that Kaitlyn is willing to oblige. With a toss of her blonde locks, Kaitlyn dives right in. "That's good, real good. But first, let's go get something to drink before I die of thirst." For the first time in a long time, Kaitlyn feels connected to someone, and it's a good thing.

Saphyre jumps up from the swing to lead the way. "Sure, we can raid the fridge. I know that there is milk, sweet tea, and soda in there all the time." She too feels the connection being made between her and Kaitlyn. If nothing else, it will be good for her to have a friend her own age around the ranch. Soon, they will learn how much common ground they actually share.

Inside the front door, Kaitlyn stops for a second to look around the interior of the house. This is a place out of a painting set around Christmas time, with the big fireplaces and antique furnishings. "Let's move, soldier, so we can go report to the commanding officer," Saphyre orders, as if she was some kind of drill Sergeant.

Dumbfounded by Saphyre's statement, Kaitlyn asks, "What are you talking about?"

"Oh nothing, I'm actually just being stupid." Looking up to the second floor balcony, she sees the open doors to Billy's room and doesn't want their conversation to be overheard. "Come on, and I'll explain in the kitchen." Taking Kaitlyn's hand, Saphyre forces a speedy trek through the house so that she could tell her new friend a secret. "See, there was this incident where Taylor told a police detective that she and Billy were the Confederate Soldiers. I haven't told anybody else this, but I think it would be so cool if we were like some kind of superhero team, and this killer ranch is our base of operations!" She walks over to the cabinet to gather a glass for Kaitlyn's drink. When she turns around, Saphyre sees her new friend committing the ultimate sin. "Oh damn, I really do wish you hadn't done that."

Kaitlyn finishes off the two liter bottle of Mountain Dew and gives Saphyre a puzzled look before asking, "What?"

Chapter VI

"Hey you," Taylor says softly while brushing his hair away from his face. "Are you still with the land of the living?"

Billy opens his eyes a little more, to see the red headed beauty of his dreams sitting beside him. He's alive, but Billy isn't quite sure how he pulled that one off. The last thing he remembers is New York, with the explosions going off behind him in the penthouse. Regardless of how he survived, or how he got home, the last thing Billy expected to see was her sitting beside him. After all he put her through, and everything that happened to her in New York, he truly expected her to be as far away from him as possible. And that's if she and the others made it out alive. "How are you?"

"How am I?" She's held back the tears for almost three hours now, a personal record for her, over the past two days. "You're the one who's been dancing at death's door." That's long enough. With tears of joy streaming down her cheeks, Taylor looks to the doorway and sees Saphyre and Kaitlyn standing at the door. Taylor jumps up from the bed and says, "Girls, go find JD and tell him that Billy is awake!" Embarrassed by her excitement, Taylor sits back down and stares into Billy's blue eyes, "I thought I lost you."

That's funny. Billy has been thinking the same thing about her for the past two weeks. He looks into Taylor's eyes wanting to tell her everything, but all that comes out is, "I'm sorry." It isn't much, but it's the best he can get out at the moment. He tries to shift his position to see her better, but the pain of it all is too much to bear. Of course, when the girls return with JD, Billy tries again to see them, only to have the same result as before.

For the moment, JD lets his worries rest. There is so much that needs to be said, but that can wait until Billy is stronger. "Hey, brother man, how are ya doin'?" He looks at Taylor's tears of joy and feels the need to crack a joke at Billy's expense. "Dang bro, you've only been awake for a second or two, and you've already got all three girls crying for you?" He points at Saphyre and Kaitlyn who are moved by Taylor's emotional outburst brought on by her love for Billy. The girls, standing on either side of him, turn and punch him on his shoulders for the remark, but he gets a smile from Taylor and Billy all the same. "Seriously, how are you doing, Billy? You had us all pretty worried about you for a while there," he adds, putting his arms around the girls' shoulders.

"Only for a while, huh?"

"Yeah, bro, we got bored and decided to play Yahtzee instead." Again the girls punch JD for his remark.

He knows that no one expects anything from him at the moment, but Billy is overwhelmed by the need to start making amends, "JD, thanks for everything you did for me. I knew I could count on you." Billy looks back at Taylor and asks with a sorrowful expression, "My mom didn't make it, did she?" Taylor just bows her head, saddened by the answer she must give. After a moment of silence, she answers by shaking her head no. Billy closes his eyes trying to hide the pain of what he already knew to be true. Does anyone know why Scotty's friend Clovis was mixed up in all of this?"

Saphyre immediately pulls away from JD and kneels beside Billy's bed, being that she is the only one with the answer. "After it was all over, I heard him telling Commander Ryker that some men showed up at the Auburn campus, looking for your friend."

"Brother, he is my foster brother," Billy corrects, with the emphasis on brother.

"Yeah, well, thinking that he was protecting his friend, your BROTHER, Clovis said that he was Scotty and punched two of them in the nose, before they could get him in the car."

"He was good at that," JD adds, caressing his wounded nose.

Billy eases himself back down, and then rolls his head over to face his friends again. "Okay, who is gonna fill me in on what happened after the building blew up, and who is gonna bring me my bottle of Mountain Dew?"

Saphyre turns and looks at Kaitlyn, knowing that she was the one who finished off the last bottle in the fridge. Without offering a defense, Kaitlyn grabs Billy's Camaro keys from his bedside table. "You're all out. We'll run to the store and grab you a few bottles," she explains, while grabbing Saphyre by the arm and pulling her to the door. "One fresh bottle of Mountain Dew coming right up, sir." The girls hurry from the room dying to take a joyride in the hotrod.

"Saphyre, tell your grandfather to come see me," Billy calls out taxing his wounds in the process, and then looks to Taylor and JD as if asking whether they thought Saphyre heard him or not.

Kaitlyn is a lot like JD in the fact that she wants to keep herself occupied, to keep her mind off the loss of her father and her life. Racing from the house, they show their immaturity, acting like kids in a candy store, anticipating driving the beast again. Saphyre quickly regains her composure though, and urges Kaitlyn to do the same, when she sees Isaiah standing by the barn door. "Hey Grandpa, Billy's asking for you, and he's thirsty. So we're going to the store to get him something to drink. You should go in to see him."

"You girls better be careful in that car. You know that's his baby, Saphyre. He'll skin you alive if you so much as scratch the paint."

Back up in the bedroom, JD and Taylor begin to fill in the blanks about what happened. "Billy," JD takes on a more somber appearance, "First of all, I want to say how sorry I am about your mother. Man, we got her out of there as quick as we could. Hell, Taylor carried her like she weighed nothing. And, those DSC guys, they really did all they could to help her. But, those shots she took from Crossfire really messed her up inside." JD closes his eyes wishing he could retract the last statement, "sorry bro."

"Ryker's people took care of your mother's burial," Taylor explains, seeing how the news report was tearing JD up inside. "He used his authority to get everything pushed through so that she could be put to rest. She wasn't alone, Billy. Me, JD, and Isaiah, went to be with her when she was laid down beside your father. Officially, the reports say that she died of a heart attack."

It's funny how life has a habit of showing humor to us, and judging by his friends' expressions, Billy needs to explain the smile on his face. "I'm sorry, but I find that funny, because my mom was a Cardiologist."

The pain on Billy's face from saying that saddens JD's expression even more. Billy knows that JD didn't mean any harm, and that his friend really did do the best he could to save Billy's loved ones. There was no way JD could have prevented Sarah's shooting, and no one ever handed out guarantees that everyone would walk away. Would Billy trade his life for his mother's death? That's a definite yes, and the main reason why he went to New York. Unfortunately, there is nothing that Billy can do to change the outcome now, so he must find a way to move on. "Don't sweat it, JD. I'll never be able to repay you for what you did." Billy looks into Taylor's eyes, trying not to be too presumptuous, and says, "You brought my girl home." Right on cue, Taylor starts to cry again, after hearing the words she has wanted to hear since being freed from her captivity.

When he got back from Florida, Billy never thought he would see her again. After all of the lies, all of the deceit, after everything that has happened to her, here she sits where Billy can stare into her gorgeous green eyes. Even the truly blessed must bear their pain for what they must do. "I don't know what else to say, except I'm sorry. I want you to know that I will do whatever it takes to get your life back for you. I hurt you, and abandoned you, to pursue a fruitless revenge. You didn't deserve that. I heard it in what you said, and I understand completely." The time has come. He has to face the great unknown and let her go, if it is what she wants. This, he has already come to terms with, no matter how much it hurts to say the words. Truth be known, part of him would have rather never to have seen Taylor again, just so he could keep from saying those words to her.

Taylor turns her head and wipes away her tears. Staring out at the stables through the balcony doors, she takes a second to regain her composure before addressing Billy's statement. Turning back to face him again with an almost angered expression, she replies, "If you're talking about the last phone call I made; they made me keep calling you to say those things." Be strong, Taylor. It takes everything she's got to hold back the tears. "I don't know what happened to you in Florida. I just don't care any more. All I want to know is, do you want me in your life, or not?"

"More than you'll ever know, baby," he replies, reaching up to touch her face. Could this really be true? Is it really possible that this could all be over, and he and Taylor can start their lives together? There's no doubt that his quest for vengeance died with Antonio. He has no reason to go out any more and run the streets as a masked vigilante. Anything else that comes their way they can face together.

Seeing the scar in the center of his palm brings another question to her mind. "Baby, what did you do to your hands?"

"It happened in Florida, and you don't wanna know, trust me," he replies, remembering the humiliation of being crucified to the floor of that rundown apartment.

Remembering what she just said, Taylor chooses not to press the issue any further. "I love you, Billy. I don't ever want to leave you, or lose you again. I can't have a life, if you're not in it. What I want most of all is for you to get better, so that we can start our future together. I need you. I believe that with all of my heart." She points to JD, and the girls returning from the store, "We all need you. Who else is capable of taking care of a group like this?"

That is the question of the century. Poor Kaitlyn just lost her father, killed by the same murdering bastard that killed her mother, and apparently, both of Billy's parents as well. As painful as it is, at least he and Kaitlyn had that in common. JD, has got to be lost in a whirlwind of shit with what he faces getting his life back on track. Surely, Taylor is bound to have some scars showing up from this, sooner or later. And then there is little Miss Saphyre. Judging by the way she is staring at JD, Billy can see a whole different kind of trouble heading for her and his friend. With everyone crowding the room, Billy has a strong desire to change the topic and the mood of the conversation. "Who was driving?"

"I was," Kaitlyn, answers bashfully.

"Next time, shift out of second sooner. It's not a little four banger that needs to be wound out. Now, will someone please tell me the rest of what happened?"

Picking up on what Billy wanted, JD takes the stage to oblige his friend. "Dude, it was a race against time trying to get out of the building, and we were running in last place. Then, if things weren't bad enough, we were dead in the water, as far as where you took off to with your pursuit. That is, until Kaitlyn stepped up to provide us with the address to Callistone's building. Then, that DSC team, Omega Corps, showed up and all hell broke loose again. Thinking that they were there to try and apprehend you, Taylor took off like a bat outta hell to find you, but leveled the Corps team in the process. Luckily, one of Commander Ryker's boys was able mark her with a radioactive tag that allowed us to follow her pursuit of you. Man, you should have seen the carnage she left in her wake. Later on, Ryker said that the tag was unnecessary, and that all we really had to do was follow her path of destruction. There were cars stomped on, a bus shoved into a store front, light poles knocked down, not to mention the numerous wrecks from drivers trying to avoid her rampaging pursuit. Oh, and did I mention that she jumped through an entire building to get to you?"

Billy slowly turns his head to see Taylor's response to JD's accusations. The glowing red of her blushing cheeks tells him that JD is pretty close to being dead on with his report. "Those things were in my way," She replies with a bashful defense.

Saphyre nudges JD, "remind me to never get in her way."

"Any way, a helicopter took off from the rooftop of the Cornerstone Building, but it was damaged by the explosion, and forced to crash land in Central Park. Your boy Antonio, was blown out of a window, and found seventy feet away from the building, in the trees that line the park." JD pauses for a moment as Billy summons the girls to bring him his soda. "Now I have a question for you. What happened up there?"

Before answering JD's question, Billy has to ask one of his own. "What about the bodies in the helicopter? Have they been identified yet?" Billy tries to sit up, but it feels like someone has nailed his chest to the mattress with railroad spikes and they are still in there, holding him in place.

"The pilot was killed on impact, but there wasn't anyone else in the cabin, and no witnesses saw anyone fleeing the crash site."

The little voice in the back of Billy's mind is finally catching up to the present, and the information being processed doesn't add up to the big finale that he was hoping for. Perhaps sharing the insight of his actions might shed some light on what happened to Margaret and her lackey, Carlton. "As for what happened to me, I basically stepped right off into the world's largest dog turd. If nothing else, I'm one hundred percent positive that this was more than just an old man seeking revenge for his son's death. In fact, Antonio wasn't even running the show, and was double crossed by his own daughter who set him up for a fall along with me." Fighting through the pain, he forces himself to sit up on the side of the bed, craving what the girls hold in their hands.

Kaitlyn, poor Kaitlyn; she has suffered as much as Billy, not counting the three gunshot wounds to his chest. Was there a chance where Billy could have rescued her father, to prevent her from becoming an orphan? At this point in time, there is no way of ever knowing the answer to that question. In his heart, he will force himself to make it up to her, consciously or not. That's just who Billy is. For now, she graciously twists the top off of the soda and hands him the bottle. Her gratitude, for the moment, is based on not being alone right now. She'll deal with her losses in her own time.

For now, she can disappear from the world and feel content in Billy's home. These new friends of hers actually seem to care about her, and her welfare. It's something that she is unaccustomed to, and yet has always wanted.

In his hands he holds the nectar of the gods, or at least that's what it is in his eyes. It takes him a little time and effort to get the bottle to his mouth, but when he succeeds, it only takes him a few seconds to down the entire one liter bottle. The bite of the carbonation, along with the citrus flavors brings him back to life a little more. "Unfortunately, I think we were part of something even bigger than a hostile takeover. The problem is that I don't think it is over yet." Billy starts to get out of bed to test his strength, only to remember the mixed company in the room. "Taylor, baby, would you take the girls downstairs, and fix me something to eat? I need to talk to JD for a minute. We'll be down before you know it, okay?" He does his best to hide his weakened condition to keep them from worrying, but some things can't be kept secret.

"No secrets," Taylor suggests, with a loving tone. She sees through his attempt, and yet forces herself to go and fulfill his request. leaning over him, she gives Billy a gentle kiss, and whispers, "If you're not down in a few minutes, we'll be back up here looking for you."

"I promise," he replies, motioning for Kaitlyn and Saphyre to go with Taylor. Facing JD, Billy points at the dresser, "Hey bro, can you grab me a pair of sweat pants out of the middle drawer?" He tries to sound as if he were ready to return to the living but it all comes across as a joker's ploy.

"Yeah, no problem, but do you think you should be up and moving around so soon?" JD opens the drawer, grabs the pair of pants, and tosses them to Billy.

"No," Billy replies grimacing from the pain inflicted by the pants hitting him in the chest. "But if I do it real slow,

I should be alright." Lifting each leg to put the pants on is a painful feat in itself, forcing him to take a breather before exerting himself any more.

"As long as you do WHAT real slow?"

"Anything," Billy answers with a smile. With his pants on, Billy takes JD's hand to help himself up off the side of the bed into a standing position. "See? That wasn't so bad, He says with gritted teeth. "Listen; in all of your dealings with Nick, and that stuff you went through in Japan, did you ever hear the names Sytaine, and/or Jezana?"

Is this JD's big chance to open up about what he's seen? He's been dying to say something since he and Billy first met. Now that has to be added to what he's seen during their efforts to free Billy's family and friends, or vice versa. He knows that there is something going on, and that it's connected to Nick and his destiny. The one thing JD doesn't know is if he should bring it up now, or not. "I don't think so, or at least not the first one any way. But, now that you mention it, the second name sounds familiar. I could check Nick's journal to see if I saw it in there somewhere. Why do you ask?" That's it JD, that's a perfect lead in to what you need to say.

For a split second, Billy flakes out remembering bits and pieces of the dream he had. It troubles him and makes him want to drop the subject of Nickolas Landry. "It's no big deal. We can talk about it later on, okay? My mind is still trying to sort all of this out, so that I can see which way is up." Slowly, Billy makes his way over to the dresser and stares at his reflection in the mirror for a second. He notes the three healing scars that look like someone had tried to use his chest as a cigar ashtray. "I don't think this is over, JD. I'd like it, and really appreciate it, if you would hang around for a while, at least until I'm back on my feet again." Billy watches as JD looks at Billy's feet, taking notice to the fact that he is already standing up. "Shut up, you know what I mean." He thinks for a second, about what Saphyre said referring to Scotty's friend Clovis. As soon as Billy finds his phone, he needs to call Scotty.

JD smirks, and then laughs. "No problem, brother man; Commander Ryker didn't want any of us to leave any way, believing that there is safety in our numbers, right now." JD offers Billy his arm to lean on, "You want some help getting down the stairs?"

"Naw, I'll be alright. Like I said, as long as I take it slow." No matter how bad he wants to forget about Nick and the man's crusade to save the world, Billy can't close his mind to it. There are two names that have been burned into Billy's mind, mainly because of the ghastly occurrence that took place with Pantera's body. The problem is that Billy just isn't comfortable enough with the situation to talk about it, yet. No, that's not the problem. The problem is that Billy is having a hard time admitting to himself that what he saw was real, to himself, much less to anyone else. He knows that what he witnessed sounded like it came from JD's book of scary secrets, but Billy just doesn't know how to strike up a conversation about something he doesn't believe exists?

Chapter VII

After a treacherous journey down the stairs to the living room, Billy surprises the girls by actually joining their gathering in the kitchen. "What'cha cooking, good lookin'?"

"Billy, I can't believe you're actually down here?" Saphyre looks at him, surprised as hell that Billy was standing, much less walking around downstairs. Not three days ago, he was barely hanging on to life, and now he looks like he is just sore from playing a game of backyard football.

"Homemade burritos, just the way you like 'em," Taylor replies, happy that Billy was able to make it down to be with them. It's a legitimate sign that he is going to be alright. The sight of him laid up in his bed is more painful for her to see than his actual wounds. Billy's not the type to be kept down. It's like tying a thoroughbred horse down to the ground, instead of letting the beast do what comes naturally, run.

On the other side of the kitchen, Kaitlyn catches herself staring at Billy's chest. Admiring his muscular features is one thing, but her focus is on the three healing scars. She can't help but ask, "Do those hurt much?"

"Taylor quickly interjects, "He's got a matching set on his back." Referring to the exit wounds made by the same three bullets.

Billy tries to ignore the remark, knowing Taylor's sense of humor. "So, any way, getting back to what happened in Chateau Callistone, This guy Crossfire, he was working for and with, Callistone's daughter. She's the true snake in the grass. I remember coming to, after everything was over, and I could hear Ryker filling y'all in on some of the other stuff that happened. If all of Callistone's loyal followers were taken out, then she has been given the crown and keys to the Callistone Empire. With no one to oppose her, she'll have it all."

"Yeah but," JD jumps in, "what you're not thinking about is how she got rid of all of Callistone's pigeons. Commander Ryker believes, just like Kaitlyn's dad did, that she was framing you for that part of her scheme. By the way, he said for you to call him when you came around. Do you want me to dial him up for ya? I've got his card right here."

"Naw, he can wait a few more days," Billy replies. "Ya know, if you think about that for a second, you'd have to admit that she's been working on this little scheme for quite some time. No matter which side the players involved stood on, if they were in line to oppose her, they earned a bullet. Kaitlyn, your dad was betrayed by his partner. If I'm not mistaken, that is who was in the lobby of the building where me and JD found y'all. She had Crossfire and his team do all of the dirty work, which ultimately earned him a couple of bullets as well. The guy impersonating me: he was gunned down. Major Delaney from Darkside Command; he earned a bullet for his contribution to her father's organization. From that point of view, you'd have to admit that there doesn't look like there's anyone left to stand against her."

"You're still alive," Kaitlyn declares, fantasizing for a second about running the rooftops with Billy and Taylor.

"Yeah, I know. That's why my gut keeps telling me that this isn't over yet."

"How about you fill me in on that?" A voice says from the dining room outside the kitchen. Everyone in the kitchen turns to see Commander Ryker. Everyone except Billy, that is. In the shape he's in, it wouldn't matter if it is President Obama himself, Billy isn't turning around. "My medical officer is surprised to find you awake, McBride. I have to say that I'm not completely shocked to find you up and out of bed." Steven Ryker continues into the kitchen and walks up behind Billy. "Were you expecting me? You don't seem as surprised by my arrival as the rest of your little clan," Ryker adds, referencing the way everyone else in the room jumped at the sound of his voice.

"I saw your reflection in the big pot hanging over the island cabinet."

Ryker smiles at the young man, impressed by Billy's awareness. "Let's see if I remember the damage report. There were three gunshot wounds to the chest, matching exit wounds in the back…"

"I told ya," Taylor interrupts.

"…From the gunshot wounds alone, your heart, lungs, and stomach were compromised. Somewhere between being shot, blown up, and the splashdown in the pool, you suffered a broken arm, three fractured ribs, and a muscle tear in your right bicep."

"That explains why my arm hurts," Billy interjects.

Ryker shakes his head, "Let's get back to my original question. Please, elaborate on why you feel the way you do about this case."

Billy slowly spins his barstool around as Ryker motions for his medical officer to enter the kitchen. Taylor quickly turns around to face the stove, not caring to see another woman touching her man. As Karen checks Billy out, he sees her giving Kaitlyn the evil eye, and Kaitlyn returning the gesture. "What's up with the two of you? Do you know each other?"

After a few seconds of silence, Saphyre pipes in, "Oh I know this one. The doctor girl's pissed at Kaitlyn because she won't go to the DSC guys for sanctuary. Kaitlyn is pissed at the doctor girl for a whole bunch of reasons I don't even want to get into right now."

"Like What?" Karen asks, losing her focus on Billy to take on her little sister one more time.

"Like, the way you screwed up my life, that's what! After mom was killed, dad went nuts after you stormed off to follow in her footsteps! He died, still despising the way you walked away from us to join Darkside Command. Then he turned my life into a prison so that he wouldn't lose all of his women!"

"Don't give me that shit, Kaitlyn! I've told you plenty of times that all you had to do is wait until you turned eighteen. But no, you had to have everything your way, and right now!"

"All you had to do is talk to him, and help me out of that living hell! You know how overprotective he was for me! Maybe he wouldn't be dead right now, if you had just spoke up for me, just once!"

"Don't you get it, Kaitlyn? You're the reason he's dead! When are you going to quit acting like a spoiled child?"

"Bitch!"

"Stupid."

In unison, Billy and Ryker yell out, "Hey, that's enough!" Shaking off the embarrassment of the situation, Ryker steps up to his medical officer and asks, "Lt. Justice, I warned you to keep your head. Please don't make me regret bringing you along, and tell me how Mr. McBride is doing?"

Karen Justice snaps to attention, not sure how that little spat escalated so fast. "Sir, McBride has exceeded my expectations. The damage to his internal organs has healed as if nothing had happened to him. The broken bones are healing nicely, but there is nothing to be done about his personality," she adds trying to inject a little humor into the mix.

"Thank you, Lieutenant. Now to avoid any more conflict, will you wait for me outside?" Ryker looks around to see that he isn't the only one unsettled by the banter. Walking over to Billy, he asks, "Can you answer my question for me now?"

"Sure," Billy replies. "Antonio's daughter made a comment about how it wasn't supposed to happen the way it did. Antonio's man, Smithers, mentioned New Orleans, as if he was telling me where to go next." More and more memories keep unlocking to help Billy put all of the pieces of the puzzle together. The frustrating part is the missing clues that continue to elude him. What is the missing factor? There has to be a common denominator that ties all of this together.

"What do you know about little rebel flags that were left at each of the murder scenes?"

"Only what Agent Justice told me. The best I can figure, she was planning to frame me with the murders, and then take the credit for eliminating her father's killer. This gains her the loyalty of the men left in the organization, who will take up her banner and follow her lead. It really is the perfect hostile takeover." Billy welcomes the bottle of Mountain Dew that Taylor brings to him, and then gives her a quick kiss as a sign of appreciation. "I've got a question for you. Who was the guy impersonating me?"

Ryker gives Billy a confident smile. "Well, I'm glad that you've got it all figured out." Then, just as quickly, Ryker takes on a more somber expression. "As for your doppelganger, He was my youngest brother Paul. Simon had recruited Paulie to join his team, tempting him with fame and fortune. He, being

STACY WRIGHT

Paulie, was the main reason that I responded to Jonathan's beacon." Ryker tries to maintain his composure over the loss of his brothers. "I thought that if I could stop Simon, there might be some way to save Paulie from himself. I guess some people can't be saved. But, on the other hand, some can." Walking over to the doorway, he motions for someone to come join him in the kitchen. It is his teammate, code named, Ranger, who is carrying a couple of bags containing Kaitlyn's belongings. "I need you to do me a favor, McBride. I want Kaitlyn to stay with you, until further notice. Technically, besides her sister, you're the closest thing to a relative she has. Evidently, she has no desire to go with us to Darkside Command, and I don't want her out in the system where she can be found."

"Kaitlyn is welcome here as long as she likes, Ryker. I've already made that point clear. Now, I have to ask you one more question. Why don't your people move forward with what I've already told you?"

The war veteran nod s his head as a sign of appreciation. "Darkside Command is in the middle of a political upheaval at the moment, and I'm going to be tied up for days, maybe weeks, while all of this is worked out. Delaney's involvement has compromised our security protocols, and has left a lot of people scratching their heads. Not to mention the fact that my involvement with your situation is not on DSC's records. Keep an eye on Jonathan's little girl for me. Take care of yourself, McBride, and watch your back while you're at it." Then, before exiting the kitchen, he turns around and hands Billy a disc, "Sorry, I almost forgot."

"What is it?"

"It's your mother's last request."

The last thing Taylor wants is any more time wasted about what happened in New York. As far as she is concerned, the sooner the matter is forgotten the better.

Billy's already got her worried about all of this talk regarding this nightmare chapter of her life not being over. "Lunch is ready," she declares, nonchalantly notifying Commander Ryker that it was time for him to leave. She's grateful to the man, there's no doubt about that. Ryker's team is the reason Billy is still in her life, or so she believes. Still, that doesn't mean that his welcome hasn't been worn out, and she is not above tossing him out on his butt. "I hope everyone is hungry. It's homemade Tex/Mex." Taylor looks to Ryker with an apologetic expression, as if to say sorry, but I want MY time with him. Understanding her every word, Ryker gives them a casual salute and then quietly bows out of the room.

Billy turns a deaf ear away from Kaitlyn's sobbing, as the smell of sustenance rises up under his nose, from the plate of food Taylor had just set down in front of him. He doesn't mean to be cold or heartless. He just needs something to eat before he passes out again. "You know how I like it," he declares, motioning for JD to grab another bottle of soda from the fridge.

"Yep, meat and cheese, and nothing else," Taylor declares proudly. She then waves everyone over to the stove to dish up their lunches, while Billy stares at the disc that Ryker gave him.

Handing Billy the bottle of soda, JD has to ask, "What is it?"

"Something I probably don't want to look at," Billy replies.

"Are ya gonna?"

"Later on, brother man, later on."

Chapter VIII

Her Narcotic is wearing off, and Margaret is a mess. Deeds of doom and despair have taken place these past few days, and the culprit and accomplice to the crimes rushes into the women's restroom to hide her agony from the eyes of man. Her false sense of bravery and arrogance has faded away. She needs to feel the recharge of power that she craves, and then all will be better again. Boston, she must return to Boston as soon as possible. The time has come for her to collect her treasure, but more than anything she must satisfy the craving that is eating at her. She must have her fix, and she needs it before her next encounter with her mother. In this condition, Margaret could be deemed unworthy of the gift promised to her. This cannot happen. It must not happen! She will get to Boston and make herself well again. Avoiding a confrontation with her mother's image is simple. All Margaret has to do is avoid mirrors. Of course, this isn't an easy feat to accomplish when dealing with the twelve feet of silver backed glass of the women's restroom. "My child of doom, tell me why do you avoid me?" The image of Jezana displays her dislike for Margaret's recent actions, and she expects an answer from her cowering agent. "Stop," she yells out, as Margaret tries to walk on by. "I demand an answer from you right now!"

Unsure what to do or say, Margaret stops, but hesitates to look at the mirror, or say anything. When she finally does turn to face the reflective glass, it is easy for Jezana to see the uncertainty showing all over Margaret's face. "Mother, I feel like everything is unraveling before my very eyes. I fear that all of this has been too overwhelming for me." Where did all of that come from? Has her cravings driven her mad?

"Childish mortal, do not allow your spine to dissolve now that the most difficult part of this grand scheme has already been accomplished!"

"But mother I haven't even received confirmation that our unlikely ally survived the event in New York. What if he didn't?" Margaret pauses for a moment as another woman enters the public restroom, needing desperately to find a vacant stall. Margaret quickly gives her an evil stare, as if saying to her the restroom was closed, to anyone else. When the young lady sees the horrific surroundings in the mirror's reflection, she quickly concedes to Margaret's expression, and chooses to turn and get out of there as fast as she possibly can.

"Listen to me child, and know the truth of my words. Have I not foreseen everything that has, and will, take place?" Jezana leans back against her throne of human remains and stares at Margaret with confidence.

"But Mother, what if he doesn't, or can't, produce the effort to accomplish our goal? This crippled boy is not of McBride's blood line, nor is he held in high regard as the others."

"You are mistaken, my child. This one is held in higher regard with your unlikely ally. This McBride will go to the ends of the earth to save this one helpless soul. That it what heroes do. Do not falter from my plan, and you will find success. You will find that allies have taken the place of the slain members of your crime syndicate. They will serve our needs from here on out, and will be loyal to you. Find your spine amongst the swill of this room and move forward with the next stage of our plan. No matter what, do not display this sickening weakness in front of me again. Once I am freed from my warden, you will receive the power and glory I promised to you. Now be gone from my sight!" The reflection in the mirror reverts back to the image of the restroom facilities behind Margaret, returning her to her dreadful reality.

Looking back into the mirror, Margaret is actually happy to see the image of Jezana gone. After straightening her hair and dress, the Callistone heir exits the restroom and ignores the looks and stares that she is receiving in the upstate New York airport. If everything is taking place as proclaimed, soon this will all be over and she will receive what she deserves.

"Margaret, is everything alright?" Carlton hurries over to her side doing his best to ignore the grumbling patrons of the airport, as she exits the airport terminal to board her jet. When all of this started, he believed that his life was going to change for the better. Since Antonio Callistone's untimely demise, Carlton has felt completely the opposite. If he is to follow his own plan and scheme, he has to keep himself consciously aware of her plans and motives.

"Dig my phone out of my bag. We need to leave right away, but have the pilot change our flight plan to stop in Boston first. I have a small business matter to address before we head south, but you will need to stay with the plane. Have my car waiting for me at the Boston airport." Reaching the cabin door of the small jet, Margaret stops for a second to look inside where she sees a young man with a crippling affliction strapped down in his chair. "Oh Scotty, I do apologize for the treatment," she declares as she enters the plane. "I promise that as soon as the plane takes off, I'll have my boys remove the restraints. You don't have a problem with flying do you?"

"Lady, the only thing I have a problem with is being able to kick your ass myself. Lucky for me, I can take comfort in knowing that Billy will happily do it for me." Scotty watches as Carlton closes the hatch. If she is still following through with this plan of hers, then that must mean that Billy is still alive and kicking. That also means that there is still a chance that Scotty will still get out of this mess alive. "Let me ask you something, lady. Have you ever seen an old fighting dog who just doesn't know when or how to quit?"

"I suppose this is an analogy of your friend, right?"

"Good, then you do know what you're in for," Scotty replies, and then out of the blue starts laughing to himself. "Here's something you might find funny. I've had my suspicions about my friend for a long time now. Ain't it kooky how the way I'm proven right, is by him having to save me from the likes of you."

"Watch your mouth kid. I'm not above beating on a handicapped fat mouth." Carlton reaches out with Margaret's phone with one hand, while dumping his armful of belongings into the seat beside her. "Here's your phone, Margaret. Give me a second to get the Captain to change our flight plan. It shouldn't take long for us to get under way."

Out of nowhere, Margaret's personal flight attendant appears in front of Scotty to deliver a piping hot, fresh and juicy T-bone steak dinner. Okay, so the service isn't so bad after all. Besides, it isn't like anyone has roughed him up or anything. Still, that doesn't mean that Scotty is willing to cut Margaret any slack. "I hope you're not trying to earn brownie points with me, thinking that I'll tell Billy to go easy on you. Because, sister, I'd love to see him kick your ass, his ass," he adds, pointing at Carlton, "and anyone else that works for you, all over the place."

Back in Alabama, Billy awakens to find himself alone in his room, sprawled out across his king size bed. In a way, it's kind of nice to find Taylor not sitting over him worrying herself sick over his condition. He's feeling better, but should probably remain in bed for the rest of the day. Of course, Billy has never been known to do what's best for him. He takes the stairs slowly and makes his way into the family room, expecting the gang to be hanging out, and getting to know each other. Instead, there is no sign of the girls, and Taylor's nowhere to be seen. Mainly because she's stretched out on the sectional, out of view, dead to the world from her vigil at Billy's side. Not to mention the latent fatigue from what happened in New York is finally catching up with her. JD seems to be caught up in his thoughts as he stares at the pictures of Billy's grandfather's prize horses, oblivious to Billy's presence. Spooking his friend, Billy asks, "Where's everybody else?"

"Oh, hey bro," JD responds. "I didn't expect to see you for the rest of the day." He points to Taylor asleep on the sectional, and then replaces a framed snapshot to the fireplace mantle. After leading Billy out of the family room, JD turns to face his friend, and says in a hushed voice, "Man, your grandfather sure loved his horses, didn't he?"

"Yeah, well those horses paid for this ranch and property. So in a way, we all love those horses." Billy takes a couple of steps up the stairway and begins to point out the money makers. "It was my dad who was the one to start boarding horses here, to perpetuate Isaiah's job. Otherwise, Isaiah and his wife would've been out on the street. With Saphyre's grandmother's health fading, there was no way my father was going to do that to them. Isaiah and Millie are like part of the family, and we don't do that to family."

Outside the house, a pair of prying eyes watches Billy and JD through the family room window. Pulling a phone from his pocket, the mystery man dials a number, and then steps back into the shadows of a large oak tree. "Hello? Yes ma'am, he has awakened and is now walking around amongst the living. Yes ma'am, I'll be ready." With no other reason to remain, the mystery man hangs up the phone and then vanishes from the McBride ranch.

Suddenly, a phone ringing upstairs catches Billy's attention. At first, Billy appears to be perplexed by the sound, but JD has no way of knowing why. "What's wrong?"

"It's Scotty's phone, up in his room," Billy answers, as a sinking feeling settles into his stomach. Why now, is beyond him, but Billy suddenly remembers what Margaret said to him in New York. Was he really out of it that bad, to where he couldn't figure out that Scotty is who Margaret was referring to? Is Billy jumping to conclusions? Maybe, but the only way to know for sure is to go answer the phone. Without offering an explanation, Billy forgets about the pain he is suffering and takes off for the stairs with JD in hot pursuit.

JD stops at Scotty's bedroom door, as Billy enters the room to make his way over to the phone. "I don't get it, Billy. What's the big deal?"

"This is Scotty's phone, his personal phone line. No one would be calling this number while he is in school up in Auburn." It rings again but Billy just stares at it. "I know who it is," He explains.

"Well, are you going to answer it?"

Billy shakes his head and replies, "No." He lets it ring again, and then one more time before the antiquated answering machine picks up the call. "Scotty has it set up to ring a butt load of times before the machine picks up. That way it gives him more time to get to the phone." Then, Billy pauses for a moment as he has a slight realization about the conversation. "Oh yeah, you don't know him, do you? Scotty's on crutches for life," he explains.

They listen to Scotty's corny recording, and then wait to see if the caller will leave a message. When it happens, Billy is disappointed to know that he is right, but not surprised. "Hello Mr. McBride, are you home? It's Margaret calling, dear. I hope this finds you well and in good spirits. If so, please let me rain on your parade. As you have probably figured out by now, I have your foster brother with me, and we are having the time of our lives," Margaret informs with a gleeful tone. After a short pause, she continues, saying, "I'm sorry; let me get right to the point. I am about to fly to New Orleans after a brief stopover in Boston. In fact, we should be taking off any minute. I expect you to meet me there in the big easy, so that we can finish this once and for all. If you don't, key evidence will be handed over to the New York Police, and the FBI, that will implicate you, your friends, and your family in what happened to my loving father and his associates. If you are able to walk away from this encounter, you will do so a free man. Just so that you know, there won't be any outside interference from DSC this time. That little problem has already been taken care of, or at least for now. However, you are more than welcome to bring all of your cute little friends. You know what they say; the more the merrier." The line goes dead, and the answering machine switches off.

"Ya know, bro, ya really need to step up into the present with your electronics," JD suggests as he tries to inject a little humor into the situation. When he sees that it doesn't help, he has to ask, "What's next?"

"I'm going to New Orleans."

"Whoa, whoa, you're in no condition to be going back downstairs, much less to Louisiana." JD shrinks back a little when he sees Billy's disapproving stare, "Alright, I know I don't have any right to contradict you like that, but don't you think it would be smarter to at least change your statement to you and I are going to New Orleans?"

"No, the smartest thing to do would be for him to say that WE are going to New Orleans," Taylor's voice sounds out, from the doorway to the room. "I just got you back, and barely in one piece, so if you think I'm gonna just let you wander away again, you're outta your goddamned mind!"

Slowly, JD and Billy turn around to see Taylor's displeased appearance. "Hey baby, I didn't know you were awake," Billy declares as she enters the room. He knows that this is about to get very complicated, very fast. "Just so that we can clear the air, I'd like to ask both of you to hold on a minute so I can finish my statement. Remember, I'm the guy who is stuck in slow motion right now, so you have to hold back with jumping to conclusions. I think that all three of us know that there is no way I am going anywhere without the two of you. The real question should be how and when do we do this?" Billy sits down on the edge of Scotty's bed, needing to find a way to relieve the pain that reminds him of his delicate condition.

"Well, you've got that right, mister!" Taylor finally enters the room and walks right up to Billy with her hands on her hips. "Look at you. How do you think you could save anybody in the condition that you are in? Before you go getting' all high and mighty about how you're responsible for everything, just remember that Scotty is my friend too!" This is the last thing that Taylor wanted to do, but at the same instant, there is part of her that can't turn away from the situation. Not to mention the fact that there isn't a force on Earth that is going to separate her from her man.

JD may not know Scotty as Billy and Taylor do, and he is nowhere as exuberant as his female associate, but he shares her feelings about the situation none the less. "Billy, you know I'm with you for the long haul, but even I have to wonder how much you have to offer for this."

As much as he would like to admit to his friends that they are right, Billy knows that this is something he can't walk away from, now or later. "I'll be ready to go in a little while," he replies, as he reaches up for Taylor's assistance to stand up. Billy knows that the two of them are just trying to look out for him, but at the same time he can't help but feel like he's being dismissed as inferior due to his injuries. "Where are Saphyre and our new guest? If nothing else, I want them locked down here at the ranch, while WE are gone. The three of us will go to the big easy, rescue Captain Crutch, and put that bitch Margaret Callistone out of her misery once and for all."

"I thought her name was Stanford?" The look coming from Billy for JD's question quickly changes the young man's approach to their conversation, "Okay, then tell me what you know about the Callistone organization in New Orleans, and do you have a plan to fit?" Before answering his question, Billy and Taylor exit the room, sending JD rushing after them. "Hey, wait up, guys!"

Billy waits for JD to catch up with them at the top of the stairs, and then answers JD's question, "To be honest, I don't know squat about her, or her associations with New Orleans. But, the plan is to go down there, kick their asses all over Louisiana, and then bring Scotty home. It's as simple as that," he adds, while grimacing from taking his first step back downstairs.

"It's never as simple as that," Taylor corrects, all too familiar with how Billy works.

To her surprise, her negative comment only makes Billy laugh, "I know, and that's why I want the two of you with me on this one," he explains as they walk into the kitchen. "I want to leave as soon as possible to try and get the jump on her. There is an unknown that she has to deal with that works in our favor. As far as I can tell, she has no way of knowing when I would receive the message; therefore she has no way of knowing when I would be arriving. I'm sure that they have preparations in place for the big event, but if we could slip in without notice, there could be a chance for us to gain the upper hand." Billy rolls his shoulder to test his pain levels and do his own assessment on his injuries. "Baby, would you grab me that bottle of Dew out of the fridge?" It may not seem like it to his friends, but his mind is working away on this latest turn of events.

At the moment, Billy is stuck on the part about how and why he didn't connect the dots sooner. Margaret told him that he missed one. Then he realizes where he dropped the ball. Earlier, he was told that Scotty's friend, Clovis, was involved simply due to a case of mistaken identity. Billy's screw up was when he assumed that if the bad guys had Clovis believing he was Scotty, then Scotty must be safe, right? This would be feasible if two separate parties made the snatch and grabs. But anyone who invaded the ranch, and saw Scotty's room, would know that Clovis was the wrong man. The walls of the room are covered with pictures of Scotty and Billy. Each one was hung with pride, as if they were trophies representing the unforgettable events that took place between Scotty and his best friend. "I won't let you down again, Scotty," Billy says silently to himself.

"Hello, earth to Billy, hey do you even hear me?" Taylor taps Billy on the shoulder, trying to get his attention. "I said, what about the kids?" You told Ryker that they would be here under safe supervision. I just don't think we should be running off like this." To show her feelings for Billy to make him understand her concern, Taylor takes on a more sorrowful expression for what she is about to say, "Maybe you should let me, and JD, take care of this, while you recover. I'm sure the girls would spoil you rotten with their bedside manner." After all that she has been through, Taylor can't believe how easily she just volunteered to lead JD to New Orleans, without Billy. Is she really that serious about keeping Billy in her life, or has the chaos and madness of past events clouded her thinking?

Right away, JD sees a storm brewing because of Taylor's suggestion. In many ways, he agrees with Taylor about Billy's condition. JD doesn't want Billy to think that JD is stepping over any boundaries, but on the other hand, he doesn't want Taylor to think that he doesn't have any faith in her, either. Humor, levity, that's what is needed in a situation like this, "Ya know, Billy, that's really not such a bad idea. After all, she can break anything and anyone, and if need be I can protect her with my force field. Let us go down and find your friend. Ya gotta admit that it would throw Callistone's daughter way off her mark, if you didn't show up at all."

"No, that won't do at all," Isaiah, declares entering the kitchen. "Billy has to go and finish this." No matter what the topic of conversation is, the old man always has a way of propping himself up, as if his only purpose is to share his words of wisdom. "The young ladies are down by the pond, having an aggressive conversation. JD, why don't you run down there and fetch them up to the house? I need to have a private conversation with these two."

Down at the pond, Kaitlyn and Saphyre sit inside the tree house over the edge of the water, killing some time with a little girl talk. "So, Kaitlyn, what makes you tick? Saphyre asks, as she crosses her legs in the middle of the floor.

A cold wind blows through the top of the tree causing the small wooden house to sway and creak within its branches as the clouds race across the sky. "I can't believe Ryker and his goons didn't bring me my coat with the rest of my clothes." Shivering from the cold, Kaitlyn moves over to the corner seeking shelter from the wind blowing through the windows, before she tries to answer Saphyre's inquiry. Only, to keep the spotlight off the massive pain and heartache that has enveloped her life, Kaitlyn tries to change the subject by asking a question of her own. "You like JD, don't you? It's easy to see that he likes you."

"Do you really think so?" Saphyre is so intrigued by Kaitlyn's question and statement that she forgets the other topic of conversation to hear what Kaitlyn has to say. "Because, girl, I've heard stories about how people, okay girls, have fallen for the guy that rides in to save the day. Hell, movies have been made about that for years. I didn't think I had to worry about anything like that, being that Billy was the one who was coming to save me. Don't get me wrong, because the man is fine, but for me, it would be like kissing my brother." Saphyre laughs right along with Kaitlyn at the remark, but still feels the need to explain, "You know, because I've known him for so long."

Kaitlyn can't help but tease Saphyre a little about how cute Billy is, but Saphyre just leans back and closes her eyes to remember the first time she saw JD. "No, back in New York, when I saw JD drop out of the air and land on the floor, I knew he was the one I had to worry about. The way he took control of the situation and never backed down an inch drove me wild inside. Then, when he pulled his mask off his face, I knew that I had just joined the list of statistics."

Kaitlyn giggles at Saphyre's enthusiasm for stating the obvious. "That's good," she proclaims, "I think the two of you would make a cute couple."

"Really? Oh man, I sure hope so. I'll tell ya one thing. He sure does change my outlook about this place." She slides over closer to Kaitlyn and confides, "To be honest, in a way, I'm in need of a place to stay for a while, and I was hoping that Billy would let me hang out here. If JD is as interested as you think he is, then he might be able to help me out with my little dilemma."

"Yeah, well I have the same dilemma, and I don't have a potential new boyfriend to give me a reference." Kaitlyn's tone suddenly becomes as depressed as her change in attitude.

"Don't you worry about a thing, Kaitlyn? Billy is not the type of guy who would turn you away, especially after giving his word. Me, on the other hand, I'm the one who screwed up my situation at school. I'm the one who needs someone standing in my corner."

"Oh, don't give me that," Kaitlyn scoffs, "If Billy is the guy that you say he is, then he wouldn't turn you away either."

"I know, but I was trying to keep from sounding pathetic by riding your wave in here." Seeing movement out the corner of her eye, Saphyre whips her head around to see JD's head rising up through the trap door in the floor. She jumps to her feet, almost hitting her head on the low ceiling and demands, "JD Johnston, were you eavesdropping on our conversation?"

Laughing to himself about her close call with the ceiling, JD quickly regains his composure to throw his hands up in defense, and declare, "Whoa, I just came out here to let you know that Billy wants to see y'all." Catching himself, JD climbs on up into the cramped space. "Seriously, I didn't hear what you were saying. Isaiah said that you were down here, so when I heard you talking I climbed up." Then he says to himself, "But don't worry, Saphyre, I'll stand in your corner."

Saphyre, wearing a devilish grin, motions for Kaitlyn to join her at the window. Knowing her new friend's capabilities, Saphyre watches JD look around and reaches out the window to grab a rope while he wasn't looking at her. When he finally looks back, Saphyre gives him a warning in a playful tone, saying, "You just better watch your step with us, mister!" With that, she leaps out the window allowing the rope to lower her slowly and safely to the ground. Kaitlyn follows Saphyre's lead, leaping through the window to the ground below with ease.

With the mechanics of the tree house in proper working order, Saphyre's action secures the trap door in the floor, when she hooks the knotted end of the rope on a forked branch below. Laughing at JD's problem, the girls take off running to the house, laughing harder all the way.

Kaitlyn motions for Saphyre to wait for a second, while she catches her breath on the other side of the pasture. "Hold on," she instructs bending over while trying not to laugh. "How did you know how to do that?"

"Billy did that to me, a long time ago," Saphyre replies, while trying to curb her laughing as well. "To be honest, I've waited about nine years for a chance to use that on someone."

Chapter IX

In Boston, a black Mercedes races through town from the private air field, heading for Margaret's downtown penthouse. Looking at her watch, she is trying to keep a careful check of the time, knowing that everything must be kept on schedule. She taps on the privacy screen between her and the driver to get his attention, as the car pulls up in front of her building. "Wait right here, Stewart. I'll be right back out in just a few minutes," she instructs before the window's fully down.

"Yes Ma'am," the driver replies, knowing that he is going to be getting another parking violation while waiting for her.

Out of the car she hurries, nearly catching her jacket with the car door, and then nearly breaks her leg, when she twists her ankle in her high heeled shoe. "Easy there, Ms. Stanford," the doorman warns, rushing to her aid. Sure that she was alright, he opens the door and asks, "Other than that, how was your day?"

"To be honest with you, Lawrence, the best part of it is that this day isn't over yet. Unfortunately, I'm running late as usual." Her anxiety for her unusual time restraints is not uncommon sights to the building's employees. They know Margaret to be the busy Corporate CEO that she is, and her trips rushing through the lobby are an every day occurrence. She stops at the elevator and pushes the call button before turning around to see the concierge watching her from behind the main desk. She gives her a cordial nod, and the act is returned before Margaret enters the elevator to take her trip up to heaven.

She inserts her key card into the appropriate slot on the elevator control panel and pushes the button, anxious for the doors to be closing. By using her card, the elevator is sent on a nonstop journey to her penthouse home in the clouds, avoiding any and all delays and interruptions.

This time is different though. Margaret isn't late for a board meeting, or is hurrying off to some social affair. No, she has but one reason for this little side visit to Boston of grander scheme and profit. There is something here that she needs for the trip to New Orleans. A trinket, or bauble, and nothing more really. What it is, basically, was considered to be a worthless object years ago that was discarded into the trash, not once, but twice. But to Margaret, it is the most valuable treasure in the world. It is the item that she believes has reintroduced Margaret to her mother, but more importantly it gives her what she needs.

Straight to the painting hanging over the head of her bed she goes. With no regard for the value of the framed art, she slings the painting across the room to get to the safe in the wall behind it. Once the combination is entered on the digital lock, the thick steel door swings open to reveal a single item inside. Margaret stares at the aura illuminating the confines of the safe, and then hurries to reach inside to retrieve her treasure. The moment her fingers touch the glass orb, she is washed over by an intoxicating feeling of strength and power. With a newfound sense of strength, she is now ready to carry out this part of the grand scheme.

Walking into the bathroom to check her hair and makeup, she finds her mother waiting for her, unexpected and undesired. "Where are you going with that?"

"I need its strength, for me to make it the rest of the way through this plan of yours," Margaret declares, with a tone of defiance.

"And I told you that there is no way for you to do that," Jezana corrects. "Lord Mysery is weak from trying to maintain his control over his minions, but he would sense the presence of your treasure all the same. If he did, my plot, our plot, would be discovered and end with failure. Doesn't it seem foolish to jeopardize your quest for power?" Jezana smiles at Margaret and then motions for the Callistone heir to hold her bauble out in front of her. When she does, Jezana waves her hand at the glass orb, causing it to produce a blinding flash of light. When the illumination subsides, Margaret stands even more confident and feels stronger than before, staring at the image of Jezana in the mirror. "Go now, my daughter, and fulfill your destiny. You now possess the strength you need to carry out my plan with ease."

Chapter X

In the kitchen of Billy's home, he stands firm with his decision, regardless of how Isaiah may disagree with it. He may respect Isaiah with no limit or boundaries, but this matter is simply out of the old man's jurisdiction. "I'm sorry, Isaiah, but now is not the time for this debate. If I remember correctly, you were the one who begged me to bring Saphyre home to you. And now you suggest that I take her right back into the hell that we're going to face?"

Isaiah shoves his hat back onto his head to make sure that Billy can see how he feels about this. "Don't go twistin' my words around, William. There's a difference between Saphyre going along to entertain, Miss Kaitlyn, and you dragging her into the mess you're gonna be in."

"Listen I appreciate what you're trying to say, I really do. But I gave Commander Ryker my word that Kaitlyn could, and would, stay here until everything is straightened out. I'm not about to resume my former ways of going against my word, and haul her off to New Orleans with me." Billy wants this debate to end more than anything at this moment. He stretches his arms over his head to test his limits. "Isaiah, I really need you to do this for me, and keep an eye on her. The last thing I need is to be worried about her welfare, while I'm trying to do whatever it is that I'm going to be doing. Saphyre will be here to entertain the girl and keep her out of your hair. Believe me, I've got enough to worry about having JD and Taylor involved."

"Hey," Taylor pipes in, "me and JD can take care of ourselves, thank you very much!"

Oops, a man should remember to choose his words a little more carefully when his lady is in the room, especially when she has the ability to crush him with her bare hands. Now he isn't sure if he should remove his foot from his mouth to save face, or leave it there to keep Taylor from ripping his face off. Slowly turning to face her, while trying to keep his toes off his tongue, figuratively speaking, he defends, "And I know that, baby. That's why I agreed to include you and JD in the first place. Still, that doesn't mean that I won't be worried about you. Hell, I thought I had lost you forever, and just got you back."

"Good recovery, kid," Isaiah declares seeing how Billy's words quickly returned the smile to Taylor's face.

Turning back to face Isaiah, Billy asks one more time, "Please, will you do this for me?"

Isaiah looks out the kitchen window and sees the two teen girls coming in from the pasture. "Billy, I have never led you wrong, but if you won't listen to reason, then I guess I don't have any other choice but to respect your wishes. After all, you are the boss around here." Hearing the hinges of the Kitchen door squeak as it opens, Isaiah turns around to see Saphyre and Kaitlyn walking into the kitchen. "Hello kitten, where's is Jefferson? He went out looking for the two of you."

"He should be in soon, Grandpa," Saphyre answers, while giving Kaitlyn a facetious grin. When Kaitlyn giggles a little, Saphyre redirects her attention to Billy and Taylor and asks, "JD said that you wanted to talk to us about something, so what's up?"

"Yeah, but first," Billy looks passed the girls at the kitchen door and asks, "Where is JD?"

"I'm here, Billy," JD responds, rushing in from the back porch. Billy just shrugs his shoulders wondering how the girls managed to beat him to the house. JD looks at the girls and then simply replies, "don't ask."

Looking back to the girls it's easy for Billy to see that there is something going on between the three of them, based on how Kaitlyn and Saphyre are snickering at JD's apparent misfortune. "Any way, something has come up. Me, Taylor, and JD, are gonna be gone for a few days. Saphyre, Kaitlyn, my house is your house. Saphyre, your grandfather will be here every day until we return if you girls need anything."

Recalling what Saphyre had said about them becoming some kind of superhero team, Kaitlyn quickly crosses through that open door to thank Billy for his hospitality. If nothing else, Going with them would keep her mind off her dismal situation. "Hey Billy, I just wanted to let you know that I really appreciate everything that you've done for me. In return, if there is something, anything I can do to help, all you have to do is ask, okay?" Maybe this could be a way to ease her mind. She looks over at Saphyre for a little support, but not much is offered when her new friend just shrugs her shoulders. It's not that Saphyre doesn't support Kaitlyn's offer. She just didn't know that Kaitlyn was going to throw that out there, so Saphyre wasn't prepared. What Kaitlyn sees is Saphyre's attention is focused on JD, and thinks to herself, "I guess I'm more alone than I thought."

Billy hopes that she isn't talking about what he thinks she's talking about. Not wanting to give away his suspicions, Billy simply says, "That's sweet honey, but I've got this one covered for now. Like I said; just make yourselves at home.

When we get back, we can all sit down and work out our problems together. Once everyone is back on their feet, we can worry about who needs to go where and why. For now, this place is big enough for all of us, so no one needs to go worrying about making any further plans, or at least until we get back. Unless, of course, it's what you want to do. The door to my house is always open and it swings both ways. If you don't want to be here, then don't let that door come back on you, on your way out."

Billy watches as Isaiah silently dismisses himself from the small gathering to return to his duties, but Billy doesn't outwardly acknowledge the old man leaving. He appreciates Isaiah's concern about Kaitlyn being left behind, with the girl in such a vulnerable state. But, Billy has to continue what he's started, and that is to keep as many people as possible out of harm's way. "Hey Taylor, why don't you and JD go get what you need, and we'll head out in a few minutes."

The time has come for Taylor to state her final concerns more clearly about this little venture that they are going on. With everyone else clearing out of the kitchen, she leans in close to Billy's ear and whispers, "Are you sure you don't want to at least wait until tomorrow to leave? I'm sure that another good night's rest would heal ya up that much more." She knows that Billy's urgency is just in his eyes, because of Scotty being involved now. The problem is that she can't shake the feeling that he is dismissing his own needs with this hasty decision and that could jeopardize JD and Taylor, if the perfect set of circumstances were to arise. The question of the moment is whether Isaiah was saying what he said because he wanted to be rid of Kaitlyn, or because he thinks Billy is worse off than they all think. Could they use, or need, what help the girls could offer? Was this Isaiah's way of saying so?

Waiting at the kitchen entrance, JD can see how Taylor's question pains Billy. Moving in to rescue Billy, JD grabs Taylor and coaxes her on out of the kitchen, "Come on, girl, so we can get on the road. Now isn't the time to be questioning him," he points out, pulling her away from Billy. "I saw the look on his face. There isn't anything or anyone who is going to change his mind. Maybe you might know what it is between him and Scotty that might shed some light on what we face. There is a lot more involved with this trip than you realize, and we may be the ones who need him to bail us out. I just want to get this over as soon as possible with no one else getting hurt in the process." Spotting Saphyre nonchalantly hovering around at the bottom of the stairs, JD adds, "The sooner we get back the better."

As expected, Saphyre steps up to JD politely blocking his path. "JD, can I talk to you for a second?" Her sheepish manner is spotted by Taylor, who smiles at JD and Saphyre as if she recognized what is taking place between the two of them.

"Taylor, you go ahead. I'll be up in a minute." JD sees Taylor's smile and becomes very suspicious about its meaning. Was she picking up on the energy between Saphyre and him, or did Taylor think that he was acting like some love struck fool? Seeing similar personality traits in Saphyre that Taylor recognizes in herself, she understands the necessity the young lady has to talk to JD alone. Respecting their need for privacy, Taylor heads on upstairs as JD walks over to meet Saphyre half way. "What is it, Saphyre? I really don't have a lot of time, if Billy wants to leave right away."

Saphyre can sense that something is troubling JD, which raises her suspicions about where they're going and how dangerous it will be for JD. "Okay, well would you mind if we talked while you put together your overnight bag?" The question is followed, in her mind, with the plea, "Please say yes, please say yes!"

"Alright, but just remember that I'm still ticked at you about being locked in the tree house." There, that can give him a little distance and still offer some sort of explanation about why he wants that distance between them. Demonstrating his abilities as a gentleman, he places one hand in the small of her back, and then waves her on upstairs first. With a smile as a reply, Saphyre takes off leading JD up to his room.

As if she was doing something wrong, Saphyre stops at his doorway and looks around before entering his room. The ironic part is that she wasn't sure if she was hoping no one saw her, or that someone did see her because she wanted them to. Once inside, Saphyre closes the door and steps up behind JD before he could turn around. When he does, she throws herself into his arms and gives him a long and passionate kiss. Pulling away from him, she smiles and asks, "Doesn't that make up for the tree house?"

"Y-yeah," JD replies, being pleasantly surprised. "But seriously, what was that for?" He shakes his head a little to regain control of his senses, and then hurries over to the closet and grabs a prepacked tote bag, containing everything he needs for a trip like this.

"Well, I was hoping that it might persuade you to maybe get Billy to let me and Kaitlyn go with you guys." Displaying a bashful appearance, Saphyre sits down on the side of the bed and looks back at JD. "I'll go out of my mind sitting around here wondering when or if you were coming back?" She's already convinced that she knows what JD's answer was going to be, but figured it had to be worth a shot to ask any way. If she was right, at least she made her point known about how she feels, and that might give him the incentive to make it back alive.

"That's something that I can't do, Saphyre." That almost killed JD inside to say that. He opens the bag and double checks the contents, and then continues with, "Billy's decisions on this are final." There, that should take the heat off him. He walks over to the dresser doing everything he can to keep from running back over to Saphyre to take her in his arms. "Wow, what a kiss," he thinks to himself, while keeping his back to her, mainly so that she can't see the happy expression on his face. JD knows that now is not the time to be distracted by her, but it sure does feel good. That's it. He has so much that he wants to say, and he can sum it all up with, "Listen, I want you to know that part of me wants you to come with us." He turns around to face her as if performing a well rehearsed part. "But there is another part of me that knows I wouldn't be as effective for what we have to do, if I'm constantly worried about your welfare." There, that should tell her how he feels, and state his defense at the same time.

He looks at his watch signaling that it was time for him to go. He needs to catch up with Billy, before they leave. There is so much that he needs to say to his friend about what they are going into, and the last thing he needs right now is his thoughts all stirred up by a girl. Granted, she's not just any girl, but JD still doesn't have that luxury at the moment.

Somewhat relieved by his answer, Saphyre hops off the bed and hurries over to the door. "Well, in that case, be careful and hurry home. My lips will be here waiting for you." Saphyre closes her eyes for a moment and bites her tongue. Did she really just say that to him? Opening her eyes to see him staring back at her while wearing a big smile on his face only adds to her embarrassment.

Seize the moment, JD. "Okay, well I hope that the rest of you will be here as well." Recognizing her vulnerability, he gives her a wink, and then changes the topic of conversation to let both of them off the hook. "I'm gonna take the back stairs off the balcony and go throw my bag in Billy's car. Would you ask him to meet me by the corral? Tell him that I said it is imperative that I talk to him before we leave."

"Sure handsome," Saphyre turns around and walks right into the closed door. How much more humiliation must she suffer before this little interlude ends? She grabs the doorknob and never looks back at JD, but before she opens the door she concludes with, "Remember what I said, alright? I want you to come back here and stay for a while." Certain that she had made her point crystal clear; Saphyre exits the room and heads downstairs.

Through the living room and dining area she skips and hops, proud that she went as far as she did with her pursuit of JD. Now he knows where she stands, and she has a pretty good idea how JD feels about it, and it's looking really, really, good. Stopping at the kitchen doorway, she watches Billy going through a series of stretching exercises to try and work out some of the soreness in his body. "Not to butt in, or anything, but is it possible that Taylor might be right? Are you sure you're making the right decision by going after them again so soon?"

"Do us both a favor, little lady, and don't go down that road, okay?" Billy leans back against the sink cabinet and sees Kaitlyn out the corner of his eye, walking down by the barn.

"No problem with that, Billy Ray. JD said that you have the final say in everything that happens around here, so I know when to keep quiet. He also said that he needs to talk to you, and that he is waiting for you down by the corral." Saphyre starts to walk on through the kitchen but stops to ask one more question. "Tell me something Billy. What is it that is so special about your foster brother that you would risk everything again to go get him?"

Billy looks away before answering, almost as if he was embarrassed or ashamed of what that answer is. "Let's just say that he saved my life a long time ago and I have to do this to repay that debt."

"Billy, I'm ready to go," Taylor announces as she walks into the room. Thank God for perfect timing. She walks over and gives Billy a kiss on his cheek, and looks him over one time. She can't help but notice that he appears to be getting better, but she doesn't want to let on that she notices just yet. That way, she can continue to hound him about taking it easy for a little while longer. "Are you sure you're up to this? You don't look so hot right now."

Hoping to ease her worried mind, Billy throws out a confident smile and says, "Funny that you should ask that, baby. I was just telling Saphyre how good I feel, and that I think my healing attributes might be speeding up."

"Well, that's good, baby, I think. The way you get blown up all the time, your body is probably just trying to compensate." She too gives off a false sense of relief, hoping that she can find a way to slow him down. "Just promise me that you, I mean we, won't take any unnecessary risks, okay?"

"Alright," Billy acknowledges, "To honor your request, will you do me a favor and grab the grey nylon tote bag out of the bedroom closet. I'll go round up JD and meet you at the car. Okay?" He turns to face Saphyre, who was trying to slip out the back door. "Saphyre, we'll all catch up when we get back?"

Saphyre answers with a nod and hurries off out of the house as if she had somewhere to go. This gives Taylor the opening that she needed to swoop in on her man. After giving him a kiss on his cheek, she leans back and looks into his eyes. "Tell me that you are okay."

"I will be, but keep in mind that I'm just as worried about you and everyone else, Taylor. I can't even begin to think about what happened to you. JD has some kind of major guilt trip working him over. Saphyre is almost guaranteed some kind of need for therapy, and Kaitlyn, where do you begin with her?" Billy takes Taylor into his arms and holds her close, while trying not to let on about the pain caused by the action. "JD walks around here like he blames himself for mom's death. And me, I'm the poster boy for the walking dead," his statement causes Taylor to pull away. "According to you guys," he quickly amends. "I truly believe that the best place for the girls right now is here. You and JD are older and more experienced with these matters now. I'm hoping that your veteran edge can give you the strength to look passed what happened, so that we can focus on what we have to do." He looks into her eyes and brushes her auburn red hair away from her face. "But, if it makes you feel more comfortable, I promise you that no one will take any unnecessary risks. Deal?"

"Deal," she responds. Happy to oblige her man, Taylor hurries back upstairs to retrieve the tote bag in question. His words offered her no comfort, but the fact that he forced himself to say that for her benefit, does. It may not give her a new found sense of confidence, but it does make her feel like she is making the right decision.

Now he has to go find his new best friend. The first thing he needs to do is make sure JD is up for this. JD would suck in a poker game, and it's that shitty poker face that concerns Billy the most. Even as cordial as JD has been, Billy can see right through that façade and knows that something is wrong. The problem that Billy has with that is he doesn't know if he wants to hear what JD has to say, or not.

Regardless, whatever it is, Billy has to go listen to what JD has to say. Billy owes JD that much, after all that he has done for Billy, and all that JD went through. So, out the kitchen door Billy goes, trying his best not to aggravate his wounds as he traverses down the back porch steps. He stops to look around the ranch for a moment; it's as if Billy recognizes a change taking place. Is it something about the weather, with the deep blue sky littered with fast moving clouds, or is it a feeling of change coming in his future? Could he be sensing something about what they are embarking on? No, that's not it, as far as Billy is concerned. If he can't see it, touch it, or at least get three verifications, Billy isn't going to start believing in such nonsense. This little trip to the Big Easy is cut and dried as far as he is concerned. One way or another, this ends in New Orleans.

Once he clears the stables, Billy finds JD exactly where Saphyre said he would be, standing beside the corral adjacent to the barn. "What are you doing, trying to earn favors by buddying up to my horse? Believe me; he doesn't have any clout around here." Moving closer, Billy can see the distress on JD's face. Whatever is bothering him, JD needs to get it off his chest. Billy is here and willing to hear him out no matter how painful it will be. "Hey, Saphyre said that you wanted to talk to me," he admits, walking up beside JD at the corral fencing.

Chapter XI

In the short time that he has known Billy, JD's strong suit has not been the element of surprise when it comes to matters of conversation. Today, he catches Billy completely off guard, causing him to take a step back when JD spins around to face to face Billy. The time has come for JD to spill his guts about what he knows. There is no way for him to deny how he feels about this, even though he can't explain why he feels the way he does. "I've tried to keep something from you Billy, mainly about what we faced in New York." He pauses for a moment and looks away, almost like he was ashamed of what he is going to say. "I'm sorry Billy, but I haven't told you everything. In my defense, it was because I didn't know if you would believe me." That hurts, saying something like that to the man you call friend and ally. He turns away from Billy to hide his pain of his confession, and then turns back around to offer his defense. "There were too many events that happened while we were in New York that were, or are, tied to something else. Then, something happened when we got back home from up north. I believe that there is so much more involved with this trip to New Orleans than you or I would've dreamed." Staring off at the tree line behind the barn, JD tries to gather his thoughts for what he needs to say next. For a split second, he thought that he saw someone or something moving through the shadows of the trees.

Wow, this was right out of left field, and nothing like what Billy could have expected. He thought maybe that it would be something about Billy's health, or possibly that JD had reached his limit and couldn't go this round, but not that his new friend had been keeping the truth from him. Not knowing whether he should be offended or not, Billy simply suggests, "Whatever it is that you need to say, just say it, JD. I want to leave as soon as possible." To Billy's surprise, JD walks around the corner of the barn to get a better view of the trees. "Hello, Jefferson, what are you looking at?"

"Nothing, I guess," JD replies as he turns to face Billy again. "Okay," he takes a deep breath and continues. "This is the only way I know how to say this, but your world has somehow crossed over with what Nick is involved with facing his destiny." That's the point where JD expected to lose Billy's faith, trust, and respect, but like Isaiah said, he has to follow through with this. "While we were in Atlanta, and New York, there were these incidents that took place that you need to know about. Remember in Atlanta when I had that little conflict in the garage at the mobster's house? The men, and that lady, were possessed by demon spirits like the ones me and Nick faced in Japan." On a roll, and still keeping Billy's attention, JD keeps going with his train of thought. "In New York, where we found Agent Justice, the men you saw falling off the roof were more of the same. The mercenary chick I fought where we rescued Taylor and the others, you can add her to the list as well." JD pauses for a moment as the feeling of a massive weight is lifted from his shoulders. "Now, before you start to analyze everything, let me finish. They knew who I was, like they were all part of some collective mind. They knew that I was the student of Nick, and that I still played some role in what is going to happen."

Even though he had been lulled into staring at the tree line behind the property, Billy still heard every word that JD had said. His silence at the moment is due to the fact that he was wondering if he should be expecting intruders or not. One thing is for certain though; no matter how hard he wanted to discredit everything JD said, Billy cannot deny any longer what he saw when Pantera was killed. This is one incident that he cannot explain with logic and deduction, and that irritates the crap out of him. Had he not seen Pantera's unholy resurrection, Billy would probably turn and walk away from JD and never look back. Instead, without facing JD, Billy asks, "Is there anything else?"

Now there is the question of the hour, and Billy just gave JD the biggest opening he could ask for. Not sure which way Billy expected this to go, JD just continues on his path already taken and proceeds to throw it all out there. "As a matter of fact, your buddies I met on the side of the road, before you showed up, they too were warriors of darkness. Before you and I met, I had a dream that Nick's teacher came to me, to tell me that my destiny is to serve as the conscience of the unlikely ally."

"Well, you know what they say; if the shoe fits, wear it," Billy suggests, never looking back at his friend.

Looking over at Billy, JD sees that his friend is now staring at the woods too, and is inclined to return his gaze to the trees while asking, "What are you looking at?" JD asks, now unsure if he did see something earlier, and now Billy sees it as well.

"I was trying to figure out what you were looking at." Billy walks back over to the corral fencing and leans up against it. He stares at JD's face trying to figure out what is truth and what JD believes to be true. With what he knows weighing in on his silent debate, everything Billy sees tells him that JD is telling the truth, no matter how hard it is to believe.

"Correct me if I'm wrong, but you don't seem to be shocked and surprised by all of this, are you?" JD expresses, taking notice to Billy's undisturbed attitude.

Billy chuckles and smiles at JD as if he had some kind of small confession of his own. The time has come for Billy to give up his secrets as well. "Remember those two names I gave you?" Billy looks away as if he can't believe that he is gonna go there. "Well, here's how I came up with them. Do you remember the big black guy that was sidestepping with Crossfire?"

"Yeah, judging by his accent, he was British, or maybe Australian," JD answers, curious to where Billy was going with this.

"That's the guy. Any way, he and I got into a scuffle when I took chase after Crossfire." Billy looks at JD with a straight face devoid of emotion. "I put the guy down, JD, and I mean in a way that you don't get up from, ever. Now, I'm not bragging about that, but during the fight, he went to the floor and was skewered through his chest by a broken chair leg." Looking at the ground, Billy tries to hide his embarrassment for what he is about to admit. "Seeing the guy down, I figured that I should resume my chase after Crossfire. Then, that dead sonofabitch in the room literally came back to life and gave me some kind of crazy hoo doo warning. Brother, I've seen some crazy shit since I started this Kamikaze crusade, but I've never seen anything like that, ever! To be honest, I'm still having a hard time with it, and I saw it happen with my own eyes." Billy turns away and faces his horse to scratch the magnificent beast's nose. "JD, the thing that crawled out of Pantera's body referred to me as the unlikely ally, and that I couldn't stop what is inevitable to come. Your stories about Nick, and what the two of you faced, seem way over the top.

But now, I find it hard to discredit any of it, no matter how hard I try. Then, to top it all off, you come up with that same name tag, and it's like a slap in my face." This time Billy is the one who looks to JD to see if he is the one disbelieving.

"Okay, that brings me to the dream sequence I had the night we returned from New York. To be honest with you, I was almost ready to write it all off, trying to believe that it was my mind playing tricks on me." Looking towards the back of the house to see Taylor exiting the back porch, after the screen door slams shut. With her heading their way, JD sees the necessity to speed up his pace of explanation. "It was a warning, and I'm almost sure that it is about our trip to New Orleans. The voice said that we can't prevent what will happen, but you most of all must not fall to the dark forces waiting for us.

Billy turns around to look at JD for clarification, and sees Taylor approaching. Lowering his voice, Billy mutters a single name, "Masamoto?"

"Nope, this guy said his name was Hyldegaarn, but I think that him and Masamoto hang out together," JD replies as Taylor walks up. He looks to Billy for a topic suggestion, unsure how much Billy wants Taylor to know about this. She should know, or at least JD feels that way, if she's going off into this mess with him and Billy. Still, JD respects the fact that it is Billy's call to make.

"Well, all of this makes it sound like a no win situation. You know how I feel about that, don't ya baby?" Billy asks her with a smile. Together, he and Taylor chime in together, with Taylor a little less enthusiastic, saying, "Captain James T. Kirk once said that there is no such thing as a no win scenario."

Her first priority is Billy. She can't deny that he seems to be doing better by the minute. Walking right up to him, she gives Billy a kiss, and then looks at JD as if he is the cause for the delay. "I've been waiting for you guys by the car for the last five minutes. What are y'all talking about?"

"But we saw you walk out of the house," JD defends.

"That's because I had to go back inside and pee," she declares to justify her actions. She looks back at Billy and wishes they could just go back into the house together, so that he could make her forget everything that has happened as of late. But, she knows that this is what Billy has to do, and it must be done before she and him can resume their lives together. "Are we ready to go?"

The little voice in the back of his mind tells him to latch onto her and never let go. The problem is that right now he has to stay focused on what is going on with Scotty. That's already a tough thing to do, especially after the conversation he has been having with JD. Never the less, he returns her kiss and puts his arm around her shoulder. "Come on, we'll fill you in once we get on the road." Looking back at JD, Billy finishes off their conversation with, "We go at this with Scotty as our first priority. Anything after that will just be the next in line." Out the corner of his eye, Billy can see Isaiah standing at the corner of the barn watching the trio make way for their departure. Billy wishes he could make the old man understand why Billy has made the decisions in play. It is then that he sees Taylor staring at the woods. "What is it, Taylor? What are you looking at?"

"It's probably nothing, but I thought I saw someone watching us from the trees. It was probably Kaitlyn wandering around down there. I feel really bad about leaving her here alone." Taking the lead, Taylor starts for the stable where Billy parks his car.

Billy and JD however look at each other for some kind of confirmation, and then say in unison, "Oh, it was Kaitlyn." Billy looks back at the barn to see that Isaiah had vanished again, as he usually does, which is good for Billy this time.

He had hoped that he could avoid another confrontation with the ranch manager, mainly because deep down inside part of him thinks that Isaiah may be right. On the other hand, hearing what JD had to say only added strength to Billy's stand about the girls' involvement. Even though it didn't come out in their earlier conversation, Billy knows that Isaiah has plenty to do around here besides babysitting two teenage girls. If JD is right, then New Orleans is the last place those girls need to be, and Billy isn't about to put the Saphyre and Kaitlyn in any more trouble.

Chapter XII

Standing just inside the barn doors, Saphyre suddenly feels the looming presence of her grandfather walking up behind her. Stepping over into the shadows, she thinks that she has avoided his detection and watches as he stays just out of sight on the other side of the barn, as Billy and the others walk by. Feeling that he was as guilty as she was, Saphyre walks on over to Isaiah wanting to get the drop on him first. "Hey Grandpa, what'cha doin'?" The fact that the old man doesn't even flinch isn't surprising to her. In fact, she isn't sure what surprises her most about this situation. On one hand, Isaiah appears to be spying on Billy and the others. On the other hand, he is moving and twisting his body, as if he is offering some kind of psychic support for Taylor, when she backs Billy's Camaro out of the stable stall. Was he worried about the car, or the building around it? Then Saphyre notices how her grandfather cringes when Billy climbs into the passenger seat of the car, after JD climbs into the back. "Don't worry about Billy, Grandpa. He's gonna be just fine. You wait and see."

Her sugar coated statement doesn't hide her unexplained presence in the barn. Isaiah turns to face the young lady wearing his concern on his face. "What were you doing out here in this barn, Saphyre Marie?"

"What? Oh, I was out here looking for Kaitlyn. She wandered out of the kitchen right after you left." Saphyre bats her eyes at her grandfather, as if stating that her alibi is sound, and at the same time trying to hide her anxiety for Billy and JD's conversation. "You haven't seen her, have you?"

"Don't be inviting yourself into other people's conversations. Chances are that you might not like what you hear." Isaiah turns and walks away, but still offers the information that Saphyre needs, as he makes his departure. "As for your little friend, I saw her wandering down along the trees. If you go down there, y'all be sure to watch for snakes."

"Snakes; after what she heard Billy and JD talking about, the last thing she is worried about is snakes. What if the bad guys come looking for Billy, while they are in New Orleans? The bad guys would find her and Kaitlyn alone at the ranch, that's what they'd find. Yep, that's the deciding factor. Sure JD might be heading right into the middle of hell on earth, but Saphyre would rather be there with him at her side, instead of here alone, facing the unknown. The question now is, can she find a way to get away from the ranch, and convince Kaitlyn that it's the right thing for her to do, which is accompany Saphyre to New Orleans. Whether or not it's the right thing for Saphyre to do never enters the young woman's equation for an instant.

"To wander; to move about aimlessly with no direction or purpose." This is the best description of Kaitlyn at the moment that everyone on the ranch has pointed out. Only now, she is deep in the woods that border the north side of Billy's property and she has no way of determining her point of origin. The bare oaks and tall pines scrape and rattle their branches together, creating a woodland melody of, rap, tap, tap, scrape, rap, tap, tap. Mesmerized by the melodic rhythms, Kaitlyn soon found herself meandering aimlessly between the trees.

The air has a certain chill to it, but she is able to find warmth by moving from one patch of sunlight to the next. This act is the primary suspect for leading her deeper into the woods. Seeking warmth from the rays of the sun was her concern, and at the time she really didn't care which direction she was heading. The problem now is that her trek to follow the sun's warmth has taken her so deep into the woods, that all of a sudden the canopy of pines thickened up blocking out all of the sunlight. She wonders if this is how Hansel and Gretel saw their surroundings as they wandered through the forest.

Adding to the fairytale setting, this is the spot where she found a female deer. Kaitlyn first saw the woodland creature drinking at the edge of the stream that cuts through the woods, to empty into Billy's pond. Kaitlyn has never seen a wild animal this close to her, without it being behind some kind of fencing in the zoo. This is a first, and it is a very intriguing moment for her.

At first, the doe looked at Kaitlyn as if trying to determine her reason for being in the woods. It then proceeded to stare at the teenager for several more seconds, without moving a muscle. When it had finally determined that Kaitlyn was no threat, the deer resumed its drinking before beginning a quest for food. It stops a few feet away from the water's edge, to nibble on some tender grasses. Then, it looks back at Kaitlyn again, almost like it was inviting her to follow along.

Intrigued, Kaitlyn begins her pursuit of the deer, amazed at how it didn't seem to mind her presence. It's not like

Kaitlyn wanted or intended to frighten the creature. She had heard how wild animals would always run away at the first sight of a human. In a way, Kaitlyn found it sort of soothing that the deer seemed to accept her as just another creature of the forest, and neither posed any sort of threat to one another. This is definitely a new sensation for Kaitlyn. In a way, it's kind of sad that an animal can accept you for what you are without judgment, and humans find it necessary to pass judgment before all else.

As she watched and followed the deer, Kaitlyn pondered her thoughts of the moment, which are of her life and its outcome so far. How did everything go from crap to total shit so quickly? Her friends, what's left of her family, her home, it's all gone and Kaitlyn isn't sure how to get any of it back. Well, unfortunately she already knows that she can never get her father back. As far as her sister is concerned, Kaitlyn doesn't want her back, at least not any time soon.

Then there are her friends or at least those alive. The hardest part is that she never got to say goodbye to Toby. He has always been her best friend, being able to see Kaitlyn for who she really is. She knows that Amanda blames her for a portion of the crap, but Kaitlyn also knows that Amanda's accusations are unjust. When Amanda and Henry were arrested, Amanda is the one who lost her cool and rushed back into the conflict. Had she followed orders, Henry wouldn't have gone back in to pull Amanda out. In doing so, Henry only sealed his fate, along with Amanda, when they were taken down and into custody. There was nothing that Kaitlyn and Toby could have done. Kaitlyn had already made the call to fall back and was well on her way out of the conflict with Toby, when Amanda decided to go back in for round two. The result was simply a TKO.

Suddenly, her thoughts are drawn back to the deer in front of her, when Kaitlyn realizes that the animal was now standing there frozen with fear. Without warning the doe looks at Kaitlyn and gives her a growling snort, and then breaks to run off into the woods. Something spooked the deer to cause it to run away like that, and whatever it was, it's enough to send Kaitlyn into a panic. Not knowing the region or wildlife, she was coming up with all sorts of wild predators that could be creeping around the woods.

Looking around for any signs of danger, while trying to get her bearings, Kaitlyn takes notice to the fact that the woods themselves were looking different, almost ominous in appearance. The shadows constantly continue to change shape as the trees moved with the wind. Coupled with the sound of the trees rubbing and scraping against each other only added to her growing paranoia.

Then, to make matters worse, just as she is getting her bearings and determines which way the house is, Kaitlyn catches a glimpse of something moving through the tops of the trees, off to her left side. This fairytale appears to be taking on a darker nature. Slowly, she turns to investigate, hoping and praying that she isn't going to see some wild beast ready to pounce on her. A grateful sigh rushes from her lungs when all she sees is the trees and their changing shadows. Still, just to be sure, she continues to scan the branches just to be sure that nothing was overlooked. That's when she notices how one shadows never moves, remaining steadfast against the upper trunk of the oak tree in front of her. It is then that Kaitlyn sees a pair of red eyes appear staring right back at her.

Fear takes control as she is reminded of the pairs of eyes she saw in Bruno Campano's gym, back in New York. This is more than a big rat, and there is nothing to say that it is some kind of predatorial animal. No, this is something dark and imposing; creating a fear deep down inside of Kaitlyn that boils up and sends her running off into the woods, hopefully headed back towards the safety of Billy's house. She isn't sure about what she saw, but she is willing to bet that whatever it is, was responsible for scaring off the deer. It's definitely scaring the hell out of Kaitlyn right now.

Of course, running blind through the woods isn't the smartest thing to do, but at the moment Kaitlyn doesn't see how she has any other choice. Tree limbs slap and scratch at her face and arms as she forces her way through the underbrush of the woods. To her luck, Kaitlyn finds the stream again where she first encountered the deer. Knowing that this is the water source that feeds the Ranch's pond, Kaitlyn is sure that it will lead her to safety. Looking up she sees the ghostly shadow swoop in over her and then hover in the air in front of Kaitlyn, blocking her path of retreat.

The demon's eyes flash a brighter tone of red, and then a ghastly howl is heard echoing through the woods before it starts to move towards her again. Kaitlyn screams, as anyone would normally do, and then takes off running across the stream to get away from the demonic spirit that is haunting her. Her panic sends her crashing into the water with her feet slipping on the algae covered rocks in the stream, but Kaitlyn doesn't let that stop her. Scrambling back up to her feet, she takes off again not even noticing the frigid temperatures of the water bighting at her skin.

For the moment, no other suffering registers in her mind while she stays focused on her need to get out of these woods, and more importantly how that need outweighs everything else. As she reaches a small rise, Kaitlyn is forced to look back to see if the spirit pursuing her was still in sight. To her surprise and relief, she sees no signs of danger looking back down into the shallow gully. Unfortunately that is because the spirit chasing her had already gained ground and was now hovering in the air just out of sight above her. Fearing a trip back through the same woods that she had just run through,

Kaitlyn decides to continue on her current path, hoping to avoid any more confrontations.

As she turns to continue on, the demon spirit drops down in front of her, and lets out a horrific sound to intimidate Kaitlyn even more. Unfortunately for her, it works. The scared young lady turns, trips, and is sent rolling down the hill to the bottom of the gully, where she scrambles to her feet to continue her race for safety. But now, Kaitlyn has lost all manner of self control, as she flails about through the trees and bushes that are stationed along her path. Her tears blind her eyes. Her crying makes it hard to breath. Surely she is a prime candidate for the demon's assault.

Finally, the stream comes back into view giving Kaitlyn some small sense of hope. Forced by some primordial need to know, she looks back again hoping to see that the spirit was gone again. This time its presence is visible for Kaitlyn to see, and it is closing in on her with dark intent.

Reaching the stream at a full sprint, she remembers the slick rocks and the result of her last attempt to cross the waters. With no time to stop, Kaitlyn simply leaps into the air trying to clear the stream. Had she not been in a panic, if her focus and concentration were not on her fear and anxiety, Kaitlyn could have easily cleared the stream, and probably leapt clear of the entire forest. Unfortunately, she doesn't have that luxury at the moment, and turns her ankle on a large rock at the water's edge. She managed to clear the water, but now her landing is sending her back down to the ground where she lies looking straight up into the sky.

This gives her a perfect view of the demon spirit as it swoops in for the kill. Crawling over to the safety of some undermined tree roots, Kaitlyn can hear the howl of the demon again as it closes in, sending a cold chill down her back. Curled up in a fetal position, she hides her face away from the impending doom, saying over and over, "I don't believe. I don't believe!" Even so, she hears the demon moving through the air, as it gets closer and closer. Again she tries to convince herself, "I don't believe," but it doesn't help her in any way. Then, a cold chill washes over her, and the event ends in an instant, with Kaitlyn still muttering, "I don't believe, I don't believe, I don't believe, I don't…"

"Kaitlyn, oh my God, are you alright?" Saphyre rushes over to her friend, shocked and surprised by her condition. Fortunately for Kaitlyn, the sound of Saphyre's voice snaps the hold fear has over her, bringing the distraught teenager back to reality. Her first gesture is to grab Saphyre with both hands, and then pulls her down to the ground where Kaitlyn applies an overzealous hug. "Easy, girl, what has got you so upset?" Saphyre pulls away from her friend after a second or two, examines Kaitlyn more closely, and quickly takes notice to her emotional state. Kaitlyn was terrified of something and Saphyre wasn't sure if she really wanted to know what it is.

"We have to get out of here!" The distraught girl declares as she smears the mud of tears and dirt across her cheeks. "We have to leave here now, Saphyre, I want to go away now!" Kaitlyn stands up and spins quickly in a circle searching the trees for any sign of her ghostly pursuer. Her actions are that of a crazed lunatic, as Kaitlyn moves about as if she doesn't know where to go. What could possibly have scared her this bad?

"Sure, Kaitlyn, let's get you back up to the house so that we can calm you down. Then you can tell me all about it. After that, we'll discuss the possibility of relocating, because I've got something to talk about as well." Saphyre is becoming very uneasy as well, feeding off Kaitlyn's fear and anxiety. The sooner the two of them are out of the woods, the better. "Can you walk? You can put your arm around my shoulder if you need to."

Instead, Kaitlyn takes Saphyre's hand and urges her to lead them out of the woods. All the while, Kaitlyn constantly scans the trees for any signs of the demon presence. To Saphyre's surprise, Kaitlyn suddenly releases her grip on her friend, when the two girls break through the edge of the trees, and see the sanctuary that is the McBride ranch. At first, Saphyre is a little agitated by Kaitlyn's departure, but then realizes that if she was as scared as Kaitlyn appeared to be, then she would have probably run off like that too. Then Saphyre gets the notion that she is the one who should be following Kaitlyn's lead and get away from the trees as soon as possible.

Once up onto the back porch, Kaitlyn turns around and looks back at the tree line once more to make sure that they aren't being followed. With her paranoia is satisfied, she turns and enters the house ready to close the door and lock it before Saphyre can enter the kitchen. "Whoa there, girl. At least let me get inside!"

Kaitlyn just stands there staring at Saphyre for a moment, and then bursts into uncontrollable laughter. She doesn't know why. Perhaps it is just a nervous response for what happened to her. Maybe it's because she is happy to know that they made it back to the house without another confrontation. Maybe she's just happy to be alive. Whatever the reason, Saphyre finds it hard not to laugh along, until Kaitlyn's laughter perverts to a sad sobbing as she collapses to the floor. "I'm sorry, Saphyre, but I think I'm losing my mind. Maybe it's just the full effect of what has happened to me, to us, but I don't think I can stay here."

Saphyre kneels beside her friend and does her best to comfort her. This doesn't mean that she doesn't recognize the possible opening to state her case. "I think I know what you mean, but just to be sure, tell me what happened out there in the woods, okay? Then I'll tell you what I know and we can go from there."

Wiping her tears away, Kaitlyn looks at Saphyre and wonders how much of her story would she believe? "You'll never believe me," she declares, feeling as if her effort would be futile.

"Sister, after everything I've seen and heard over the past two weeks, I'll believe just about anything." Taking notice to how Kaitlyn was shivering from her cold wet clothes, Saphyre motions for her to stand up. "Come on, Kaitlyn," She suggests, "Let's get you upstairs and changed into something warmer. Maybe then you'll feel more like talking." Leading Kaitlyn upstairs, Saphyre takes the initiative to undress first when they reach the bedroom that the two girls share. Her clothes aren't wet, but she is more than ready to slip into something more comfortable and warm just the same. This also breaks the ice between her and Kaitlyn, giving her friend reason to follow suit.

"Ya know, you've got a great body," Kaitlyn points out. "Have you ever considered modeling?" She pulls her wet shirt and sweater over her head and grabs an oversized flannel shirt to put on. "I've got an agent, well, he's not really my agent, but he can line you up some photo shoots, if you're interested."

Slightly embarrassed by Kaitlyn's observation, Saphyre quickly pulls up her pajama bottoms and sits down on the bed. "No thanks, I get a serious case of camera shy when I know that they are pointed at me. Are you feeling better?"

"Yeah, but I still want to get outta here. I'm sorry but after what I saw out there in the woods, I don't think I can stay here." Kaitlyn slips into a pair of sweat pants and sits down on the bed beside Saphyre.

"Okay, but you have to tell me what you saw out there." Saphyre gives every possible body signal to state that Kaitlyn has her complete and undivided attention.

"Maybe you should go first," Kaitlyn suggests, hoping to delay the inevitable at least for a little while longer.

"Okay," Saphyre responds, not sure how she should go about this. "I'll be honest with you, I was eavesdropping in on Billy and JD's conversation while ago and I overheard some stuff that makes me think we might be better off if we were with them. Now I know that this might sound a little crazy, but they are headed into some deep shit down in New Orleans."

Kaitlyn sits up straight and asks, "And how do you see that it would be better to be with them?"

Saphyre knew that her statement came out wrong, and now she has to come up with something good to keep Kaitlyn from walking out on her. "Because, we would have better protection being in Billy's company, that's why. If I'm right, then we sure don't want to be here alone if the spooks and goblins come here looking for Billy." That was the key word that Saphyre shouldn't have said, but she has no idea why it sets Kaitlyn off.

"Are you mocking me?" Kaitlyn stands up off the bed and stares at Saphyre, as if she had betrayed Kaitlyn in the worst way, even though Saphyre doesn't know what Kaitlyn is talking about. "What do you know about what happened in the woods?" Kaitlyn asks as her tears begin to flow again. "Were you part of that? Was it some kind of ploy to try and win my vote to chase after your boyfriend?" Angered by the accusations Kaitlyn decides to opt out of hearing Saphyre's defense, and proceeds to exit the room.

Insulted by Kaitlyn's accusations Saphyre jumps up and chases her out into the hallway. "Now you hold on there a minute, girl. I don't know what you are talking about and frankly I'm a little offended. I don't know what happened out there in the woods to you, and at the moment, I could care less. But let me tell you one thing for sure; yeah, I would feel better about being near JD, but I would never try anything underhanded like what you're suggesting to get you to come along."

Kaitlyn stops, realizing that she might have passed the wrong judgment. Without turning around, Kaitlyn asks, "What did you mean when you said spooks and goblins?"

The question opens up all sorts of curiosity for Saphyre, causing her to think about the question for a moment before she answers. Was this based on Kaitlyn's incident in the woods? If so, what did she see out there? "I heard them talking about things that happened, evidently in Atlanta, and in New York when they were there to rescue us. From what I picked up, JD has been through something like this before, in Japan, with some guy named Nick." She reaches out and touches Kaitlyn's shoulder, causing her to turn around and face Saphyre again. "This may sound weird as hell, but they were talking about people being possessed by dark spirits and facing off some army of dark warriors led by beings who wanted to take over the world." There, she said it. Some of it was ad-libbed but the gist of the story was accurate. Now the question is whether or not Kaitlyn can and will believe her.

"Why do you think they would come here?"

Saphyre stares at Kaitlyn for a second and replies with a question, "What did you see out there, Kaitlyn?"

This has all been too much for her. Again she starts to cry, but forces out an answer all the same. "You think that they will come here, don't you?" Before Saphyre can answer, Kaitlyn wipes her nose on the sleeve of her shirt and continues her explanation. "I think you are right. I saw something in the woods that was right out of a top notch horror movie, and I'm still having a hard time believing what I saw with my own eyes." Kaitlyn leans back against the hallway wall and slides down to sit on the floor. The more she talks, the more hysterical she gets about the subject. "It looked like a ghost; you know like in the movies, only this one was black, wispy like a cloud of vapor, but as it moved it also took on the shape of a body. At least in some areas, but never in complete form." She looks at Saphyre kneeling down. I saw it, Saphyre, and it scared the hell out of me. The thing looked at me with red glowing eyes like it was looking into my soul. I've never been so scared in all my life, so I ran. I ran until I fell down, and that's where you found me."

She was right, and they have already made their move to locate and assault the ranch. This is something that Saphyre does not want to face alone. "What happened to it?"

"I don't know," Kaitlyn, replies between sniffles. "It was coming down at me, when I heard you calling my name. Maybe you scared it off long enough for us to get away." Then Kaitlyn realizes the true meaning of Saphyre's proposal. "If Billy, Taylor, and JD are heading into more of that, what makes you think I want to join them?"

"Maybe it's like I said. With them to help fight, and more importantly protect us, I think we'd stand a better chance than fighting alone against something we know nothing about." Saphyre looks at Kaitlyn's appearance and tries to apply it to herself. "Face it, there is strength in numbers."

"Why wouldn't we be safer going the other way?"

Saphyre chuckles at the remark, not intending to insult Kaitlyn in any way. "Well, let me put it to you this way, girlfriend, I'm heading after Billy and JD. I'd rather be on the frontline with them, than suffer some sneak attack when I'm all alone. Now you can go wherever you want, but if they tie you to Billy, what makes you think they won't keep coming after you? At least if you go with me, you'll have a fighting chance. Besides, you were the one who was so keen on building this superhero team. What about that?"

"Yeah, what about that? I couldn't believe that you left me out to dry like that, when I tried to state my case earlier." This is good. At least now she can clear the air that she feels about Saphyre's lack of support in the kitchen.

"Hey, we're kinda in this together, kid. Next time, give me some fair warning before you drop an egg like that," Saphyre replies with a smile. Has she won Kaitlyn over, and if so, can they get on the road as soon as possible?

"Do you really believe the sermon you're preaching, Saphyre?"

She laughs at the question and then takes a moment to ask herself the same thing. Saphyre then looks back at Kaitlyn wit a confident expression. "I have known Billy Ray McBride for an awful long time. Yeah, I really do think we would be better off with them."

Okay, then that's where I want to go too. The question is how do we get there?"

Chapter XIII

The clouds building on the horizon warn of bad weather ahead. "It sure seems to rain a lot," Taylor, mumbles, distracting JD from his reading. She turns on the car's headlights, looks over at her man, and asks, "Billy, are you awake?" Reaching over Taylor gently rubs her fingers against his cheek. The act causes him to shift in his seat, but he doesn't respond to her touch other than that. This is actually the sign she was looking for. After adjusting the rear view mirror, Taylor makes eye contact with JD and asks, "Listen, I was wondering if Billy might have said anything to you about me? You know me and him kinda stuff?"

JD looks up from Nick's journal, and gives her a comforting smile before saying, "yes, and no, but his actions speak louder than words. You were his primary concern in New York. Sure, he held favor with his mother and the others as well, but every time the names were mentioned, yours came out first. He was afraid that he had lost you forever, and to be given the chance to have you back again; well, I don't think the Gods of Olympus could have stopped him. What matters though, is the here and now. Right now, the two of you are together, regardless of the circumstances."

"How should I approach him about what happened?"

JD looks back at the mirror and says, "Listen, I think that the best advice that I could give you is to enjoy the moment of being together. Who knows what could happen in the next few days." Redirecting his attention to his sensei's journal for the third time, JD continues to scan the many pages he skipped through, the first time he read it.

"What were you and Billy talking about out by the corral?"

JD finally closes the book for now, and makes eye contact again with Taylor, but is unsure how he should answer that. "Is Billy awake? I think we should wait and talk about this stuff all together."

Billy is doing his best to hide his weakened condition. He has to, because Scotty is counting on him. Billy will find a way to rest when everybody is safe at home. For a second, he remembers the dream he had. Who was that woman in his dream? He remembers how positive he felt that this mystery woman was the same image that he saw in the reflection of the mirror, before going off to New York. The question is, why is he so sure? With the way the mirror was so steamed up from his shower, there was no way for Billy to make out any identifying features. But for whatever reason, he believes deep down inside that she was the one watching him.

Jezana? The name comes to mind, as if he is trying to make connections any way he can to rationalize the chaos going through his mind. Could the connection be all part of what Billy wants to deny? JD told Billy that he is somehow connected to Nick's destiny. With everything that has happened over the past week or so, it is getting harder and harder for him not to see that this is all more than coincidence happening here. And yet, he still refuses to accept that there is some all powerful cosmic force controlling his life. Everything that Billy has done was by his choice, his will. No, he may be caught up in something that isn't by his choice, but he is not being led into some role as a heroic leader.

This is all completely insane. Surely his mind is playing games with him, brought on by his weakened state, right? He's still weak from his injuries and he needs rest. Once his body has recovered, his mind will settle down, and he can process the situation better. What's the old saying, sound body, sound mind? Or is it the other way around? What does it matter? With Taylor and JD babbling on, how could he think about getting any rest? The problem is that time is short and he needs the rest to be good enough for Scotty's rescue. "Go ahead, JD, and tell her," Billy suggests, surprising Taylor and JD with the fact that he was awake. "What? You really don't think I could've been sleeping with the two of you babbling on, do ya?" Billy looks out at the growing clouds and rolls up his partially opened window.

Embarrassed for offering advice behind Billy's back so to speak, JD jumps into the new topic of conversation, "Thanks, I was getting pretty chilly back here. Listen, I found one of those names you mentioned, Billy. According to Nick's Journal, I can only find one entry that mentions her. Apparently, was the dark Queen, Mistress Jezana, and was Lord Doomsayer's mother."

"And that's the same guy from Japan, right?" Billy is sure he already knows the answer. He just wanted to make sure he was on the right track.

Taylor holds up her hand before JD could answer Billy's question, for her own clarification. "Wait a minute, who is this Nick guy?"

He's JD's martial arts instructor," Billy answers, while motioning for JD to continue.

JD opens his mouth with the full intention of answering Billy's question, along with offering some insight about Doomsayer. Taylor however has different plans. Holding her hand up in front of JD's face, she looks at Billy and asks, "You know this guy Nick? How is that possible?"

"We met in Florida," her man replies, not wanting to bring up the sore subject again.

"She looks back at JD and claims, "I guess it's a small world isn't it? Did you meet Billy in Florida too?"

"No, we didn't meet until I got to Alabama," JD replies.

"And what about the other name? You'd think that if the bad guys were named in the book, someone would make sure to give you all of the players, right?" Billy tries to turn around to look at JD for the answer to his question. In a way, he is still a little curious about what JD has seen and done. Especially, after what Billy witnessed first hand, when he was in Nick's company, while in Florida. The fact that what's happening now, and the connection to their topic of conversation, hasn't truly come to light yet.

"Okay, okay, I don't think you understood me." Taylor looks back at JD, and then at Billy before stating her case. "Just so that we are clear on one thing, I don't have a clue about who, or what, you are talking about. So, to make this easier and less painful for us all; start at the very beginning and bring me up to speed."

Billy reaches over nonchalantly and grabs the steering wheel as his Camaro starts to drift out of her travel lane. "Honey, I bet JD would be happy to tell you everything if you promise to keep your eyes on the road." Then Billy adds with a stronger tone, "Wouldn't you, JD?"

"Yeah, sure Billy, no problem," JD answers, wondering how or where to start. He is still trying to figure out the dynamics of this couple's relationship. All of a sudden, he has flashbacks to when he first explained his tale to Billy, and the skepticism he suffered in doing so. This time is different now. Billy has had his share of events take place that squelch his disbelief. The question now is how will Taylor accept the information he s about to offer. "Okay, let's see how well I can do this. When I was living in Florida, I was a student of Mr. Nickolas Landry, my martial arts instructor. Seven years ago, Nick was approached by a old, older than you would believe, Japanese man who told him that he has a destiny to save the world from darkness. After training for this destiny, after losing everything that was dear to him, Nick is now on the run from every law enforcement agency in the free world.

His statement causes Taylor to look back at him, just like JD expected. Before she can ask her question, he raises his hand to stop her politely, and then says, "I know, I know, but hold on to your questions for now. I'm pretty sure I'll answer the majority of them before I'm done, any way." Before he continues, JD opens his water bottle and takes a drink to wet his throat for this long and drawn out explanation. "As hard as this may be for you to believe, there are beings and forces of darkness that are here on this world for one reason. These beings, these creatures of darkness want nothing more than to bring hell to earth, for humanity to suffer for all times."

"Tell her about Japan, JD." Billy looks over at Taylor, only to receive a disapproving shake of her head.

"This force, this army of darkness, has tried three times to achieve their goal, only to have victory snatched away from them at the last minute, each and every time. I don't know the whole story, but I do know that they have just one more time to try again, and the time is coming soon. I've seen how real this is Taylor. I've witnessed first hand how real the threat is to humanity. The thing is I believe that we have all become part of this plot against the world, including Billy and yourself."

Suddenly, the hot rod comes to a screeching halt, as Taylor develops the need to demand specific clarifications before they continue any further. After pulling the car over to the emergency lane, Taylor shuts off the engine and turns to face Billy with a very serious expression. "What exactly have you gotten me into, lover?"

Scrambling for a defense, Billy sits up in his seat and explains, "I think what JD means is, you have had dealings with these baddest of bad guys yourself. Now, I have no idea how long they were associates of the devil before you and I met, but the men I fought at the bowling alley, were the same guys I rescued JD from on the side of the road. According to JD, they displayed attributes and knew things about what was going on that they couldn't have known any other way. So, technically, you were involved first, based on guilt by association." If one was to nit-pick around the truth, Billy's theory is sound.

Did he really say what she thinks he said? Taylor looks out the windshield at the road ahead of them, appearing to be shocked by what Billy had just said. The rain is moving in fast. She starts to count the small drops that are increasing in number by the second. "Are you talking about Jackie and his boys?" She tries to make eye contact with Billy without turning her head. Is this some kind of twisted prank that he is trying to pull? He's not really serious, is he? She has to look at him to know for sure, but part of her doesn't want him to be telling the truth. The unexplained, the supernatural, has always been a topic that Taylor wanted to ignore. With no other choice, she turns to face Billy and sees him to be very serious about the matter. "Well, I guess that would explain why those guys were such bastards all of the time. But, I still don't see what I have to do with your friend's destiny?"

This is where Billy feels the need to man up and explain his version of her involvement. Taking her hand, he feels a strong desire to comfort her, and take the blame if any need be, "To be honest with you, I'm to blame for your involvement. At least I think I am." Looking into her eyes, Billy can't help but feel a different kind of pain brought on by her concerns about the situation. "JD has had a couple of dreams that he thinks they are connected to what has been going on with me and my life. I hate to say it, but your guilt by association is with me as well, making you nothing more than a victim of circumstance."

"See, that's where I think you're wrong, Billy. I believe that it is our destinies that are coming together to face this end of times. "You met her, and then met Nick. I met Nick, and then met you and Taylor, and even Kaitlyn and the others. At this point, I would be happy not to rule out anyone that we've met, to be our allies."

"This is where Taylor's anger comes to light. Obviously, these two know a lot more about the subject, than they have ever let on. "Don't you think that this is something that we should have talked about before we are half way to Mobile? So let me see if I got this straight. Your buddy, is some kind of savior for mankind," she states pointing at JD, "And you have somehow dragged the both of us into this mess," she adds directing her attention to Billy. "So, do you think either of you can tell me what is going on right now? How is Scotty involved? What are we going to be facing when we get there? These are the kind of things a person needs to know, ya know?!"

JD and Billy look at each other wondering who should speak first. Understanding Billy's delicate situation with Taylor, and that Billy is closer proximity to the girl, JD decides to take the brunt of her anger. At least he has a force field that he can hide behind. "Just so that you know, Billy only knew a small part of this, until we had our little talk out by the corral. You asked what we were talking about; this was the topic of conversation." JD looks out the window trying to hide the embarrassment for what he is about to say. "When you get right down to it, I'm at fault for the lack of communication. As far out and wild as this stuff seems, I had a problem talking to any of you about what I saw. I should have had more faith in my friends, and I'm sorry for that."

"In all fairness, all of this has happened so fast, we really haven't had time to discuss all of the specifics," Billy points out. "Neither me nor JD know how we've been swept into this mess, or what is suppose to happen. There is no way for us to know if this with Scotty is tied to Nick's destiny or not. We have our suspicions, but no solid facts. The best thing for us to do is be prepared for anything, and be aware of all possible dangers." Billy turns in his seat again, mostly to test his mobility. "So, this Jezana chick, do you think you might find something else on her in that book?" Now it is his curiosity that outweighs his rationality. Somehow, Billy has to find the evidence to know if his dream, this Jezana, and Nick's destiny are all connected.

JD's impressed by Billy's open outlook on the possible scenarios they might face. Unlike him, where all of this is just spinning around in JD's head. Here he is, giving his spill for the second time, this time because he believes that Billy and Taylor have become involved with Nick's destiny, along with himself. His job is to serve somehow as Billy's conscience to make sure that everything moves forward with a happy ending. This JD is sure of, but has no idea which way to go with it. Billy and Taylor, on the other hand, just found out that they could be possibly linked to the fate of the world, and they act like it's no big deal. Surely this is a front to cover their true feelings, as if they want to portray themselves stronger than they need to be. His analysis of this leads JD to believe that these two are definitely who he wants standing beside him when the crap hits the fan. Getting back to Billy's question, he answers, "I'm not sure. The only thing I've found so far is that she was Doomsayer's mother, but I haven't found anything that pinpoints what happened to her."

Curious about the topic, Taylor asks, "Could she be Callistone's daughter, Margaret?"

Billy looks at her with no idea if it was possible or not. He and Taylor both weigh the possibility, but can't be certain. This leads him to look to JD for a little help. You said that Doomsayer's spirit possessed Masamoto's brother. Is it possible that Margaret has been possessed by the mother from hell?"

JD simply shrugs his shoulders and replies, "I'm not sure, but I don't think so. In every instance so far, they have always been willing to reveal their darker side. If she was truly as powerful as I suspect, these games wouldn't fit the profile. Even lord Doomsayer boasted of his true power. You'd almost have to believe that Margaret would have done the same, if she was Jezana incarnate." JD thinks for a second or two and then asks, "Did you ever notice a jittery motion to her appearance? Before Doomsayer revealed his true nature, there were times where his body seemed to jitter, or wiggle, as if he was having trouble maintaining his presence in this realm under the guise of Seko Masamoto. In fact, Nick mentioned other occasions where he saw the same thing with other opponents he faced."

Billy thinks about his confrontation with Margaret, and then with Pantera as well, but can't recall any abnormality like JD mentioned. "Naw, but everything was happening so fast that I'm not sure if I missed it or not."

With a thought of her own coming to mind, Taylor chimes in to contradict her earlier question. "I guess you're right, JD. If she possessed any kind of supernatural power, she probably would have used it against Billy right off the bat, wouldn't she?"

"I suppose," JD replies. "But in a way, that's what makes this so confusing. My dreams both referred to Billy as the unlikely ally. I don't really know how that fits into the grand scheme of things yet. But, if she isn't involved with these forces of darkness, what is her fascination with Billy? This has obviously gone farther than just simple revenge."

"That's why we have to be on our toes and ready for anything possible," Billy confirms. "It's also another reason why I'm glad the kids stayed at the ranch. At first, I was just worried about their safety, but when JD opened up to me, I'm even happier that they're not with us. It would be hard enough to deal with the situation, without the girls freaking out, if all hell breaks loose."

"Yeah, and what about me?"

He smiles at Taylor the way only he can to comfort her. "You've got the advantage of me and JD watching out for you."

Wanting to believe Billy in the worst way, Taylor has to ask, "How are we gonna do this?"

To emphasize his statement, Billy highlights his eyes with energy and says, "The only way Scotty would want me to do this."

Billy's declaration does not boost her confidence one bit. Turning around to face JD, Taylor asks, "Do you know everything he knows?" JD nods a hesitant yes. "Good," she replies, "you talk." She looks over at Billy and warns, "You be quiet." Then to soften her tone, she looks back over at Billy and smiles, "I love you Billy Ray."

"She starts up the car and checks the roadway for traffic. With a clear path, she pops the clutch and sends the Camaro rocketing back onto the pavement. Looking into the rear view mirror, Taylor clears her throat to get JD's attention and says, "I'm sorry, Jefferson, but I can't hear you."

"Hey, no problems here on this end," JD sits up straight, ready to spill his guts. "Is there any specific starting point you have in mind?"

"Why don't you start with what we might be up against?" Out the corner of her eye, Taylor sees Billy wanting to say something and immediately shuts him down with, "Don't even think about it."

The antics and gestures of his friends in the front seat bring a smile to JD's face. Glancing over at the seat beside him, JD picks up a CD case and reads the title, "The Black Eyed Peas? Billy you don't strike me as the type who would listen to BEP."

"He doesn't," Taylor, explains, "that's my CD."

"Ya know, that reminds me. When I was in Florida, they were at…"

Taylor whips her head to the side and stares at Billy. Then, she reaches out and touches her fingertips to his lips. Adding a little playfulness, she grabs his lips and twists them shut. "Now, if you would continue, Mr. Johnston."

Laughing, JD happily replies, "Sure Taylor." His following statements bring to mind the old adage, "be careful what you wish for." To start off, JD gives her the full low down on Nick's destiny, or at least all that he knows. That is followed up by his elaboration of his abduction he suffered in Japan, and all of the players that were involved. This little story includes Sonny's demise, and what happened to her after JD and Nick returned from Japan.

Knowing how Sonny was responsible for Nick's current status and dilemmas, JD wants to change topics to avoid the pain he feels for the loss of Nick's guidance. His mentor's advice is something he could use right about now. "Then, if you want to break down the ranks, we can start at the top and work our way down the line. First, there are the ones known as the originals. These were the first turned to the darkness to serve as the new army of darkness. They are the ones who attack and turn lost souls, recruiting them into the ranks. Those who can't be turned are left for the feeders, or become food for the originals. The feeders, these baddies basically consume the souls of the fallen, leaving the body as an unoccupied vessel, open for repossession. Ya see, trapped on Earth in some kind of limbo, if a dark soul loses its vessel because the body is too damaged, it can seek out an empty vessel to occupy and continue to fight."

Taylor asks with a fearful tone "You mean to tell me there is no way to save them?" JD can see the pain of what he's saying all over Taylor's face, but this doesn't sway him in the least. If she wants to know the truth, then she deserves to know the whole truth. "No," He answers, "Once attacked, the corrupted perpetuate the recruiting spreading like a disease through humanity. If I read this right, Doomsayer had his army of minions and was ready to take over the world instead of handing it over to some being known as the Devastator."

"Something doesn't add up though, JD." Billy can't be quiet any more. "You said that the Doomsayer dude was taken out by Nick. How or why does all of this keep going if the head guy has already fallen?"

"I know; and it's why I wish Nick was here right now." JD stares out the window wondering where his friend could be. "Any way, getting back on topic, these bad guys can sometimes find a person, who is dark in nature, and can possess the body and use it as transportation to find another vessel to inhabit. That is, unless it can take control and forces the soul out. If the demon wins, and it usually does, the soul of the person would be lost to become food for the feeders."

Taylor actually slows the car down a little and looks back at JD to ask, "How the hell do you beat something that can just move on to another body?"

"That's what I don't know. When Nick took out Doomsayer, he used the energy of the talisman. Maybe that's why everyone wants the talisman so bad."

Again Billy has to interject his opinion, "That's why if there is any outside interference from these guys, we take 'em out fast and let Nick and his people handle the rest. Keep in mind that we could be jumping the gun with this stuff. The last thing we want is to be distracted by the possibility of facing ghosts and goblins, and have some guy with a gun jump out and pop us off with no problem."

"I won't argue that one with you, Billy. But I think we both have seen enough signs to know that the possibilities are right in front of us."

Taylor steps on the gas and speeds up the car. "I think I like Billy's plan best. We get Scotty out of there, and let someone else handle the rest. Whoever, or whatever, gets in our way or tries to stop us will be put down until we achieve our goal." Feeling the need to be close to Billy, Taylor reaches over and takes his hand. "I love you, Billy."

Billy closes his eyes and squeezes Taylor's hand. "I love you too," he says, as he lays his head against the passenger door glass. "Don't wreck my car."

"We're gonna be alright Taylor," JD declares, adding, "He'll make sure of that."

Chapter XIV

Half a mile back down the interstate, Kaitlyn and Saphyre sit in the cab of the McBride ranch work truck, breathing heavy and panic stricken after the truck slides to a stop on the wet pavement. It wasn't the losing control of the truck that scared them so. It was the sight of Billy's car stopping up the road ahead of them that sent the girls into their panic. "Do you think they saw us?" The exact same question has been running through Saphyre's mind, ever since she spotted the brake lights of the Camaro. Kaitlyn was just the first to ask the question out loud.

"I don't know," Saphyre responds, never taking her eyes off the car ahead of them. "But they stopped for some reason." Maybe the rain has offered enough cover to keep the girls' presence hidden. Surely it has to be as hard for Billy and Taylor to see the truck, as it is for Saphyre to see the Camaro ahead of her. The weather is really getting rough. Maybe they stopped to wait out the weather for a little while. Saphyre has lived in the south long enough to know how these storms come through so hard that you can't see five feet in front of you. The logic is good, or at least she thinks so. Of course, they could have stopped to talk about something, and have no idea the girls are a half a mile behind them. Saphyre never saw how the car initially stopped. She just noticed the brake lights, and realized that the Camaro wasn't moving. Thus the need for her slamming on the brakes and sending the truck sliding off to the side of the road. Then again, there is the possibility that Billy and Taylor did recognize the truck following them. The question of the moment is, are they just going to sit there and wait for Kaitlyn and Saphyre to come on up and join them? One positive note is that the car isn't backing up the interstate to confront the two girls about why they are following them. Saphyre laughs to herself for a second. What if Billy really does have them stopped, just waiting for Saphyre and Kaitlyn to drive on up? Good luck with that. If they are planning on waiting for the girls to drive to them, Billy is going to have a long wait. "Hopefully, it's just the weather playing out in our favor."

"So, what do we do now, Saphyre?" Kaitlyn can't help but wonder if this little covert operation of theirs is blowing up in their faces.

"We'll just wait 'em out, I guess. I don't have anywhere else to go right now, do you?" Saphyre checks the storm clouds to the left, recognizing a break in the storm heading their way. "The sun is going down, and the break in the clouds is coming. I'm willing to bet that they are going to be heading on down the road soon, and our cover won't be blown with twilight replacing the rain. Until then, we'll just kick back and wait for them to make their move."

"Ya know, I'm a little curious about something," Kaitlyn declares, while turning in her seat to face her friend. "Why are you doing this, Saphyre? I mean, if you think about it, nothing really adds up." When Saphyre finally faces Kaitlyn, the former New Yorker explains her statement to her new friend. "First, you are abducted, an innocent bystander who was just in the wrong place at the wrong time. You were taken against your will to New York, and held captive with a promise that you were going to die. Now that you've been returned home safe and sound, you jump at the first chance to run off and get into more trouble. It doesn't make sense. Sure there is that tidbit about you and JD having the hots for each other, but most people aren't willing to run into the pit of death for somebody they just met. I know it's not because you feel some debt to Billy for saving you, or at least you shouldn't. He's the reason you got mixed up in all of this mess to begin with. "Kaitlyn pauses for a second to give Saphyre the chance to disagree. "You know, or at least have an idea of what they are going to face. I have basically substantiated your theory with my report about what happened in the woods. Why? Why are you doing this, Saphyre?"

It's a legitimate question, and one Saphyre has already asked herself. "In a way, it's because of my dad." Okay, that wasn't so hard for her to admit. "See, he was an Army Ranger stationed over at Fort Benning. He died in combat a few years ago." A tear rolls down her cheek as she turns away from Kaitlyn to look out the driver's side window. "He served his country and did so with pride. My dad believed that we all have a duty to serve one another in different ways. He felt that it was his role to serve in the military, to protect us from the bad people. He always told me that there will always be the bad guys in the world who want the innocent to suffer for little or no reason."

"You sound like you're really proud of him."

Saphyre turns back and smiles at Kaitlyn. "You're damned right I am. But more than that I love him, and miss him tremendously. My dad was the one who believed in me, and always told me that I was going to be something special." Saphyre wipes the tear from her cheek, and then rolls her eyes as if trying to hide some embarrassment for the show of emotion. "I know that I have been a real shit to my mom, and even my grandparents, lately, and I've used the excuse that I was acting out because of that loss. To be honest with you, I think he would be disappointed in me for such childish antics. So to honor him, and make amends, coupled to the other reasons that you've already mentioned, that's why I'm doing this. Maybe it makes sense to you, or maybe it doesn't. The important thing is that I now recognize it, and know it. And if you don't think that JD is worth rushing off for, you need to look him over again. Believe me, that kiss is worth it."

"Oh, you're terrible," Kaitlyn returns, shoving Saphyre over against the driver's door. Both girls laugh at the lightened situation and regain their composure after a little bit. "If I owe you an apology, I'm sorry. I guess I just find it a little strange that someone like you is willing to risk your life like this."

Suddenly, Saphyre's happy demeanor quickly fades to a more serious tone. "I'm sorry, but what does that supposed to mean? I know it isn't the race card being thrown out there, because JD' black too. It can't be because I'm a girl, because that would be so hypocritical coming from you, Kaitlyn Justice."

"No, no, no, I didn't mean anything at all by that. I was referring to your, how should I say this, inabilities." The term only causes Saphyre to raise an eyebrow. "Okay, listen; I have the ability to defy gravity somewhat, or so I'm learning. You know that. Taylor is super strong, JD has his force field and ninja shit goin' for him, and Billy, well we all know about Billy. The question is what can Saphyre do?"

It's a feasible inquiry. If Kaitlyn was putting her life into someone's hands, she'd want to know what their qualifications are. "Well, if you mean can I fly, or something like that, then no I don't have anything to offer. But, with a father who was an Army Ranger, I have grown up with plenty of knowledge on how to take care of myself. I have taken several martial arts courses and classes, and have a vast knowledge of hand to hand combat handed down from my dad. I do admit that I never thought I'd need to use any of that. So, yeah, I'm confident that I can take care of myself in a fair fight."

"Saphyre, if there is one thing that I have learned; it's that there is no such thing as a fair fight. Believe me; if there is nothing else, I have learned that I could end up dead, every time I went out playing superhero. The question you should be asking yourself is how do you deal with that moment when it happens to you? Will you be able to do what is necessary when the time comes?"

"Look, they are driving on," Saphyre says, mostly to change the subject. Still, Kaitlyn has planted a seed of thought in Saphyre's mind. The question is can she find the answer before the time comes? Before she can cross that bridge, they have to get there first. Saphyre puts the truck in gear and pulls back onto the road. Neither girl sees the pairs of red eyes on the side of the road in the growing darkness, where they were parked. At this stage of the game, it's probably better that way.

"So, what about you, Kaitlyn? Do you have some similar motive for going with me, or are you just looking out for yourself?"

"Oh, you can believe that it started out with me, looking out for myself, and I wasn't even going to get involved. But after hearing such a heart warming testimonial, I think I might have to rethink that, just so that I can save face. But, being the one with the most experience, I think we should just stay in the background until we know what is going on." The sets of red glowing eyes stare at the truck as the girls head on down the road, from where they were parked a few seconds ago. The girls never look back at the spot where they were parked. If they had, they would have seen that their enemy was closer than they thought. For now, it is probably better that way.

In the city known as the big easy, Margaret's limousine pulls up in front of her hotel where her men wait for her arrival. When the car stops, she looks across the back seat at Scotty and gives him a devilish grin. "We're here. It's time for this party to start." Climbing out of the car, she takes notice to the party goers who are starting to move about the streets awaiting the night's festivities. She, like them, is glad that the rains have let up. "Parker," she calls out, getting the attention of her man standing outside the car on the street. When he walks over to her, Margaret asks, "Who's your friend?"

"That's one of HIS people," Parker answers. "Boss lady, I've seen some pretty freaky shit since we've been down here. Are you sure this is how we want to do this?"

"Darrell Parker, I assure you that it's something that you don't need to worry about." She turns away from one of her most loyal men, and then quickly returns her attention towards him again. "There is no other way for this to happen, Darrell."

"But Ms. Stanford," Parker leans in close and whispers in Margaret's ear, "Boss lady, I overheard his woman tell him that taking our target's power will make this voodoo witch doctor sonofabitch unstoppable. The scary part is that I think the crazy bastard believes he can pull it off."

Margaret smiles at her man and pats him on the shoulder. "Don't worry, Parker. He won't get the chance." She looks around the street, and becomes disturbingly aware that one out of three people were looking in her direction. Was it her paranoia trying to slip back in or is there something transpiring that her people are unaware of its presence. "Take the boy in the limo to the meeting place," she pauses for a moment, "and be sure to take enough men with you to scout the area before I arrive. It's always better to be safe than sorry. I was told that the meeting would take place tonight at ten. Is that still the correct time?"

"Yes ma'am, this Mysery character will have his people pick you up from your room and escort you to the meeting." Parker motions for the rest of his men to get into the limousine, followed by his contact liaison. "I don't know where the meeting place is, Ms. Stanford. This gothic clown has his orders to direct us along the way. But don't worry; we'll be ready for your arrival. Me and the boys will report back to you when we have the answers you need."

Margaret leans in close, and orders, "No, I want the men to stay there, but I want you to come back here when it's time for the meeting. I do want to be briefed about what I'll be walking into. You understand, don't you, Darrell?"

"Yes ma'am," he answers before climbing into the limousine.

Chapter XV

Billy, what's with all of the weirdoes here tonight?" Taylor asks as they enter the front lobby of the hotel. The gothic costumes of zombies and monsters are a little unnerving.

Curious about it as much as Taylor is, Billy asks the Concierge, as they walk up to the front desk, "What's with the Halloween costumes, bud?"

"Good evening, and welcome to the Big Easy." The man gives them a polite smile and nods to some partiers heading out for the night's party. "Aren't the two of you here for the festival of the dead? It's going on all weekend," he looks at Taylor and offers a wicked little tone, "It's to die for, really."

"Nope," Billy answers, "we are here on business for this trip. I'm afraid there won't be much fun and celebrating for us." Billy explains, knowing full well that this isn't an excursion seeking fun and excitement.

"Well, you know what they say about New Orleans, you always find what you're looking for in the Big Easy." Getting back to the business at hand, he asks, "Do you have a reservation with us? Otherwise, I'm afraid that we are booked solid."

"Yes sir, we do," Billy answers. "The name is Billy Joe McAllister. I believe you should have two rooms for me." Billy shakes his head no, ever so slightly when Taylor looks to him for an explanation.

"Here we go," the desk manager, replies, "I have you two connecting rooms on the top floor, in the northeast corner of the hotel. Now, we do ask that you keep the partying down to a low roar and no loud activities in the rooms or halls after midnight. Housekeeping comes around the rooms about ten o'clock, and room service runs from six in the morning until midnight. There are movies for rent, with a play card stationed on the TV in the room. Is there anything else I can help y'all with?"

"Nope, just the keys please," Billy responds, not needing any of the information that the manager has been programmed to give. With a nod, the desk manager hands Billy two envelopes with card keys inside for the two rooms. Billy taps them against the counter and salutes the hotel employee, and then takes Taylor by her arm to lead her to the elevator. He isn't forceful with his actions, but she does like it when he takes charge. At the elevator, Taylor hurries to push the call button to beat Billy out of the chance. It is nothing more than a try to lighten the mood a little, and Billy understands completely. "Why you little devil," He says, picking her up in his arms and spins her around. He remembers a time not too long ago, when he didn't think he'd ever do that again. Right now, he wishes that he had thought the action through a little more, due to the tenderness of his wounds.

Where Billy's thoughts are on events of a painful past, Taylor's sights are set on the hotel lobby doors. There, just outside the establishment, stands a peculiar little man wearing a ragged looking top hat. What bothers her about this is how he just stands there staring at her like he knew who she was. With a tip of his hat, he bids her farewell and disappears into the street crowd. This troubles her enough to bring the happening to Billy's attention. "Baby, put me down. There's a little man standing at the door looking at me."

Billy is quick to oblige, and then turns around even quicker to see who this culprit is. "I'm sorry, baby girl, but who is it that's staring at you? I don't see anyone." He looks back and gets caught up in her green eyes, and just shrugs his shoulders.

Taylor looks again, but there is no sign of the little fellow anywhere. "No, he's gone now. But believe me, he was creepy, and he wore a top hat like the kind you'd see in the circus or something." The door to the elevator opens giving Taylor the escape route she needed to get out of the public eye. Pulling Billy in with her only accentuates her current state of mind.

"Are you alright? Did the little guy bother you that much?" Billy is a little surprised at how unnerved Taylor is over something so trivial. But, he has to keep in mind everything that she has gone through lately. This train of thought starts to make him wonder if bringing her with him was such a good idea. Billy loves Taylor and believes in her, but that can't prevent her from having some kind of breakdown if the chips fall against them. If she is still out of sorts over what happened in New York, there really is no way of knowing how much more could send her crashing down to the ground. "If this bothers you, I'll be fine with it, if you want to hang out in the room while me and JD do some scouting around."

"No, no, I'm fine. Maybe it was all of that spooky talk in the car," Taylor offers, trying to cut off Billy's line of doubt. "Ya know, it's bad enough that you and JD hit me with all of that stuff out on the highway, but to get here and find everyone partying like ghosts and ghouls just topped it off, that's all." She gives him a kiss and then snatches the room keys out of his hand. "Which one of these is ours?" She asks, stepping out of the elevator.

"You choose," Billy, answers, as he starts down the hall. "As far as I know, both rooms are identical. Then without looking behind him, he says, "Come on JD, there ain't no reason to be playing hide and seek right now." Billy gestures with his hand for Taylor to choose a door.

"Ya know, I'm kinda bummed that you picked up on my presence," JD admits, walking up to his friends.

"Don't be too hard on yourself, JD. I was blessed with good peripheral vision. If not, I wouldn't have seen you step back into the shadows." Billy waves Taylor into the room as soon as she opens the door, when he realizes that they are now sharing the hallway with other approaching hotel occupants. Not wanting to be recognized together, Billy hands JD the other key and hurries into the room before the small crowd of partiers walk by. Once inside, Billy opens one door between the two rooms, and then raps on the other a couple of times for JD to open up. As soon as he does, Billy turns away from the doorway and walks over to the bed. "I wanna get out on the street as soon as possible, find out where Margaret is, and where she is heading."

"What then?" JD asks.

Billy looks at his friend as if asking, really? "I think it's pretty simple after that, ain't it JD? We follow her, find Scotty, and then take him home. Anybody tries to stop us, we kick their asses." Billy pulls off his coat, tosses it onto the bed, and lays back. He closes his eyes for a second, hoping that he isn't giving them the wrong impression about his welfare. In all honesty, he's just trying to clear his head of all of the madness so that he can focus on what needs to be done. "Go ahead and get ready to head out, JD. Give me and her about five minutes to get ready, and then you find a good spot to keep an eye on us. I don't want your presence revealed unless absolutely necessary, got it?"

"Loud and clear, boss man," JD replies, wishing that Saphyre was here to keep him from feeling like such a third wheel.

Billy rolls over still feeling the wounds of his gunshots. "Taylor, did you bring up that grey tote bag?"

She walks back around the bed, picks up the aforementioned piece of luggage, and tosses it onto the bed beside Billy. "Of course, but you owe me for that. What is in there any way? It felt like it weighed fifty pounds. It isn't guns is it?"

"Oh quit your cryin', lover. I know for a fact that the entire bag and contents weigh less than twenty pounds." Billy unzips the bag and pulls out his father's old bullet proof vest. "I did the modifications to the harness myself," he explains as he grabs his costume from another bag. Laying the body armor on the bed, he begins to get dressed.

"You mean to tell me that you've had a bullet proof vest the whole time, and you think it might be a good thing to use NOW? Tell me something, Billy Ray McBride. Why do you need to be shot half a dozen times before you try to avoid the danger?"

JD steps back into the room, and asks, "Is everything alright? I thought I heard someone shouting. Hey, I like the suit. The all black suit with the blue cape says it all. But, ya know, you probably should have pulled that out for use a lot sooner, or at least the flack jacket part."

"See, I am right, Billy," Taylor exclaims, happy that JD also sees her point of view.

"Nag, nag, if y'all are ready to go, we'll hit the streets," Billy offers, hoping that the two of them will drop the subject.

A ways down the street, where the prices are lower and the service not as good, Saphyre and Kaitlyn push their way passed a drunk in their hotel hallway, pretty much forcibly entering their room while trying to keep the undesirables out. "Man, Saphyre, don't you think we could have gotten a little better room than this? My credit card has a five thousand dollar limit," Kaitlyn points out, noting the condition of the room.

"Look, I know things look rough right now, but this was the best I could get on such short notice. Every place in town is booked solid because of this festival that's in town. Besides, if we're lucky, we won't be here long enough to despise this place any way." Saphyre pulls out a pale purple outfit complete with golden yellow ribbons and shoes. "This was my gymnastics outfit that I wore for Nationals last year. I thought I'd wear it tonight, when me and you go to find Billy and the others. What do you think?"

"I think JD will like that a lot. But, don't you think it might be a little cold for such a small outfit?" Kaitlyn follows suit removing her outfit out of her tote bag, and takes notice to the blood stains and bullet holes that reopen her memories of the past. "See, even I have leggings to keep my legs from getting frostbite." She starts to disrobe and then slips into her outfit designed for her vigilante activities in New York. It's a lot different from the outfit she wore with her neighborhood watch friends. It's funny in a way, how Henry and Toby both sided with her about team apparel but Amanda was a hard sell, even though she was the one most worried about being recognized. Kaitlyn wishes her former friend's belligerent attitude was around for this little venture, and Henry and Toby too. Deep down inside, she has this feeling that she and Billy's friends are getting off into something a lot more than they're ready for. "I have to be honest with you, Saphyre. I don't know how Billy does it. I mean, he acts like this is old news to him. How does he act so strong all of the time?"

Saphyre knows that she has the answer for this, or at least she's pretty sure any way. "As crazy as it may sound, I think he draws strength from his pain of losing his father," she explains as she wraps the sash ribbons attached to her shoes up and around her legs and ties them in place. "My granddaddy told me that Billy took it real hard when his dad was murdered. "I've heard that people sometimes can draw strength from emotional experiences as strong as that. If you think about Billy's aggressive nature, I'd say that he has a lot of pain and anger inside of him, and that would make sense, if ya think about it. Standing in front of Kaitlyn in her full attire, she asks, "What do you think?"

"I think you're crazy to be going out dressed like that," Kaitlyn answers after pulling her shirt over her head. "At least my outfit has this little coat to keep me warm," she adds, grabbing it from the bed. "You do plan on covering that up so that you don't stand out in the crowd, right?"

Saphyre gives her friend a sarcastic smile, and then pulls a slinky black dress out of her bag and slips it on. "I don't look like a zombie, or nothing, but it's close enough, don't you think? So, how do we do this?"

Kaitlyn can hear the uncertainty in Saphyre's voice, and knows from experience that she needs to assure Saphyre that this is going to be okay. "First, we need to determine the best travel route that both of us can make. Obviously, you can't move like me, so I should stay with you on the street. We'll make our way towards Billy and JD, and hopefully we can run into them along the way. The worst case scenario is that we have to track them down starting at their hotel."

"Okay, we know where that is, so are you ready to go?" Before Kaitlyn can answer, Saphyre walks over to exit the room. She opens the door, and then looks back at Kaitlyn to make sure she was coming with her. To her surprise, Kaitlyn displays a look of shock, and then fear as she stares into the hallway passed Saphyre. Spinning around the unsuspecting young woman is grabbed and pulled out into the hall by two dark figures that just appeared in the darkened corridor, in front of their room. Before, Saphyre has the chance to scream for help, one of the men places a small thin round jewel onto her forehead, completely incapacitating the girl.

Something takes control of Kaitlyn Justice, something deep down inside of her. It is that driving force that perpetuated her desire to be a hero, so to speak. Is it something that is as hereditary as her abilities? Her mother passed on the gene to Kaitlyn allowing her to perform the feats of her recent past. Is this desire to serve humanity connected in some biological way? For the moment, it really doesn't matter, except for the fact that it guides Kaitlyn's actions. Recognizing this scenario from her past, facing off against the thugs and street criminals of New York, Kaitlyn tucks her fears and anxiety aside, and acts. With no fear for her own safety, Kaitlyn draws from experience, leaping towards the doorway, ready to strike a blow for her helpless friend. "Oh, no you don't," she declares, landing just outside the room, before kicking one of the attackers in the jaw.

"Oh yes we do," another of the attackers proclaims, materializing from the shadows to slap Kaitlyn back into the room. Stepping inside, he looks at Kaitlyn with red glowing eyes and suggests, "Go little one, and find your friends. Meet us in the cemetery to the west before this one is served to our master." With that, the man exits the room and waves his hand causing the door to slam shut behind him.

Kaitlyn jumps to her feet and rushes for the door. Fear, anxiety, and panic, race through her heart and soul as she finds the door jammed shut. Those men, those evil creatures, are making off with her friend, leaving Kaitlyn feeling scared and lonely. Sure she wants to do something to help Saphyre get free from her abductors, but in all honesty, it's mainly to ease her own fear of being alone. Those eyes, it's those damned red eyes. She is sure that she would feel better about finding Billy if Saphyre was doing it with her. The question now is where does she start looking? Panic clouds her thinking, sending her off on a wild goose chase without considering what she knows.

Chapter XVI

Margaret stands in front of the mirror in her hotel bathroom, staring at her reflection. She remembers the day that her mother revealed her evil plot for takeover. Margaret remembers what was promised if she carried out her end of the deal. There was a time, not very long ago, when Margaret sent Carlton to New Orleans, under the instruction of her mother, to have this voodoo witch doctor kill Billy Ray McBride. Carlton was supposed to set up the arrangement. For Callistone's right hand man, it was not a pleasant trip. She remembers how he returned, distraught about the meeting. She remembers how he told her about Mysery drawing out visions of Billy from his mind for validation. She remembers how he told of this Mysery character sounding overconfident and arrogant about how he would steal Billy's power to make himself stronger. A thought comes to mind, he never did say how Mysery extracted the thoughts and visions, and she never asked. It doesn't matter. Margaret knows better, because her mother told her that Billy could defeat this mystical maniac. The sad thing is that she can't ever reveal to Carlton how she gets her inside scoop for Billy's demise, or the corporate takeover. Poor Carlton, he has no idea that he is simply a means to an end for her. For a split second, the thought runs through her mind questioning why she is doing all of this. The answer is coursing through her body right now and it makes her feel invincible in every way. She's doing this for the power she has been promised.

"Margaret," Carlton gives the bathroom door a gentle rap with his knuckles. "I believe that our escorts have arrived. It's time for us to get this over with.

No sooner does he remove his hand from the door, Margaret swings it open and asks, "Is Parker with them? I want an update before we make this move."

"Actually, no," Carlton answers. "She, our escort, said that our men were temporarily detained until our arrival."

"Well they all weren't supposed to come back here, Carlton, so that isn't such a bad thing." Margaret points out. "Still, I do wish that Parker had followed orders."

"Carlton puts his arm around Margaret's shoulder and leads her to the front door. "Let's go get this over with, my lady. We have an empire to rebuild."

At the door to the room, Margaret is surprised to see a funny little man wearing a top hat and tails, resembling something from the turn of the century. Despite his ornate and dusty clothing, this miniscule male wears a dark and ominous air about him. This only accentuates the features of his face that only a dead mother could love. "Good evening, Ms. Callistone. Me name is Dreg, and it is my privilege to escort you to see my boss," he announces with a bow.

Margaret simply stares at the little man with contempt for his obvious shortcomings, "The name is Stanford, you little toad." Margaret turns around to face Carlton and says, "You said our escort was a she. You didn't say anything about a sack of shit in a fancy suit." In his defense, Carlton points out the thin female dressed in black, waiting by the elevator with a hulking figure wearing a dusty suit that is two sizes too small. The look on the big guy's face suggests that he is dead to the world. To add a little more "strange" to his appearance, this goliath wears a deep ruby red gemstone on his forehead, with no apparent reason for its purpose. What's even more peculiar is how the young woman appears to be trapped in a state of constant mourning, as she stands there with her head bowed, clutching a bouquet of dead flowers against her breasts. Together with the little man, the trio makes up a matched set of demented freaks. Then, Margaret catches a brief visual, of the threesome, as their bodies seemed to quiver for a second. With her mind obviously suffering from sensory overload, she dismisses the visual misperception and grabs her bag from the table. How any of this fits into her mother's plan is beyond Margaret, but she has to continue to move forward, regardless. "Let's go, Carlton. I want this over."

Satisfied that he had accomplished his task, the little man that calls himself Dreg, starts to waddle down the hall expecting Margaret's entourage to follow. To explore his perverted tendencies, Dreg stops along the way to torment a couple of female tourists who happened out into the hallway at the wrong time. Once he has successfully scared them back into their room, Dreg continues on to the elevator where he bows before the young woman. He turns around and waves Margaret on, and then gestures with his hand for her to step up in front of the leader of the trio.

"So, ya have a task for my Lord Mysery, do ya?" The young woman never removes her gaze from the floor as she speaks. "My Lord awaits your arrival, and looks forward to what you have brought him." On cue, the large man turns and presses the call button for the elevator, never showing any emotional signs of life. The young woman finally rolls her head up when the elevator doors open and says, "Come my guests, Mysery awaits."

Chapter XVII

Back down on Bourbon Street, Billy and Taylor exit their hotel and walk out into the night's festivities as the streets begin to come alive. Billy looks one way and then the other trying to determine his best course of travel. Taylor finds herself scanning the growing crowds for the little man that spooked her earlier. "Which way do we go, Billy?"

He pulls her close as a group of drunks plow down the sidewalk. "Wow, they must be early starters," Billy declares based on the time of evening and the severity of their alcohol induced idiocy. "I guess we need to find out where Margaret is. Until we do that, we can't come up with the next step."

"Oh, don't give me that crap, Billy Ray McBride. I know that you already have plenty of contingency plans for your contingency plans, packed away in that brain of yours." Taylor looks up at him with loving eyes and says, "Remember who you're talking to, Mister." God, she hopes she is right.

"I know, I know," Billy replies, mostly for pacification. His focus at the moment is really on determining where to start looking for Margaret.

"Good, then remember that it's your job to keep me safe," she says, mostly for her benefit.

STACY WRIGHT

"Evenin', y'all," a voice offers from behind the couple. "I couldn't help but overhear y'all's conversation, and would like to offer you my services."

Billy spins around quickly, and comes face to face, so to speak, with a young boy, who was maybe sixteen or seventeen. Sneaking up on Billy Ray McBride is not a good move to make, especially after the past few weeks. Seeing a young white male, who appears to be living on the street, based on his clothes, Billy takes a deep breath and exhales. The kid doesn't know how lucky he is right now. "Didn't your daddy ever tell you that it is very bad for your health to sneak up on people like that?"

"Mister, I don' even know who my daddy is," The freckled face juvenile replies. "I'm just out here trying to make a living, that's all. You're in luck though, because I am the best in my field."

"Oh really," Taylor chimes in, "and what is your expertise, my good man?" As soon as she heard that the boy was living on the streets, Taylor's soft spot in her heart opens up to him.

"At the moment, my Cheri, I believe that I am required to find someone named Margaret, am I not?"

"Easy there, Casanova, and watch what you say." Billy looks around and happily sees that no one is paying attention to them, or their conversation. "What makes you so sure you can come through for me?"

"Mister, I've got friends, you know, eyes and ears on the street. You give me some incentive and fifteen minutes, and I can get you whatever you want."

Billy thinks about the bargain for a minute, and then pulls five twenty dollar bills out of his trench coat pocket. Before he says a word, he tears all five bills in half. "What's your name, Junior?"

"You got it right," the boy replies, drooling over the sight of a hundred bucks. "It's Junior."

"Alright Junior, you've got ten minutes to find out for me, where a Margaret Stanford is staying. Here's your incentive," Billy hands the boy on half of the bills. "You get the rest when you take me to where she is."

"I said I needed fifteen minutes."

Billy gives the lad a devilish grin, "and I said that you get ten. Do it in five, and there's another hundred in it for ya." Billy steps back away from the street with Taylor and motions for the boy to go fill the order. Now he is standing here, waiting for someone he doesn't even know, to do his dirty work for him. If JD is on top of things, he saw what happened and hopefully followed Junior down the street. Billy knows that Scotty is depending on him and every second wasted puts Scotty one step closer to danger.

Taylor looks around, and then steps back to the corner of the intersection and looks around some more. Loud music was playing from every balcony and doorway, and everyone walking the streets were laughing and yelling as loud as they could. But Taylor was sure that she heard something. Now that it has caught her attention, she doesn't hear it any more. The side street is void of activity as far as she can tell. Was this all just a figment of her imagination?

Billy looks around and quickly takes notice that Taylor wasn't at his side any more. The last thing he needs right now is for the two of them to get separated. He sees her at the corner and hurries over to state his distaste for her vanishing like that. "Baby, you've got to give me some kind of warning when you're going to do that."

"I'm sorry Billy. It's just that I thought I heard something," Taylor explains as she continues to look around. It's not that she was intentionally ignoring Billy's rant, but she heard the sound again. It was closer this time, a little louder, and a little clearer. It was the sound of a woman screaming.

Taylor continues to scan the surrounding area, hoping to determine the source of the scream. Looking down the side street again between the hotels, Taylor notices how an eerie veil of fog was drifting down the street. What's puzzling about that is she didn't see it just a few seconds ago. Then the source of the scream makes her presence known, as a woman and a man exit the alley way on the other side of the deserted side street. Obviously the two were in serious peril; by the way they stumbled and fell out onto the pavement. Running for their lives, they continue on into the next alley as the woman is heard screaming again.

When Taylor sees the condition of the woman's clothes, something goes off inside her and she has to act. After what happened to her in New York, Taylor Lewis will never let anyone do that to her, or anyone else, ever again. She knows what Billy just said to her about running off, so she looks back for him wanting to honor his request, by reporting what she saw. Looking back to the alleyway, Taylor sees the three punks that were harassing the couple. One of them stops and looks directly at Taylor, and then points a knife at her. "Oh no, you did not just do that!" Taylor takes off running, accepting the challenge laid down to her.

Believing that Taylor was at his side walking with him, Billy continues to nag about possible outcomes. Then his manner changes dramatically when he sees Junior moving through the crowds towards Billy. He can't hear Taylor trying to get his attention. He isn't aware of her absence. "You're back pretty quick there, sport. You better have something good."

"Better than that, Mister. I know where she's going." Junior looks around and then asks, "Hey mister, where's your lady?"

Billy looks around and can't believe that she isn't standing right behind him. Did he rant and rave about how much he is worried about her, for nothing? "Quick, tell me what you know, kid."

"The lady has a room three blocks down. Better than that, she was just spotted getting into the old funeral coach from the cemetery over there." Junior points towards the west, and then jogs his hand to the right. People don't go around that cemetery any more, Mister. You should stay away from there too," he adds, taking on a more sinister air.

"Yeah, yeah," Billy replies, worried about Taylor and wanting to get to her as quickly as possible. "Here kid, take the rest of the money and get lost." Billy turns away, seeing Taylor down the street at the alley entrance. Not knowing what is going on, he begins to push his way through the oncoming foot traffic, only to be stopped by Junior pulling back on Billy's arm.

"Hold on, Mister," the boy replies. "Maybe I can help you find your missing woman too. What's her name, and I'll have her location for you in ten minutes, for a fee." This only delays Billy even further, causing him to lose sight of Taylor running down the alley. Irritated by the boy's interference, Billy snatches his arm away from Junior's grasp, and then hands the boy another hundred dollar bill, just to be rid of him. "Thanks Mister," Junior replies, as he turns his back to Billy, allowing his eyes to glow bright red. Once he checks to make sure all of the pieces of the money are counted for, the boy vanishes into the crowds.

Billy darts around the corner of the building just in time to see Taylor running at full speed up the alley behind the hotel. No matter what the reason is, this isn't going to end with a high note. He hates the fact that her increased strength also increases her speed. With a two block head start on him, Billy will play hell catching up to her.

"Alright now," The thug talking is the same one who had the balls to point the knife at Taylor. "I suggest you hand over all of your money, or we are gonna mess up your lady's pretty face." The other two punks laugh with a devious tone at their leader's threatening remark. One grabs the woman, lifts her up while the other reaches out, and grabs the gold chains around her neck.

A simple tug snaps the gold links, sending a diamond pendant down into the woman's dress. "Ooh, let's go fishin'," he says with dark overtones. The woman tries to pull away from the man that holds her, while kicking at the one reaching down her dress. Unable to watch this any longer, the husband jumps up to fight off his wife's attackers. The leader steps in and halts the husband's assault by thrusting the blade of his knife under the man's throat. "Hold it right there, pal. Don' go tryin' to be a hero. Try anything like that again, and I'll give you a new smile." The attacker's voice sounds out deeper, darker in tone, adding to the apparent danger of the situation. Looking over at his associates, the leader demands "Pick her up Sluggo. I want this poor sap to watch her take a beating!" He waves his hand over at the third of his trio, commanding him to help. "Don't just stand there Killer, help him get the bitch up!"

"Yeah, sure, Demon," Killer replies. The one known as Sluggo has no problem with the request. He reaches down and lifts the woman to her feet, but that is as far as he gets. Surprising the three hoodlums, Taylor runs in and blindsides Killer and Sluggo, driving her shoulders into the two men's abdomens. Caught completely off guard, her two victims can do nothing except fold in half, before she plants them into the side of the building."

"Bitch! I'm gonna cut you up!" Demon, the knife wielder, exclaims. He can't believe what just happened to his friends, but for some reason, Demon thinks he has a chance against

Taylor. The flash of his knife blade causes Taylor to hesitate with her attack, this time. A quick flash of her stepfather threatening her with his straight razor crosses her mind. "That's right, you know that you don't stand a chance, don't ya? Darlin', I'm gonna carve you up and serve you to the Master, and your boyfriend has been held up, so he ain't around to stop us!"

"I don't think you've got your facts straight," Billy disputes, as he walks up out of the shadows. Before Demon has a chance to do anything, Billy fires an energy blast at the thug's weapon, melting it in Demon's hand. With a calm but dark demeanor, Billy steps up to the would-be villain and lays him out with an uppercut charged with energy. The attacker is sent flying back where his body is buried in a mound of trash bags piled up at the back of the nearby building. With no cause for hesitation, Billy doesn't stop there. No, instead he walks right over to Taylor and is ready to lay into her with a verbal assault for running off from him.

Taylor quickly diffuses the situation by turning her attention to the couple. "Are you alright?" Taylor asks as she helps the woman up off the ground.

"God bless you, man!" The husband exclaims as he jumps up to shake Billy's hand. "Who knows what could've happened if you hadn't come along! Thank you, thank you, thank you," he adds, shaking Billy's hand furiously.

"Don't thank me, pal. She's the one looking to be the hero." With this little episode over, Billy wants to be moving on to a place with more private surroundings, where he can thoroughly chew Taylor out.

"Let's go, Taylor," He mumbles as he walks passed her. Even in a hushed voice, she can hear the disapproval of what happened. As he starts down the alleyway, Billy sees JD on the roof above, giving Billy a thumb's up sign. Billy nonchalantly nods to his friend, and then JD is gone again.

Taylor walks away from the couple and heads after Billy, knowing that he is really pissed. Regardless, this is something that they need to get out of the way, before they go any further. Right or wrong in her methods, Taylor isn't going to back down from him on this. Looking back for the couple, Taylor sees nothing but hundreds of glowing red eyes in the darkness staring back at her. Needless to say, this changes everything. No matter how pissed Billy is, it can't be as frightening as what she just saw.

When she catches up to Billy, Taylor grabs his arm and holds on tight as she walks right beside him. He has to stop and wants to lay into her something fierce, but when he looks at her face, Billy can see that something has troubled her. He looks back up the alley to find that the couple had vanished from sight. There's no way that they pulled themselves together that quickly and took off to seek help, is there?

Suddenly, Billy gets the urge to start walking again. This time he's the one who grabs Taylor by the arm to lead her away. Why does he have that feeling like the hairs on the back of his neck are standing up? What was it that Taylor saw that upset her so? He wants to ask, but isn't sure if he should. Obviously she hasn't volunteered the information, so it's safe to assume that she might not want to talk about it. On the other hand, if that is the case, maybe Billy should press the matter to get it out of the way. Focused on his thoughts, Billy walks them to the end of the alley, where their only option is to take the adjoining alley headed towards the gulf, away from the target Billy was given.

That's it; that's what has him so rattled. That kid, Junior, mentioned the cemetery. That and all of this festival of the dead crap that's taking place have basically given Billy a case of the heebee jeebees, or at least that's where he's putting the blame. None the less, he can't let his fear show. Taylor and JD are counting on him to be the strong leader, unafraid and unwilling to accept defeat. "Come on, Taylor. Let's see if we can find a way out of this rat's maze."

Just ahead, a thick cloud of steam rolls out of the building's vent system, clouding the alley and blocking their view of what's ahead. Fearing what could be waiting on the other side of the fog, Taylor looks back again, hoping to see nothing following them. This time, luck is with her, but it still doesn't make her any more comfortable about what lies ahead. Wanting to end this fear of the unknown, Taylor breaks free from Billy and rushes into the fog to face her fears.

Surprised by her actions, Billy quickly takes chase to find out what has gotten into Taylor. Once through the fog, his eyes quickly focus on Taylor standing in front of a fortune teller, who was seated outside her quaint little shop. As odd as the sight may be, Billy walks up as the old woman begins to shuffle her deck of cards, wanting more than ever to get back on track. Appearing to be as old as the merchandise on the shelves inside her shop, she looks up at Billy's approach, but refuses to greet him. Instead, she lays down five cards in front of Taylor, and then starts to flip the pasteboard circles over one at a time. "Believe in this man, child. He is a being of great power, but is forced to balance the fate of the world on his shoulders."

The first card turned face up is the card of true love. "There, do you see? It is your love for him that gives him strength." As if intrigued by her proclamation, the old woman hurries to turn over the next, revealing a pair of twins. "Ah, this card is a warning for the first. This card says that the very love I speak of could be his undoing as well."

Taylor looks at Billy, concerned by what the woman said. Looking back at the fortune teller, she could see that the old woman was hesitant about turning over the next card. This only drives Taylor crazy with anticipation. No matter what it is, she has to know what the card means. "Well, go on and turn it over."

The fortune teller looks up into Taylor's eyes as if apologizing for what she is about to say. The flip of the card reveals a picture of a skull, surrounded by a multitude of smaller skulls. "Go home, William," she warns, "so that you may live to fight another day. You cannot prevent what will happen this night."

"Yes, well thank you very much. That was all very intriguing, but we must be going now." Billy reaches into his coat pocket and fishes out a couple of bucks to toss onto the table. As if dismissing any credibility to what the fortune teller said, Billy motions for Taylor to move on. They have already lost enough time as it is.

The old woman hands Taylor the card of true love, as Billy pulls Taylor away from the fortune teller's table. "You may mock me, soldier of the south, but if you don't heed my warning, peril will befall your group this night. One will perish, and yet be reborn. Three will become five, and five will become many. How you will lead those followers could determine the fate of the world."

Okay, now she has hit a sensitive spot with Billy. There is no way some dime store hack could know that much about him. Stopping dead in his tracks, Billy turns around only to be surprised to find that the alley was not only dark but empty as well. He can't believe what he sees, and has to rush back over to the fortune teller's shop for proof that he isn't going mad. The table where the old woman was sitting is now leaning against the building, missing a couple of legs, weathered, and decayed. There was no chair, no old gypsy woman, and no sign of life anywhere inside the shop either. Inside the storefront window, just over the table outside, was a lamp burning that illuminated the fortune teller's workspace and should have at least warmed the single pane of window glass. Using his investigative skills, Billy lays his hand against the pane, expecting to feel some measure of heat. But instead, the glass is as cold as the night air.

Taylor peers inside through the door window and is astonished to see empty shelves where she remembers seeing jars and books just minutes ago. Curious, Taylor takes notice to the padlock and chain on the front door, but tries the doorknob any way. "Billy, what's going on?"

"I don't know and it doesn't matter either. We've got other things to worry about right now." Ready to move on, Billy wants to put all of this behind him so that they can get back on track. He takes off for the next cross street hoping to get some good bearings for possible course changes. This doesn't mean that if he had the chance, he wouldn't ask JD what he saw in front of the fortune teller's shop.

Taylor just stands there for a second, and looks at the tarot card she is holding in her hand. Not understanding how or why she has it, Taylor stuffs it down her shirt and positions it over her heart. Hey, it couldn't hurt, and to her it's the place that makes sense where she should keep it.

Chapter XVIII

What are they doing? Not an hour out on the streets of New Orleans, and they've already had three outside encounters of the creepy kind, if you include Taylor's "little man" sighting. In a way, it's a shame that Billy Ray McBride is the man that he is. Otherwise, he could just take the advice of the fortune teller and pack it up to go home. "That's it, JD, let's reel it in so that we can clear out of New Orleans," he thinks sarcastically to himself. That's if Billy was any other kind of man, but he's not. There is no way in hell that Billy could walk away from Scotty when he needs Billy the most. Billy owes him that much, and so much more. Scotty once made comment that he didn't mind his crutches so much any more, because he knew that he would always have Billy to stand up for him. "Don't worry, kid. I'm here and I'm coming for ya." Billy looks around, wishing he knew if JD was within sight at the moment. A quick regrouping could do them some good.

"What did you say, baby?" Taylor asks.

"I said that I'd like to regroup with JD for a minute, but I'm not sure where he is off to."

It doesn't matter at the moment. JD's focus is on Kaitlyn, who just dropped out of the sky, to land on the roof in front of him. It's obvious that she knows who he is, and there is no way for him to mistake who she is. The funny thing is that her knowing it is JD under the mask makes him a little uncomfortable for some reason. "JD, oh my God am I glad I found you! Saphyre is in some real trouble and we have to get to Billy right away!"

JD is completely blown away by Kaitlyn's statement. The first question coming to mind is, what are the two girls doing in New Orleans in the first place. The second has to be, what has happened to Saphyre. "Are you out of your mind?! If Billy finds out you're here, hurricane Katrina would be considered a simple rain shower compare to Billy going off! Now where is Saphyre, and what have you gotten her into?"

Kaitlyn's attitude quickly takes a defensive turn, when JD makes his accusation. "Let me tell you something, Mister! I'll have you know that she was the one who dragged me down here, because SHE wanted to feel safer with YOU, lover boy. So, don't you dare go pointing fingers at me like this was my idea, alright?"

JD takes a step closer to the edge of the roof and looks down into the alley, hoping to see Billy and Taylor. Finding them gone from view, he quickly begins to scan their surroundings, until he sees Billy climbing up the roof ladder of the building next door. "Come on," he commands as he takes off running for the next roof.

He knows why, or at least he thinks he knows why Billy is climbing up to the roof. It's because JD has failed in some way and Billy was now looking for him. To a small extent, JD admits that he has failed Billy in that he was distracted by Kaitlyn's arrival when he was suppose to be watching Billy's back. With the distraction of Kaitlyn's arrival, he lost sight of Billy momentarily, which could have resulted in a bad outcome. Granted, nothing seems to have happened, but the point is that it could have, and JD wouldn't have been there for Billy and Taylor.

After stepping away from the edge, JD spins Kaitlyn around and stares at her for a second to get his point across. "The best thing for you to do is stay at my side, understand?" Walking across to the center of the roof, JD turns and starts to sprint towards the hotel next door, with Kaitlyn hopping and bounding right along side of him. Both of them reach the edge and leap together, clearing the narrow alley below with ease.

By the time Billy and Taylor reach the top of the roof ladder, JD is standing there waiting for him, with Kaitlyn hidden behind his back. "There you are," Billy acknowledges as JD offers him a hand up onto the roof. "I need you to tell me exactly what you saw when we were at the fortune teller's table, down there in the alley."

JD shrugs his shoulders and steps to the side, revealing Kaitlyn's presence. "I had something in my eye." Once Billy sees Kaitlyn, JD explains, "The worst thing is that she said that Saphyre is here too, and somehow the bad guys know who they are, and took Saphyre hostage. To top it all off, they told Kaitlyn to bring you to the cemetery somewhere to the west of here."

The sight of Kaitlyn standing in front of Billy infuriates him to no end. In any other situation, he would probably just go off in all directions. Instead, he mumbles, "The fortune teller's suggestion is looking better and better." He grabs Kaitlyn by the arm and pulls her over close to look her in the eyes. "What in the hell were the two of you thinking? Now Saphyre has gotten herself in a heap of shit, for what?" Billy looks back at JD and offers his portion of information that Junior gave him. "Evidently, this cemetery is a happening spot tonight. According to a local source that me and Taylor met back on the street, Margaret is headed there too."

Feeling an overwhelming need to defend her presence, Kaitlyn offers, "Well, before you go getting everything distorted out of focus, let me just say that it is Saphyre's fault we are here. After what happened at your farm, I was willing to go anywhere instead of staying there. She's the one that decided to come looking for you guys." Kaitlyn crosses her arms and stands there ready to defend herself from Billy's next onslaught.

After looking to Taylor for some sort of input, JD returns his attention to Billy. "What are we going to do, Billy?" Seeing a dilemma brewing here, JD suddenly finds himself weighing in on what happened with Saphyre. Regardless of why she's there, or what she's gotten herself into, they have to do something. More importantly, JD has to do something.

Billy looks at Kaitlyn and asks, "What happened at the ranch? Better yet, I don't even want to know." He directs his attention to JD, and answers, "We continue on with the original plan. I'm here to rescue Scotty. If you feel the need to break away to save your girl in the process, then good luck." He takes off walking towards the front of the building and gets his bearings. "Okay, I've now had two different people tell me that what we seek is in a cemetery," Billy points out, gesturing with his hand to the west, and then jogs his hand sideways, the way Junior did earlier. He then turns to face Kaitlyn. "Here's the key to my room. Don't go back for whatever you have at the other place. Get to my room until we come back. Do you understand?" Billy hops up onto the short parapet wall, and then looks back to Taylor and JD to see if they are coming with him.

After everything that has happened to her, this is not the way she expects or wants to be treated. If Billy wants her out of their lives, then so be it. Kaitlyn may not stop at the hotel room and stay put like Billy said. She may just keep right on going to wherever her feet take her. As she starts to walk away, Kaitlyn looks up and sees hundreds of red glowing eyes in front of her. This time the sight strikes her down with a fear never felt before. Without thinking, she leaps backwards, screaming, "Oh my God! They're everywhere!

Her terrified reaction sends her right at Billy. He was looking down at the crowds on Bourbon Street below, as a parade passes by. Billy didn't see what Kaitlyn saw, nor did he witness her reaction to it. But before JD or Taylor could offer a warning, the young girl collides with Billy, sending him off the parapet wall and down onto the clay tiled balcony roof. Could this really get any worse?

The clay half barrel tiles crumble under Billy's weight from the impact. This doesn't stop his descent, but it does slow him down enough to allow him to see the telephone wires stretched between the two buildings. He hopes that they are telephone lines instead of electrical cables, and that they will stop his descent, as he reaches out to grab them. Snaring one in his grasp, the sudden stop wrenches his shoulder, but it's better than trying to pick himself up off the sidewalk. So far, the only people that see Billy's predicament are Taylor and JD. He shakes his head and reaches up to grab the other wire with his good arm, to take the weight off his wounded shoulder. It isn't serious as far as he can tell, but it is uncomfortable at the moment, and he wants a little relief. No sooner does he get a good grip, the old phone wire snaps under the strain of Billy's weight, sending him swinging out towards the festivities.

As luck would have it this night, a mounted patrol man walks his horse right into Billy's path. "Look out!" Billy warns, but it is heard too late. The police man turns just in time to see Billy collide with the officer, knocking him from his saddle. Luckily, the cop is sent crashing onto the float that was passing by, preventing him from suffering serious injury. Billy on the other hand swings right through the main character of the float, causing the grim reaper to explode into hundreds of chunks of paper and plaster.

Ripping through the chicken wire skeleton of the float decoration, the collision breaks Billy's grip on the wire, sending him crashing down to the sidewalk on the other side of the street. Slightly dazed, he looks around to see that half the crowd was cheering his rebel antics, while the other half just stares at him with red glowing eyes. The eye part doesn't seem to register, or Billy just chooses to ignore it. What bothers him is the jittery wiggling that was going on with their bodies. This he can write off as the effects of a blow to the head. He closes his eyes hard trying to clear his head. No matter how much he hates to admit it, Billy knows what all of this means. To the east he hears a bunch of cops blowing whistles trying to regain crowd control, and those same police are moving in on him. Unlike other encounters with law enforcement, this is a welcome change for Billy.

Billy looks to the west, which makes sense, being that it's the direction he needs to go any way. What surprises him is the sight of a little man, even shorter than Harley Preston, wearing an antiquated top hat with matching tuxedo jacket complete with tails. This has to be the same man Taylor saw earlier. The little man tips his hat to Billy, and then turns and runs off into the crowd. It has to be the same person. What are the chances of there being two creepy little bastards dressed alike? It doesn't matter. He's taunting Billy on, and that is a mistake that could prove to be fatal for the dwarf.

Things have changed in the past few moments for Billy, psychologically speaking. He has tried to maintain control of his explosive personality, but how can anyone expect success when so many people keep getting in his way. No, the time has come for him to embrace his aggressive nature and take the fight to whoever stands against him. The time has come for him to find Scotty and take him home, the only way Billy

Ray McBride really knows how. His growing fear is an added opponent, adding to the odds being stacked against him. Regardless of how the monster inside of him approaches the next unfolding events, he must maintain his control over the fear. He has to be strong for all that are now involved.

Billy may be able to deny what he saw, but Kaitlyn, Taylor and JD can't, when the crowd below turns their gaze to the trio on the roof. "Oh fuck, there are more of them!" Kaitlyn has had about all that she can stand of people with red eyes and twitching bodies. "I'm sorry," she says, "But I've gotta go." The desire to follow her calling is still there, but even this is too much for the young girl to handle. Without further explanation, Kaitlyn leaps into the air and disappears over the building across the street, leaving Taylor and JD dumbfounded by the action.

Again Taylor's hearing picks up a sound, only this time it was something being kicked across the roof deck. Realizing that they aren't alone on the roof, Taylor grabs JD's arm and turns him around. To their surprise, there were the people that Kaitlyn saw, when she knocked Billy off the roof. Only now, they are moving in on Billy's friends with intimidating intent. With his eyes glowing bright red, the closest one to Taylor asks, "What are y'all doing up here, when the party is going on down below?"

Seeing the distorting features of the approaching mob, JD knows who these people are. He has dealt with their kind before, in Japan. He was right. God damnit he was right, and here they are right in the middle of this shit. That's okay. JD knows how to handle a situation like this. "Taylor, can you jump to the street below, without injury?" Her nodding yes is all JD needs. "Then jump," he tells her, as he projects his force field forward, sending the foot soldiers of darkness flying back across the roof.

They hit the street together, ready to take off running, but now the police force was quickly moving in on their position to shut the streets down. When one of the officers spots JD and Taylor, he draws down on them quickly with his riot gun, but never manages to get off a shot. Instead, the police man is tackled to the ground by several members of the crowd with gnashing of pointed teeth and growing claws from their hands. What is even more shocking is how they savagely and brutally rip the man's chest and throat open without care or worry right there in front of JD and Taylor. Taylor looks around and sees more of the same carnage. The police force is being decimated right there for everyone to see, as the street scene is turned into a slaughter house with the attacks now falling on the rest of the party crowd. One attacker stops and looks at Taylor, and then simply points his hand down the street, as if telling her where she had to go.

JD grabs Taylor by the arm and snatches her away from the madness as fast as he can. He knows that now more than ever, they need to reunite with Billy because there is strength in numbers. Deep down in his gut, JD knows that something big is happening here, and every sign and warning is coming true.

The first thing they need to do is get off the main street. More and more of these henchmen of darkness make their presence known by trying to slow JD and Taylor down. With the street crowded ahead of them with sets of glowing red eyes, the time now is as good as any for them to make their move. JD deploys his force field to halt approaching aggressors, while Taylor lashes out with extreme prejudice at the ones closest to her. Seeing that their path was clear for the moment, JD deploys his force field around him and his friend, and then pulls Taylor up a side street to further their retreat. The first thing they need is distance between them and the mob chasing them, so that JD can figure out which way to go next.

Seizing the opportunity, JD grabs Taylor, pulls her up into a doorway, and allows the mob to run passed. JD watches as the pursuers didn't seem to be too worried about catching their prey. Instead, the mob seemed like they were more intent to drive JD and Taylor north, as far away from Billy as possible. "How did you do that, JD? It was like they couldn't see us standing here."

"It's a little trick that Nick taught me about hiding in plain sight. Ninja assassins mastered the art almost nine hundred years ago." JD looks around and sees that they had the all clear. "Come on so we can go find Billy." Nick, now there is a person that JD wishes was here. This entire event has become a flashback of what happened to JD in Japan. "Where are you Teach? I sure could use your help and guidance right about now."

Taylor follows JD's lead with no hesitation. The last thing she wants is to stay in one place for those maniacs to come back around. The mere thought of how they ripped and chewed the throats of the police officers out is more than she can handle. Innocent people were slaughtered as if life had no meaning. JD is right about one thing. They do need to find Billy as soon as possible. That is the one thing she wants the most. This is something that Taylor isn't sure if she can handle.

When they come across an antique funeral carriage, both of them know that they are on the right track. The down side is that it goes without saying, how the sight of the old carriage adds to the eeriness of it all.

A thousand miles away, or so it seems, Nickolas Landry sits at a corner table, in some run down, middle of nowhere, beach bar in the Jamaican Islands. He appears to be nothing more than a man who is down on his luck, much like the rest of the patrons of the bar. They, the drunk and desolate souls of the establishment, seem to ignore his existence, and that is exactly the reason why Nick likes the place so much. Right now in this time of his life, he prefers to be a ghost in the shadows, nursing his bottle of water.

"Guardian," a voice echoes through Nick's mind.

After taking a swig of water, he looks around, just to make sure he can't see his old teacher. "Get outta my head, Masamoto," he mumbles, drawing the attention of the drunk at the table next to Nick's corner booth. He looks over at the old Jamaican man, and then shakes his head in short motions, as if telling the old drunk to go away.

"You think that you can turn your back on your destiny and to the Council' guidance. But, my question to you this day is can you turn your back on your protégé? The voice of Masamoto asks.

Nick takes a drink from his bottle and says, "I haven't got a clue about what you're babbling on about, Masamoto. The way I remember it, the council wasn't interested in guiding me anywhere except into a grave." Nick sits back, but the old man at the table next to him decides that it was time to leave, just in case Nick was possessed by some evil spirits. The elderly Jamaican has no idea how close he is to being right.

"The rebirth of the Dark Queen Jezana is upon us, your student will be caught in the middle of this tragic event, and your unlikely ally will be the cause of their demise." Masamoto's voice pauses for a moment, to allow what he had said to sink in to Nick's consciousness. "You must go to them, Nickolas. The unlikely ally must not fall into the hands of our enemy, and the rest shall be drawn together for these coming times, under your leadership."

"So why don't you just send in your crusaders then, and let them handle the situation," Nick returns with a slightly higher tone, brought on by his rising anger. "Never mind, as I recall, they probably aren't up for it." Nick looks around noticing how several more patrons were becoming agitated by his louder and louder outbursts. Deciding that the time had come for him to leave, Nick asks his former teacher, "Where are they, Masamoto?"

"They are at the festival of the dead."

"How do I get to them, and where is this festival being held?" Nick is stopped by several uneasy drunks who feel the need to express themselves.

Masamoto's only reply is, "You have the power of the talisman; figure it out."

Then, all is silent in Nick's mind, which in a way, only adds to his frustration about the episode he just experienced. On the other hand, he doesn't want to take it out on these misguided fools standing against him. Before anyone has a chance to state their claim, Nick decides to end the standoff as quickly and as nonviolently as possible. To do so, he lets the yellow eyes of the dragon spirit inside of him show forth through his own eyes. Then to accentuate the moment, he lets the pointed fangs in his mouth show slightly, sending the inebriated patrons of the bar scurrying for their lives. By the time some of them get the courage to look back, Nick is gone from sight.

Billy has run for blocks, allowing the monster inside him dictate his actions. When he came across the carriage in the parking lot, he knew that he was on the right trail. When he found the dead men dressed in suits with automatic weapons, Billy wished he was in the wrong spot altogether. He's tried to do this the right way, or at least as right as possible. All that has gained him is heartache and misery. So, if they want the rebel vigilante, they're gonna get him. Billy loses his trench coat and returns his mask to its rightful place. The vest of modified body armor gives him a sense of relief, if bullets are involved, as he pats the palm of his hand against the Kevlar plates on his chest. "You want this man so bad? Be careful what you wish for."

"JD, do you think he went over there?" Taylor points at a group of lights on the other side of the trees in front of them. "It sounds like its some kind of carnival." The only response Taylor gets is JD walking off into the fog between her and the carnival lights.

There is no way she is going to be left alone out here in the dark, after what she witnessed while ago. Taylor takes off running after JD, and quickly finds him standing just in the fog with Billy of all people. "What are you doing?" She asks in a whispered tone."

"Hiding," Billy answers, "from those guys over there." Billy pulls JD and Taylor down into a squatted position. "Something is going on, people. I ran across one of Margaret's men, or at least I think it was. Any way, I get the feeling that there could be some kind of double cross taking place here, so watch your backs, and your fronts. Things could get real stupid around here twice as fast."

"Really, do you think?" Taylor has to wonder if Billy has been paying attention for the last few minutes.

Chapter XIX

The light seen glowing through the trees is not a carnival, festival, or any other kind of light hearted event. This Margaret Stanford can see all too well. Lighting the scene are seven large bonfires burning bright. What appear to be entranced cult members are dancing and leaping about the center fire as the ceremony begins. Mysery's woman leaves Margaret's group and takes her place perched on a headstone above a mound of broken earth. As Margaret and her entourage is ushered along, Saphyre and two other girls are brought out strapped to large crucifixes, completely oblivious to the world and what is happening around them. As the men lay one crucifix down on the mound of dirt, the other two girls are stood up at the head of the earthen mound to wait their turn. Margaret has to ask the question, "Excuse me, but do you intend to sacrifice those young girls?"

The young woman stops the progression and turns to face Margaret with a devilish smile, "Why Ms. Stanford, you of all people must know the value of sacrifice, don't you? Sure you do, that's why you're here aren't you? If you don't want to watch, Dreg can take ya on down to meet the master." She raises her hands, and silences the crowd. But before she continues, she turns back to Margaret and says, "Just remember that this is all for your benefit."

Jezebel motions for Dreg to lead Margaret and her men on their way, and then she rushes out to dance and frolic with her followers around the fire as the macabre celebration continues. The toad of a man waddles on off with Margaret dreading this more and more as she follows him. She has come too far to turn back now, even if she could. Her addiction is starting to wear off again. They have got to get this over with as soon as possible. "Carlton, no matter what happens, no matter what I say or do, don't let me try to back out of this." She looks back at him for reassurance, or at least support.

To play the role, Carlton reaches up and lays his hand on her shoulder, and then gently rubs his fingers against her cheek as she continues on this mad trek. "You're the boss. Don't worry, Margaret. Everything will be alright." She feels the comfort in his touch, and hears it in his voice. What she doesn't see is the red hue of his eyes, as he walks along behind her.

Dreg waddles along whistling a happy upbeat rendition of the funeral march as he leads Margaret and her bodyguards deeper into the cemetery. "You've come here to see the Master, yes? You want the master to do something for you, yes?" Dreg turns and faces Margaret. "Something evil, isn't it?" The dreadful little man stops at a large mausoleum and turns to smile at Margaret. "Me thinks that it is something truly evil indeed." He pushes the massive door open with no effort at all and rushes inside cackling with a maddening laughter.

Margaret looks back in the direction of the sacrificial ceremony and sees a glow of energy being expelled. Suddenly, she feels as if she is being placed between a rock and a hard place as she and her entourage enters the white stone structure. Once inside, they find Dreg standing against the wall on the opposite side of the octagonal room, where he motions for them to stop. Beside him, about five feet above the floor, is a wrought iron torch holder mounted to the wall. "Reaching up to grab a section of tattered silk cloth tied to the torch, he says, "Follow me, if you will, to see the master." He tugs down on the silk, pulling the torch holder down to activate the ancient mechanisms. The sound of stone grinding against stone echoes from the mausoleum as the stone sections in the center of the floor begin to fall away, forming a spiral staircase, obviously leading into the pits of hell.

Margaret looks around the room as the torches stationed on the walls ignite on their own. In the light, she can see coffins laid open with the bodies inside hanging out, as if they were greeting Margaret and her men. Dreg walks over and takes her by the hand, brandishing a devilish grin, and says, "Come Mon Cheri, Lord Mysery awaits."

Back out at the edge of the cemetery, Taylor looks around as the fog clears out a little, and then grabs Billy by the arm and asks, "Billy, do you know what this place is?"

"Yeah," he answers quietly. "It's the cemetery we were looking for."

"Well who in their right mind throws a party in a cemetery?" Then, everything goes silent through the crowded home of the dead. They can't see what is going on, but they can hear voices talking to one another at the center of the ring of fires. This was not what Taylor expected when they left Alabama. Sure she was warned, but even after what JD told them in the car on the side of the interstate, she still didn't think it would be anything like this. After the attack back there on Bourbon St, she wondered how much worse it could get. Why are they being lead through this horrid ordeal? Everything going on right now seems all out of place, like a bad movie with a terrible plot line.

Suddenly, two thugs jump up in front of Billy and Taylor, from behind a large headstone, with black skulls painted on their faces and wearing raggedy clothes. Their purpose is to serve as sentries for the ceremony taking place. Immediately, Taylor and Billy check for glowing eyes, although Billy would never admit it. The two hoodlums should have chosen better when they tried to use their scare tactics on Taylor. Her reaction is a straight punch to the closest sentry's jaw that almost takes his head off.

Before Billy has a chance to eliminate the other, two more sentries appear out of nowhere, closing the circle around Billy and Taylor. "Where's JD?" Billy asks himself. It sure would be nice to have him make his presence known right about now. Okay, so maybe Billy might have come across a little hard while ago, but at the time he never thought that JD would've taken Billy's suggestion serious. With no other choice, Billy takes a defensive stance and readies for the next round of battle. "We should probably try to keep this quiet," he suggests in a whisper to Taylor.

On cue, JD drops down from the tall pines above, and replies, "not a problem," as he takes out two of the sentries right off the bat. Pressing the button on his baton, the ends extend out creating a full length staff. It is a souvenir from his ordeal in Japan, and his weapon of choice. JD twirls it around over his head, and then one more flip of his wrist brings the end of the staff around to connect with the third sentry's head. "Never mind," Billy says out loud, as he reaches out offering JD his hand. "Let's go find our friends, amigo." Billy starts towards the bonfires, only to see five more opponents have stepped up for the challenge.

A young woman's scream cuts through the night air. "That's Saphyre," JD points out. She's definitely in trouble and he has to go to her. Billy just said let's go find our friends. JD looks to Billy for confirmation.

"You gonna die, masked man!" One of the combatants declares. Unfortunately for this wasted example of humanity,

Billy has other plans. The hour glass has run out. The camel's legs have buckled. This is the last straw. As far as Billy Ray McBride is concerned, he's already thrown down his gloves, and it's time for these covert actions to cease as well.

"You want the monster, then so be it!" Without warning, Billy charges both hands with energy and unloads on all five opponents, ending the standoff completely. "I didn't think so," he disputes as he walks between the trembling bodies that were blocking his path. "I bet you weren't expecting that, were ya?"

Taylor looks at Billy and is a little unsure who his question was directed at, his downed opponents or her and JD. She surely wasn't expecting him to go off like that, that's for sure. Looking at JD to state her concern, she isn't comforted when he just nods and points for her to follow Billy.

The trees create a natural perimeter around the cemetery's original plots. Inside that circle are rows of headstones and grave markers that surround the makeshift ceremonial ground with a stone crypt as its centerpiece. "Let's go," Billy commands. If you need to know where someone is, the direct approach is always the best method to use. Billy's plan is to directly approach the first person he sees, and then proceeds to kick the shit out of everyone he meets, until someone tells him what he wants to know.

"Billy, that isn't music playing, it's chanting. Taylor can see the shapes dancing around the center fire at the base of the mound. "Please tell me that they aren't doing some kind of voodoo ritual, are they?"

"Don't know, don't care," Billy responds, as if he was unaware that she was standing beside him. If you think about it, it almost sounded like he didn't that know if she was beside him or not. Be careful soldier of the south.

Weaving through the graves and headstones, Billy acts like he doesn't have a care in the world as he tries to get a better view of what they're up against inside the ring of bonfires. There are horseshoe shaped rows of people standing awestruck by the ceremony taking place. At the center of the horseshoe is the center bonfire at the foot of the earthen mound. As he gets closer, Billy can see Mysery's woman had taken her place on a large headstone to conduct the ordeal. What he can't see are the faces of the female sacrifices, or the rather large demonic canines hidden off in the shadows.

Walking up to the closest cult member, Billy taps the guy on the shoulder, and then asks, "Do you know Margaret Stanford?" He then punctuates his question with a quick jab to the man's face, as Billy sees the next person looking his way. "Do you know who Margaret is?" The woman screams out a warning and charges at Billy like some kind of wild animal. He reacts just as fast, and back flips her into the rows of onlookers behind him.

"Oh, this isn't going to be good." Taylor grabs JD's arm, and then points out how quickly Billy is being outnumbered by his opponents. Unfortunately, JD's attention at the moment isn't on his friend. He is pretty sure that Billy can handle his own. No, JD is more concerned about a certain young lady, who is tied to a crucifix. "JD, are you with me? We've gotta help Billy!"

"You go to him. I've got to help Saphyre," he explains, pointing at his potential girl friend tied to the large wooden cross. He nods at Taylor as if saying it will all work out, and then twitches his head sideways a little, as if hoping she would understand. Then, he simply takes off headed for Saphyre.

Something is wrong with Billy, and Taylor doesn't have the opportunity to find out what it is. At the moment, she believes that he needs her, or is it possibly that she needs him? Taylor's greater problem right now is that she is so focused on Billy that she fails to recognize what is really going on.

Draped over headstones are Margaret's men, either dead or dying, positioned as if they were being forced to watch the ceremony until their dying moments. Billy and JD gave warning about something like this, but deep down inside, there is doubt about her really believing the threat existed. None of that matters now. Whether she believes or not, all Taylor can think about is getting to him as fast as she can, so they can get out of this nightmare once and for all. In her mental developing state, nothing else matters.

That isn't going to be as easy as Taylor thinks. Billy has already started to move through the spectators, and his path has closed behind him with the onlookers crowding in around him. The gathering may think that his trek through their ceremony is at an end, but for Billy, it's easy. All he has to do is release an energy blast and five or ten obstacles are cleared from his path, as he demonstrates over and over. When he reaches the inner circle, Billy is forced to halt his onslaught when he sees the young girl tied to the wooden cross on the mound.

"Believe it or not, rebel warrior; this is all for you." In that split second, Mysery's woman, Jezebel, leaps from the headstone brandishing a long thin bladed knife. She lands on top of the mound and sinks the blade into the girl's throat. The young victim's blood rushes from the wound and pours onto the earthen mound, where it is sucked down into the soil. Jezebel turns her head sideways and gives Billy an evil grin. "Everything is transpiring as my master has foretold," she declares. "The taker of life will rise and come for you." Suddenly the ground underneath the sacrificial female begins to move as two withered hands dig their way out of the broken soil. Reaching up, they grab hold to the girl's arms and quickly drain the very essence of life from her body. In mere seconds, she is reduced to a withered corpse, crumbling and falling away from her crucifix.

"Oh hell no," Billy says, staring at the result of what happened. Awakening in time to see the gruesome demise of the young girl, Saphyre screams above him from her cross, as does the third girl hanging to Saphyre's right, as more followers stand the crosses up at the foot of the mound. Having an open shot at Jezebel, Billy fires an energy blast at her that melts the knife blade and sends her flying off into the shadows.

Then he abandons his true nature and focuses on Saphyre, as the spectators return their attention to subduing Billy. Perhaps they were right about him, and he does care more about others than he pretends. Unfortunately, this diversion from his plan proves that Billy was right. He knew that the risk of friends and family would affect his actions as he pursued this futile quest. At every turn he has been proven right. From Barbara and Harley, to Taylor, his mom and Scotty; everyone connected to his life has suffered because of their association to him. Here it is, happening again, with Saphyre's name being added to his list of interference. Had he remained focused on his goal, without any deviation from his mindset, Billy would still be on his way to finish this crusade. Instead, he has given his enemies the opportunity to gain the offensive against him. The more he fights off, the more opponents take their place two fold. In a matter of seconds, Billy is taken to the bottom of the pile.

The overwhelming odds snap Billy out of his compassionate stupor, and return him to his previous state of mind, even if it is a few seconds too late. "Are they serious?" Billy is almost insulted at the attempt against him. Without thinking about it, he unleashes an energy blast that erupts from under the pile of followers, sending their bodies flying into the air. This gives him the chance to look around and catch his breath, before the next waves arrives in a second or two. What he sees are some of the followers trying to push the other two crucifixes over onto the mound. Billy charges towards the two men pushing on the closest cross. The fact that it is the one Saphyre is tied to, doesn't even register to him. Billy hits the two men from the side and tackles them to the ground. Several violent punches delivered, and the two adversaries are out of the fight. The next victims for Billy to face are three more of Mysery's minions, working on toppling the other cross. He takes the fight to them, not because of the threat to the young woman, but simply because they are the closest. A knee to the stomach of the female adversary, and a punch to another man, leaves Billy one on one with the third opponent. He hits the man hard and takes him to the ground, but there is nothing Billy can do to help the other girl before she lands face first against the mound of dirt.

When the dust settles, the college coed finds herself staring at the face of a dead body, that appears to be forcing itself to breathe. That is, until it opens its eyes and stares back at her with black hollow eyes. Terrified the girl screams again, only when she does, the withered undead corpse grabs the sides of her head and sucks the life force right out of her mouth. This in turn causes Saphyre to scream out again, knowing that if somebody doesn't do something fast, she is the next in line for the kiss of death.

Billy's right there and he's ready to do his part, not for her, but for his own gain. But before he can, one of the zombie decorated thugs drops down out of the sky right in front of him. "Nice makeup, pal." Billy unloads a right cross that should take the man's jaw off. When it does, he is stunned by the result of his punch. "What the hell?" Billy is forced to stand there and stare at the man who is showing no sign of pain or suffering from the blow. Instead, the man just grabs Billy during his moment of vulnerability and throws him out into the masses again where he is enveloped by a flurry of hands and red eyes.

Taylor is turned around several times as she is attacked by blows coming from all around her. It's all happening so fast that she can't set her sights on just one target. As much as she is unwilling to admit it, there is just too many of them. Finally, she just sticks out her arms and spins around quickly, knocking almost twenty opponents to the ground, as they charge in to meet their fate. Some try to get back up, while others simply back up to figure out their next move. Taylor just wants to know how she wound up alone again, and wants even more to correct that as soon as possible. There is no sign of Billy and JD has vanished again. More and more attackers gather around her, not getting close enough for Taylor to lash out, but building a barricade of bodies just out of reach to prevent her from running. "Come on, then, if you think you can take me!" Her fear, panic and anxiety have festered into a life defending rage. Now that they have cornered the predator, how will they take her down?

A few yards away, JD watches Taylor as she goes into action. It's not that JD abandoned Taylor in any way. In his defense, they were separated by outside forces. Once JD had fought himself free, Taylor had simply moved on without him. Now his sights have to be set on one Saphyre Colton, hanging helplessly on a cross. He leaps over the crowd at the base of the crucifix and grabs onto the cross member with his arms wrapped around Saphyre. "Hang on; this might be a bumpy landing." He deploys a force field bubble around them, as the cross leans over and falls to the ground. "That wasn't so bad, was it?" Under the protection of his force field, JD frees his potential love, only to have her jump into his arms. Then she turns away from him displaying the same anger and expressions that Taylor developed just a few minutes ago.

She may not be like the others, possessed with special gifts or abilities, but Saphyre does share common ground with them for the way she has been treated. Like Taylor,

Kaitlyn, and the others who have suffered at the hands of others, she has reached a turning point in her life where she will no longer be a victim. If she is going down, then it will be on her terms and she will do her damnedest to take as many with her as she can. She pushes away from JD and rushes at their opponents. JD drops his force field just in time to keep her from running into it and hurting herself in the process. Judging by the look on her face, he doesn't want to be blamed for something like that. Instead, it's the ones on the outside of the energy bubble that receive her violent backlash, with Saphyre sending bodies flying left and right. This act gives JD something else to admire about his lady, and more than one reason to join into the fight.

Just across the gathering, no one is prepared for the backlash of Billy Ray McBride. From underneath the mountain of dark minions Billy erupts with an energy blast that sends bodies flying in all directions and levels most of the most of the onlookers as well. He knows that he caught a glimpse of Margaret walking off through the cemetery. Wherever she is, he should find Scotty. Forsaking all others, Billy takes chase after Margaret, believing, or at least convincing himself that JD, Taylor, and Saphyre will be alright.

Jezebel sits in the shadows, stroking the thick coats of her two demon dogs, and watches as Billy sprints off into the darkness. "Go, my pets, and make sure he gets to where he needs to be." The two oversized canines both growl out a response and then take off into the darkness after Billy. Now for her next step. Jezebel sets her sights on Taylor and then leaps into the air. With her target distracted by the mob that she is facing, Mysery's witch swoops in and rakes her extending claws across Taylor's back. Taylor falls to one knee and screams out in agony from the blow. It felt like acid filled the wounds inflicted and no amount of Taylor's strength can withstand that pain. Jezebel moves in and drives the red headed heroine to the soft soil of the earthen mound.

Jezebel's fast as light abilities and extraordinary strength has Taylor at the disadvantage. Mysery's woman reaches over and plucks a gemstone from the sacrificed girl's forehead, and quickly places it on Taylor's brow. Immediately, Billy's woman collapses to the ground, unable to move, or speak. "You will make a grand feast for Sepulcher. With your strength combined with your man's power, Lord Mysery will be unstoppable." Looking for the life stealing zombie, Jezebel calls out the creature's ungodly name, "Sepulcher, come to me and take this offering for our master."

JD was glad to have the undead thing being called away, but hates the fact that it's for Taylor's demise. He can see her lying on the ground helpless, but at the same time he has got to protect Saphyre with his force field, and now the numbers against them is out of control. "Saphyre, we have to try and move towards Taylor!"

"Where's Billy?" Saphyre asks, quite happy where she's at behind JD's force field.

"He went that way," JD, answers, as he watches the undead creature moving towards the helpless Taylor. Then, just as Sepulcher reaches Taylor, Kaitlyn drops in out of the sky, landing on the two attackers moving in to guard Sepulcher's assault. A guilty conscience is a bad thing to have at a time like this, but the way Kaitlyn abandoned her friends the way she did has forced her to return to make amends. After drop kicking the life stealing zombie away, Kaitlyn latches on to the next opponent rushing in on her. She lifts the surprised attacker high into the air, and then simply releases her grip on him. Needless to say, her return to earth is far less traumatic as his she lands beside Taylor as Sepulcher approaches again. As the zombie closes in, Kaitlyn grabs her paralyzed ally, and takes Taylor off into the air seeking safety.

This eases JD's mind a little, but then he is reminded that he and Saphyre are the only ones left to stand against Jezebel's followers. With Saphyre seeking her revenge for her abduction, JD is forced to face off against the majority of Mysery's minions, on his own. His first priority is to work his way over to his woman. Even with his force field as a weapon, JD is finding that the task is harder than he expected, with her opponents pushing the two would be lovers apart.

At first glance, Saphyre appears to be holding her own, but JD recognizes that her opponents are merely toying with her to accomplish their goal, divide and conquer. The dark ones that crowd around her push and taunt her, driving Saphyre further and further away from JD, but this act isn't a success without casualties. Each blow she lands is executed flawlessly with devastating results. "Come on you red eyed bastards! I can do this all night long!"

With her directly in his path, there is no way he can deploy his force field to move obstacles without affecting her too. Still, they haven't demonstrated their full intent, so JD pushes on hoping that Saphyre can hold on until he gets to her. The problem is that once he is close enough to reach her, the attacking minions reveal their true nature and intent and direct it solely at Saphyre. JD has to act fast. He drops his force field momentarily, and then deploys it again encircling Saphyre and half a dozen of her opponents. One against six is a bit much, but two against six are easy enough odds to overcome, especially for these two, while JD is able to hold off the rest with his energy field. With the last of their victims falling to the ground around them, JD looks to Saphyre and asks, "Saphyre, sweetie, are you ready to run, because we have to get out of here!" Expanding his force field outward, JD clears a path for their retreat, sending the crowding minions scattering and falling away. He looks around and takes notice of the fact that Billy, Taylor, and Kaitlyn are nowhere to be seen. "Come on, baby girl, we need to regroup in a safer place." Grabbing her hand, JD runs off into the darkness with Saphyre in tow.

Jezebel watches as JD and Saphyre make their escape, knowing that Kaitlyn and Taylor can't be far away. "Find them, and bring them to Lord Mysery alive. He will want the power of these mortals as well." With sepulcher in tow, she leaves the scene above ground to join her master in his lair.

Chapter XX

Margaret stares at the walls of the narrow corridor, where shallow shelves have been carved out to display the death and decay beneath the cemetery. "What sort of place is this, little man?" She asks, while trying to keep the stench out of her nose.

Why these are da 'combs," Dreg answers while pushing a body back into its final resting place. "Sometimes, they just try to get up and walk around," he adds, as if trying to explain his actions. After offering a laugh to show that he isn't totally serious, Dreg turns back to the corpse and slaps her hand as if scolding her moving.

"The what? Margaret asks, not understanding any of the gibberish that is coming out of Dreg's mouth.

"Da catacombs," he answers, this time a little more clearly. "Ya see, they built these catacombs for the plague bodies," he adds with a grin.

"The plague? What kind of plague?"

"No one knows for sure. It came in on a French frigate in 1782 and wiped out almost three quarters of the settlement. This is where the bodies were buried. Dreg gives her another smile, this time trying to ease her tension. "Oh, don't worry; I know what you're thinking. They quit being contagious after a hundred years or so." To prove his point, Dreg grabs the hand of a groom who was laid to rest beside his bride of many years ago. After shaking the husband's hand roughly, Dreg leans in, gives the bride a kiss, and says, "Congratulations," to the happy couple. "You made it to the 'til death do us part, part." It's more than obvious that the little man is right at home in these catacombs, with Margaret and her entourage quickly becoming the opposite.

To make matters even more morbid, Margaret takes notice to the condition of the twisted corpses. It's not the death that bothers her. It's the fact that they were chained in place with shackles around the bride and groom's wrists and ankles. Dreg starts to move on, but Margaret has to stop him and ask, "Hold on, little man. Why were these bodies chained down?"

Dreg spins around and bounds up one side of the corridor, so that he can look into Margaret's eyes. "Stop calling me, little man!" Then he stops for a moment, as if he sees something in her soul that he should recognize. "Why are you here, Margarite?" As if his point had been made by letting her know that he is on to her little game, Dreg returns to his more jocular but sinister nature. As he descends back to the damp muddy floor, the little man resembles a monkey exiting a tree.

Looking back at Margaret with red glowing eyes to make sure he has her attention, Dreg continues his tale with morbid intent. "In da end, everyone who displayed possible symptoms was brought here to die. It is said that it was the only way that the settlement could be sure that the plague for good. Legend has it that the survivors were haunted by the moans and cries of the dying for two weeks before the reaper silenced them forever." Dreg looks back again to reveal how the mentioning of the suffering invigorates him. "Wait, that's not the best part! See, the women of the settlement were a tight bunch, and the remaining of the lot became so guilt stricken over what they had done, over half of them hung themselves or swallowed poison. One woman went as far to slit her wrists and walked out into the gulf confessing her sins as a murderess. Is that a hoot, or what?"

"You mean to tell me that people were brought here to die, just because someone thought that they might be sick! That is some pretty strong and morbid paranoia. You never really know how barbaric people can be." Margaret has stooped pretty low in her life, but if she had someone killed, they had it coming.

"You should know, eh? If you think that is morbid, wait until you get a look at what's down the way." Dreg scurries down the narrow corridor and climbs up into a middle shelf. "Come here and take a look at this one. I call him Willie the wolf. Can you see how he tried to chew his hands off, so that he could get away?" Dreg lifts the corpse's arms to prove how the hands had been gnawed off at the wrist. "I guess he bled out before he could figure out how to get to his feet." Despicably, Dreg reveals one of Willie's hands hanging from the little man's belt. "I always keep one of them with me," he pauses before giving the punch line, "just in case I ever need an extra hand!" Dreg starts to laugh, but sees all too well that Margaret does not have a sense of humor at the moment. "Oh well, so much for trying to lighten the mood."

Out of frustration, and annoyed by his disturbing and macabre antics, Margaret pushes passed the little man and then stops to address her dislike for the current situation. She can see the exit to the corridor just ahead. Time is wasting, and she wants this to be over. "I have had about enough of your delay tactics through your personal haunted mansion. I demand that we conclude this sightseeing tour of yours, so that I can be finished here once and for all! Do you understand me? I want what's coming to me, and I want this over now!"

"How did you know this place is haunted?" Dreg gives Margaret a devious grin. "You're a tough one, aren't ya? The master has chosen well. Come, Lord Mysery is just ahead." Stepping passed Margaret once again; Dreg walks on down to the exit of the corridor. There he waits for her to join him, and then enters a large underground mausoleum.

Margaret walks through the doorway and is amazed at the grandeur of the ancient structure. Though aged by the years, she could see that this place was built for the wealthy. Its perimeter walls are laid out to make an octagonal designed structure. Its domed ceiling was constructed of white marble, with drapes of roots that have penetrated the stone enclosure over the years. Small showers fall to the marble tiled floor, from the rain water of days past that has found its way down into the mausoleum. Directly across from her, Margaret can see another entrance barricaded by a stacked pile of wooden church pews of high quality. Well, almost four hundred years ago, they were probably the best that money could buy. What she finds disturbing, is how her men's bodies were stationed on the highest pew, as if they were given the best seats in the house for what is about to take place.

More of the wooden pews were stationed around the centerpiece of the extraordinarily large room, four rows aligned with the compass to create a large cross, all facing the center stage. At the head of each row was a statue of an angel that also faces the pulpit. All of this seems normal, at least to an extent, but what is strange about the arrangement is what now resides within the circle of heaven's warriors. Years and years ago, the exaggerated statue of Atlas holding the world on his shoulders, was stationed up above ground in the cemetery. The weight of the statue, the weakness of the soil, and gravity, caused Atlas to fall through the domed ceiling to land on the Reverend's pulpit, and the small pipe organ. Needless to say, the fancy furnishings didn't survive, but it appears to have been enough to keep the statue from shattering. Looking up, Margaret can make out Atlas' globe still wedged in the opening of the ceiling. It too was overgrown by a netting of roots, but Margaret could swear that she sees the form of a person lying inside the wrought iron framework of the globe.

Returning her focus to the center of the room, Margaret walks around to the side of the center stage, where she finds the most disturbing sight. There, stretched out on a lounge sofa built of human remains and dry dusty corpses, is the man she has come here to see, Lord Mysery. Rising up, he wears a long black coat, a shallow hat with a large flat brim decorated with bones and skulls of small creatures, and a cane that appeared to be his pride and joy. This Lord Mysery is the perfect example of a voodoo priest from some B movie, and yet more formidable than Margaret could ever know.

He turns to face her, revealing all of his sinister glory, and says, "Don't you agree that there is far too much extravagance here not to be utilized?" His face is pale white, with a darkened silhouette of a skull covering his face. She isn't sure why, But Margaret gets the feeling that he isn't wearing face paint. With a wave of his hand, he casts aside his morbid throne, and topples one of the angel statues, just so that he can have full view of his guest. "So, you are the one who seeks my attention?" Mysery points his left hand at Margaret, and then slowly raises it; causing Margaret to rise up off the dirt covered marble tiles of the floor. Did you know that," he inquires, "this place once stood above ground, and was constructed as the funeral chapel for the region's rich and famous. Great minds saw the future potential of the area and knew that people would come here. People would come here to live, and people would come here to die. However, the plague of 1782 changed the plans of the founding fathers. Those gutless leaders saw fit to bury the entire cemetery once the catacombs were constructed to forever seal the plague away from mankind." Mysery smiles at her reaction to his little history lesson. "I know different though. They buried the cemetery so that the cries of the dying couldn't be heard. Allow me to introduce myself. I am known by many names, but you can call me, Lord Mysery."

From her new perspective high in the air, she looks around to get a lay of the land, so to speak. The only other thing that seemed out of place was the iron spiral staircase over against a wall to Margaret's right. It was obvious to her that it was not part of the original design of the structure, due to how the doorway at the top of the stairs appeared to be hacked into the domed ceiling and recklessly stuck in place. Suddenly, Margaret grows a pair of stones, and speaks to him as if she was in charge of this operation. "Sorry magic man, but you will have to do better than this if you're trying to impress me." Margaret struggles to get free, but quickly concedes to the fact that she is his prisoner for now. "See here, your highness; I have gone through a lot of time, money, and preparation to get to this point. I want your word that you will end the life of this rebel vigilante once and for all."

Is that so?" Mysery returns, letting another smile cross his painted face. "You will tell me if this is a better attempt, yes?" He swats at the air in front of him with his right hand. The act causes the rest of Margaret's party to be flung across the room, with their lives ending as they collide with the marble tiled walls. Carlton was the lucky one to be able to dive clear from the attack, but Margaret can only follow Mysery's will, as the dark Lord summons her over to him. "How was that?"

"Tiring," she responds, showing no fear. "Can we get on with this? I have a corporation, and a crime syndicate to run."

Mysery's confidence is borderline arrogant when he chuckles at her demand like it holds no weight at all. "My dear, Ms. Stanford, I'm afraid that you have been mislead in believing that I was working for you." The dark Lord twirls his cane around in his hand, as he walks around his captive audience. "You really don't understand who you are dealing with, do you? I on the other hand have the same problem, but I have the means to change this, for my benefit." He reaches out and places the palm of his hand against Margaret's forehead. Reading her mind, the dark Lord smiles and then opens his yellow hued eyes once again. "Are you hexed girl? There are portions of your thoughts that are blocked from my perception. Could you truly be more evil than I, blocking me from your mind? I am far more than you know or believe, my dear. I have lived countless lifetimes over the past eight hundred years. I came to this land under the guise of a deity, with my followers believing that I was the great voodoo god, Papa Ghede, though over the years I have managed to lose the top hat," he explains, pointing to Dreg wearing it proudly. "Bringing my followers with me, I began to consume the life and possibilities this land had to offer. You see, I was the plague that came here."

"Please," Margaret says with contempt, "Is all of this really so necessary?"

"Did you really think that I didn't know what was going on? Your people did not find me; I found them. I knew what your father was dealing with, and I knew of the plot you had against Antonio Callistone. Realizing that this warrior that stands against you is a being of tremendous power, I knew that I could become invincible if I could tap such a power source. I had full intent of approaching Callistone about his little problem, before you interfered. It was of no matter though. All I had to do is set my sights to you, and continue with my plan. That is why I lead you here, so that you would lead him to me."

Margaret struggles to get free, but there is no way for her to combat the force that holds her in mid air. "But I thought the boy was the bait for this. Surely you can see that our gains are separate and that both of us can benefit from this venture. Now that I have my father's empire, all my goals have been achieved. If you take out McBride, and I really don't care how you do it, then the only threat to my empire will be erased."

"The boy," Mysery explains, "Was merely the means for you to get my prey's attention. By abducting the boy, you simply made yourself the bait. However, I believe that there is some kind of hidden agenda wandering the halls of your mind. The problem I now face is that I cannot read those thoughts. If I cannot read your mind, then I must believe that you cannot be trusted. Since I believe this to be true, I want you out of the way until this episode is concluded." He waves his hand that suspends Margaret in mid air, sending Margaret flying across the massive hall, until she collides with the wall high above the barricaded entrance.

"Where is Scotty McAllister, and whose ass do I have to kick to get him back?" Billy stands at the corridor entrance to the mausoleum with his eyes glowing with energy. He sees Margaret pinned to the wall, and he sees her men slaughtered in the center of the floor, and really could care less how any of that happened. Since helping Margaret down isn't on his agenda, Billy directs his attention towards the man in the center of the room. The only thing that matters right now is finishing this so he can go home. "I bet you're supposed to be the guy who can take me down, right?"

"Yes, warrior of light, I am that guy," Mysery answers, displaying his skepticism for Billy's chances at success.

"Let's find out, and then you can tell me where Scotty is." Billy charges further into the room with all of his fury on display for everyone to see, ready to meet Mysery head on. The first two of the dark Lord's minions to confront Billy simply fall to the floor as he delivers a vicious twist to each of their necks. Without missing a step, Billy doubles another raving lunatic over, delivering a crushing knee to the beastial man's abdomen as Billy sidestepped the assault. Then with no regard for the man's welfare, Billy shoves the injured attacker back into four more approaching combatants. All five men go down to the floor in a twisted heap, but that really doesn't matter to Billy. He feels no threat from these that rush to meet their fate. Each one is simply an annoyance trying to keep him from his prize.

Again he starts for his prey, but on cue, Jezebel's demon dogs leap in from the shadows and tackle Billy to the ground. The first of the two beasts able to land a successful attack latches on to Billy's arm and bites down. This time, it's Billy who howls in pain as the razor sharp teeth of the monster penetrates his skin. Without thinking about it he charges his entire arm with energy, burning the demon dog's mouth and face, but the damage to Billy has already been done. The demon staggers around and collapses to the ground, but the threat to Billy isn't over yet. The second hell hound moves in and latches onto Billy's leg, inflicting pain that is down right crippling. He has no choice but to drop to his knee as the beast hangs onto his other leg. As soon as he does, the demon dog pulls Billy off balance, sending him to the floor to be drug away by the beast.

The destination of this fallen hero appears to be the life stealing zombie known as Sepulcher, who was entering the mausoleum from the main entrance. This was one spook that Billy didn't want any part of. To avoid the threat of the life stealing zombie, Billy has got to get free of the demon dog.

Drawing up his energy, Billy unleashes it at the back of the beast's head, eliminating the threat once and for all.

Favoring his new wounds, Billy charges Mysery again. The dark Lord scoffs at Billy's valor and launches an energy blast of his own, as he points his cane at the approaching vigilante. "Foolish mortal," he declares, when Billy is blown across the room, scattering Margaret's dead gunmen and the pews that they were sat upon. Like a pit bull, Billy scrambles to get up again to take the fight to Mysery, surprising all onlookers including the dark Lord Mysery. "Are you insane? You don't stand a chance against the power I possess!"

With his sights set on Lord Mysery, and an unbridled rage driving him on, Billy is oblivious to the threat moving in on him. This time he is broadsided by two of the minions, snatching Billy out of the air to drive him down onto the dirty marble floor. Injuries are received, but Billy is still able to gain the advantage, snapping one minion's neck while crushing the other's head between his boot and the floor. Turning around to face Mysery again, Billy's appearance assures the dark Lord that his opponent is not finished yet.

"Die mortal," Mysery commands, pointing his cane at Billy to release another energy blast, stronger than the last. Even though it is a painful attempt, Billy leaps clear of the blast as the antique pews are splintered by the explosion. As Billy slides across the smooth floor surface, Mysery turns to Jezebel and demands, "Release Sepulcher upon him now. My power is weakened."

"M' Lord, I'm afraid he is still too powerful to risk Sepulcher being damaged."

"Then call down the children to finish him off. I..." Before Mysery finishes his statement, Billy hits the dark Lord with an energy blast, wounding his enemy and weakening the foresaid power even more. In response to Jezebel's call, the room is suddenly filled with more of the dark Lord's minions to protect their wounded master, as Jezebel sees to her fallen leader.

Billy has lost all control of conscious thought and reasoning. It doesn't matter how many more are brought in to stand against him. The killer deep inside Billy has been brought to the surface, and he is willing to do whatever it takes to get to Mysery. One dark warrior is back flipped into others. Then Billy crushes another's wind pipe with a devastating punch to the man's throat. On and on this goes with the bodies piling up around Billy's position. More step up, raising the challenge attacking two and three at a time. Billy is ready for them all, whether he beats them into submission, or blows them out of the equation with his energy blasts, he really doesn't care. In a matter of seconds, the minions have backed away and begin to circle Billy as they lick their wounds and seek the right time to strike again.

Mysery forces Jezebel away from him, and uses his cane to rise back up to his feet. He realizes now that this mortal is far more powerful than originally thought. The power of Billy Ray McBride will truly make Mysery unstoppable, this he believes. Even with his own followers in his sights, Mysery fires another blast of energy from his cane that blows Billy and several of the minions from their stance.

Young McBride collides with the stone wall of the mausoleum again and falls to the floor. This time he suffers a head wound that sends a trickle of blood running down his face. His thoughts are scrambled and regaining clear vision seems to be impossible at the moment. Trying to stand up, he grabs hold of the dingy red velvet curtains that hang on the walls, and tries to pull himself up, until his weight pulls the curtains down. With his enemies moving in again, Billy has no other choice but to clear them out with his energy. He looks up at Margaret who seems to be content watching everything unfold from her place pinned to the wall. Billy can't help but wonder what her part in this could be from here on out. Surprisingly, for the first time since this began, he remembers who Taylor and JD are, and how he wished that they were here.

Kaitlyn sits quietly in a dark and damp little crypt, scared out of her mind, with Taylor lying peacefully on the floor beside him. Normally, she would be spooked by her surroundings, much less being in a graveyard. But at the moment, she fears the people wandering around outside a lot more. "Why won't you wake up, Taylor?"

Looking at her more closely, Kaitlyn sees the thin gemstone on Taylor's forehead and tries to pluck it off. When she does, Taylor's body cringes and Kaitlyn receives an electrical zap that runs up her arm. Not wanting to cause Taylor or herself any more harm, she concedes and assumes that the gem is the cause of Taylor's affliction.

Sitting down, Kaitlyn looks at Taylor and whispers, "I'm sorry." Her apology is for the way she bailed out on Taylor and Scotty earlier tonight. The shame and guilt of her actions finally set in on her when she was a few miles away. Overwhelmed by the need to redeem herself, Kaitlyn made her way to the cemetery hoping to get the chance to beg for forgiveness. When she found the battle in progress, and JD tending to Saphyre, Kaitlyn set her sights on Taylor who was down for the count. The problem is the strain she has trying to carry Taylor while she makes her jumps. Thus the reason she sought out the shelter of the crypt.

She sees movement out the corner of her eye. Was it Taylor waking up? Kaitlyn looks over and finds Taylor still in the same position as before. Then she sees the man's shoe beside Taylor's arm, and for a split second, thinks it seems out of place. Then she realizes that someone is wearing that shoe. Looking up, Kaitlyn is horrified to find one of Mysery's minions looking back at her. Acting in a fit of panic, she uses her ability but in reverse, sending the dark warrior flying across the crypt knocking the coffin from its pedestal.

The result surprises her, having never attempted that maneuver before. She shifts her weight and runs into another pair of legs. Could it be the same person? Kaitlyn looks down and thinks, "Nope, they're different shoes." Whoever is behind her hasn't reached down to grab her yet. Seeing this in her favor, Kaitlyn attempts to put some distance between her and the closest minion, only to be backhanded back down to the floor. "Grab the females and take them down to Lord Mysery. We will continue to look for the others. They are nearby. I can smell the female's fear."

Hiding behind a curtain of overgrown ivy behind a monument was never part of JD's plan when this started. His whole mental picture of how this would go, has him standing at Billy's side, and fight when need be. Of course Saphyre and Kaitlyn were never part of the scenario. Somehow, he needs to find Billy and the others with hope that they have a chance to regroup.

Seeing Kaitlyn come in to save the day for Taylor the way she did, was a welcome surprise and somewhat a relief. She was definitely the last person that JD expected to see. At least she was able to get Taylor clear of danger for the time being. He can't help but wonder about what happened to Taylor. Occupied with Saphyre, he missed what Jezebel did to Taylor to take her out like that. All he knew was that Taylor was down and very vulnerable. Strength lies in numbers. He knows that if he could find the girls, he'd stand a better chance of resuming his duties at Billy's side. Whether they all take up the search together, or they wait behind while he moves with freedom, doesn't really matter to him at this point.

Realizing that the foot traffic has died down around them, JD decides to take a peak. Saphyre quickly grabs his arm, believing that he was leaving her alone. Looking back, she has now got exactly what she came here for. JD motions to her that he was just looking around. Using his fingers, he slowly lifts a section of the ivy to give him a view port. Right away he sees Taylor and Kaitlyn being drug off through the cemetery. This kind of blows his plan of building some kind of support group. He wants to run out there and try to save them, but he knows that there is no way he could get both girls to safety, and might even jeopardize Saphyre's safety as well. No, for the moment, they may be better off where they're at.

What does he do then? He could follow them. Yeah, but that would only get him to the outer perimeter, before he is spotted or has to do something drastic. No, he needs a way to get to the center of the situation where he can do the most good for everyone. Then it dawns on him. "Saphyre, I have a job to do. Do you trust me?"

"JD, I know you're not going to just leave me here, are you?"

"No," JD replies, "You and I are going to give ourselves up together."

Saphyre stares at him with confusion and anxiety setting back in. "Are you serious?! JD, there's no way!"

"I know it sounds crazy, but I need your help to pull this off," He explains.

"I can't do this, JD," Saphyre confesses. "Fighting them to get free is one thing, but to walk in and give myself back to them is insanity!"

"Do you trust me?" He knows that time is running out and they need to act fast.

"Yes," she answers reluctantly.

JD takes her by the hand and leads her right out into the waiting arms of several minions, who had overheard enough of the conversation to get a fix on the two behind the bushes.

Chapter XXI

Ah, good," Mysery proclaims. "My children, the rest of the guests of honor have arrived," he declares, while looking over at Margaret pinned high up on the wall, as if he was mocking her. Mysery then lowers his attention to the doors opening beneath her, as JD and the others are led into the underground chamber.

To everyone's surprise, and even his, in an odd sort of way, Billy relinquishes the offensive to his opponents, allowing the embattled minions to apprehend him in a very aggressive manner. He shows no sign of weakness or pain. There is no worry or cause for alarm. Instead, Billy just stands there as if waiting for the executioner to pass judgment.

"Please, tell me that you aren't planning to make it that easy for me, are you?" Mysery asks in a dark tone, as if he expected more of a conflict from Billy. "Do you believe that your surrender will save your loved ones? Good warrior vigilante, you will have to battle for their freedom. But be warned, it is a fight to the death will be like no other experience. For you to fail would guarantee your friends the same painful outcome you are about to receive."

Billy looks over at JD and gives him a subtle nod. JD on the other hand has no idea what Billy is planning, but acknowledges Billy's signal with a subtle wave of his hand, stating that he will be ready for whatever happens next. Surprising the two friends, Mysery raises his jewel capped cane, points its head at Billy, and then unleashes a blast of dark energy, directed at the unsuspecting McBride. At the last possible second, Billy drops to the floor pulling himself free from his captors. Their demise is soon after delivered, as the two minions take the full brunt of Mysery's attack, vaporizing the demon spirits within.

Free from the minions, Billy jumps up and charges Mysery with the full intent of finishing this before it goes any farther. Without taking his focus off his target, Billy launches a massive burst of energy right at his friends. JD is ready and deploys his force field around the girls to allow their captors to receive Billy's attack. This is where Billy turns his attention to see the result. To his surprise, the large ominous escort of Jezebel drops down in front of Billy and stops the rampaging vigilante dead in his tracks.

Something deep down inside of Billy tells him that a snappy remark should be said, but before he can make his statement of sarcasm, Mysery hits Billy's hulking opponent in his back with another blast of dark energy from his cane. The massive being isn't budged by its master's assault. Instead, he just looks down at Billy with dead eyes. "Monquar," Mysery calls out, "show this upstart the nature of the power that you possess!" After turning his head to face his master, the huge man snatches his head back around to look at Billy once again.

"Yep, this might not be good at all," Billy mumbles, as his large opponent throws its head back and begins to shake violently, while its form begins to distort and expand. Like JD and the others, Billy is forced to stand there, caught in a stupefied gaze as the large man transforms into an even larger demonic beast. "You must be Monquar," Billy inquires before hitting the monster in the chest with a violent blast of energy. The demonic creature, Monquar, howls out, but it is as if it is more irritated than harmed. It looks back at Billy as if to state that its defeat will not come that easy. "I was right," Billy confirms to himself, "This is definitely not going to be good at all."

As the creature continues to swell to take on its new form, curled horns like that of a ram sprout from the sides of its head. As the horns grow longer, with the tips of them framing the beast's face, the head starts to spread wider and its mouth is filled with long sharp pointed teeth. With the red gemstone still centered in the middle of the demon's forehead, bony knots begin to protrude, running the length of the beast's crown. Continuously, this Monquar lets out howls and snorts as if the pain of the transformation is unbearable.

This is Billy's opening, if there ever was one. Taking another shot while the demon finishes its restructured appearance, he then charges his large opponent. Several feet from his target, Billy leaps into the air and dropkicks this one called Monquar right on its knee. Billy figures that if his energy blasts were ineffective, he'd try good ol' fashioned brawling techniques. The demon monster howls out again from the pain inflicted, and then looks at Billy as if he was condemning the action. Billy hits the ground as expected, and then scrambles to get up and gain a defensive stand. This is one instance where Billy can't move fast enough.

Off to the side, JD has watched enough of this to know that he has to act now if he is going to help his friend in need. The minions that were guarding the group of would be heroes were scattered by Billy's assault, but they are recovering to find him and the girls protected by JD's force field. Protected yes, but with the growing numbers moving in around them, JD isn't going nowhere with Saphyre and the others like this.

Pulling a sixteen inch baton from his waist sash, JD pushes a small circular button on it, causing the ends to extend out to become a four foot staff. "That's really cool, JD," Saphyre admits. "But what in the hell are you going to do with it?" She asks, as she looks to Kaitlyn and Taylor's needs.

"This, JD replies, dropping his force field just long enough to swing the staff outward, making contact with the heads of the four closest aggressors near him. Then, before a response can be given, he slips back under the safety of his force field deployed around the girls. It isn't a lot, but at least he's lowered the odds on the outside of his bubble, to help Billy as much as possible. "Come on, Billy." Then, JD simply performs the act again, taking out three more of the dark Lord's followers.

Across the room, Monquar adjusts its leg back to norm with no effort at all, and then reaches down and grabs a hold of Billy's cape. "I knew I should have left the flag at home this time," he thinks, as Monquar swings Billy around, and then lets him go. With no way of stopping himself, Billy flies through the air towards a row of the wooden pews, and splinters the first on impact. This slows his momentum down enough that he only topples the next ornate bench, and then scatters the two or three more. From a distance away, both JD and Saphyre grimace at the collision, knowing that the results can't be good.

Still, Billy rises up to his hands and knees, and gingerly shakes his head. "That hurt," he admits to himself, as he feels the floor vibrate under the palms of his hands. He knows that it is Monquar stomping towards him again. Rolling over to a seated position, he assesses the situation and takes his shot. Mysery's minions are holding back from joining in the battle, so all of his focus is directed at the lumbering monster closing in on him. Monster. Has Billy finally given in to the truth about what he is mixed up in? If he has, this powerful young man is doing a very good job not allowing it to affect his efforts. His mindset at the moment sees this dark creature as just another opponent. Big Ed was almost as big as this thing in front of Billy, when he won the title from the big wrestler. Ed wasn't pulling his punches that night in the wrestling ring; much like this monstrosity is doing tonight. Still, if Billy could take down Big Ed, there is no reason he can't take down ol' Monquar here. Billy just needs to figure out how to do that, before Monquar gets the best of him.

Before Monquar revealed its true form to Billy, it was just a man; a very big man, mind you, but it was still just a man. So, Billy is hoping that Monquar still has the same vulnerabilities as before. Launching a blast of energy from both hands, Billy hits the monster right in its fur covered crotch, with a devastating blow that causes the demon to double over and howl out in pain.

The injury doesn't put the big boy down for good, but it does give Billy the chance for an offensive strike. Focused on his target, he takes off running right at his oversized opponent. Calling on his wrestling experience, he leaps into the air and flips his body around, just short of the monster's position. As he flies feet first over Monquar's head, Billy reaches down and latches his fingertips onto the edges of the gemstone centered on the demon's forehead. Figuring that it was the only common denominator before and after the transformation, Billy hopes that it is a key to the demon's strength. With his body flopping down onto the beast's back and his elbows wedged against Monquar's horns, Billy pulls at the jewel with all of his might.

First, a howl from the beast sounds out, and then Billy can hear the disgusting sound of the jewel being separated from the demon's skin. Giving everything that he's got, one last pull from Billy rips the jewel free, causing Monquar to vanish in a flash of blue and black flames. Acting unimpressed at the attempt to defeat him, Billy throws the cut jewel to the floor, shattering it. Stepping from the unearthly fire, he states boastfully, "I do hope that wasn't your grand finale." To hide his growing fear and worry, Billy launches another blast of energy at the dark Lord and his minions to keep them at bay.

"I'm afraid there are many levels of this test for you, upstart." Mysery brushes off the attack and smiles at Billy. "Do you know why you went through this elaborate ruse to get here?" He asks, as if Billy poses no threat to him. You are an obstinate fool for believing that you are here by your choice. There are great plans in store for you, my young warrior."

"Big words," Billy replies. "I'm not impressed, so why don't you enlighten me." At the moment, this is merely Billy's play at stalling the madman he faces, at least until he can come up with a better plan.

"Look at her, full of fear and ignorant to how I played her, "Mysery points out, gesturing at Margaret pinned up high on the wall. "Everything that has transpired as of late has done so according to my plan. You see, I am able to maintain this mortal form by consuming the power of others. You have been on my radar, so to speak, for quite some time. To consume the power in you William will make me the strongest of all."

This is getting too weird for Billy. If this guy wants Billy's power so much, he can have all that he wants, and then some. "To bad you're gonna be disappointed," Billy explains, launching a massive energy surge right at the dark Lord again. Reacting to the attack, Mysery simply waves his hand at several of his followers, sending them directly into the path of Billy's assault. "Do you not see the futility of your actions?"

"Looks like you'll need some more followers, if you keep doing shit like that," Billy points out as the demons escape the dying bodies.

"Oh, you haven't seen nothing yet," Mysery boasts. To prove his meaning, Mysery summons one of the young followers over to his side with but a wave of his hand. With no remorse or concern about the young girls' life, Mysery sinks his teeth into her neck to feed on her life's blood to strengthen his health, but it's the energy of her soul that gives him the power he needs to heal his wounds.

Looking back at Billy, Lord Mysery is genuinely surprised to see that Billy isn't fazed by the act at all. "Brother, you're gonna have to do better than that," Billy explains. "Man, I was a Professional Wrestler. I've seen my fair share of raving lunatics." Billy picks off another one of Mysery's minions that was trying to get the slip on him. Without even looking, he sends one little concentrated energy blast into the possessed man's chest, vanquishing the demon within, and freeing the poor man once and for all.

"Do I look like a raving lunatic?" Mysery asks, wiping the girl's blood from his mouth and chin.

Billy lets his energy flow around his eyes, almost as if he was warning Mysery that this was about to get real serious. "You know what they say about the shoe, right?" With that, Billy lunges at Mysery and body blocks the dark Lord to the tiled floor of the mausoleum. Apparently, Billy's estimation was right about getting the drop on Mysery like that. But the upper hand is his for only a short time. With a well rehearsed move, Billy delivers a crushing elbow to Mysery's chest, before rolling over to the side.

As fast as it is gained, the offensive is taken away from Billy, but not before he can charge his hand with energy.

Once Billy concentrated all of his attention on Mysery, it allowed several of the minions to move in. One of them grabs Billy by his right arm, halting his downward motion with his energized left hand. Adjusting his trajectory accordingly, Billy delivers the punch to the unfortunate soul that decided to stop him. The minion's head explodes with the impact of the energy enveloping Billy's fist. The body jerks around for a second or two, before finally collapsing to the floor, allowing the demon within to escape.

This is where Mysery reclaims the offensive while Billy is distracted by the sight. It's not the first time he's seen that. Still, he is distracted enough to let Mysery have a wide open shot. With a swing of his cane, Mysery sends Billy flying back where his impact punches a hole through the marble clad wall of the mausoleum, and depositing the rebel vigilante into the catacomb corridor on the other side.

To the dark Lord's dismay, a blast of energy exits the hole Billy just created, stating that the rebel vigilante isn't down yet. Caught by surprise, the blast hits Mysery full on, driving the mad man to the ground, as Billy steps back through the hole in the wall. To Billy's surprise, Mysery rises to his feet unscathed by Billy's assault. The time has come for the dark Lord to remove the fight out of this crusading upstart. Experience has taught Lord Mysery that the easiest way to defeat an opponent is to crush the man's soul. The dark Lord knows exactly how to do this in Billy' case. With a wave of his hand, Scotty's crutches slide out into the middle of the floor between Billy and Mysery. "Do you recognize these?"

"Mister, you just sealed your fate," Billy proclaims, charging his hands and eyes with energy.

"No," Mysery corrects, "But I am about to seal his fate as well as yours." A gesture of his hands in unison causes the iron representation of Earth to fall from above. Billy can see that it is Scotty inside the spherical prison cell, but there is nothing he can do in time to save his friend.

Looking away, Billy can only assume the worst when the globe crashes to the marble floor with a mighty clang. His rage grows even more, forcing him to look back to see his friend's demise, only too be surprised to see Scotty floating in mid air in front of Mysery. "With a devious grin, the dark Lord asks, "Are you ready for this?"

Before Billy can react, Scotty's body takes off flying through the air at blinding speed and slams into the statue of Atlas, resulting in the creation of a brilliant flash of light. For lack of a better term, there is no other way to describe it. Billy is frozen in place; horrified and awestruck at what he has just witnessed. This gives Mysery the clear opportunity to walk over and touch the tip of his cane to the back of the statue. "Did I mention that I know the little secret the two of you shared?" The mere mention causes Billy to drop to one knee. Let me see if I have this right," Mysery continues, "I believe that you were responsible for the death of his father, and young Scotty took the blame to keep your shining reputation untarnished, is that correct?"

"It was self defense, and the dead guy was his low life foster parent," Billy corrects through gritted teeth.

"Yes, but for his sacrifice, you swore that you would never let anything happen to him. It appears that you have failed, Mr. McBride." This is too easy for Mysery to find his joy in Billy's tragic loss. "I'll have you know, that he kept your secret right up to the very end." As Billy stands once again, the dark Lord finds cause to taunt his adversary even more. "I have something special for you, William. Your best friend, your little foster brother," Mysery says with a condescending tone, "isn't dead yet."

There were only two people in the world who knew what Mysery was talking about, Billy and Scotty. Billy honestly never thought that he would hear that statement spoken aloud, ever. That was his and Scotty's great secret. It's true, and Scotty did what he did, to protect Billy and his future. Now that sacrifice has cost Scotty his life. Hate driven rage begins to boil up inside of Billy. Yes, he failed Scotty, and it was Billy's shortsighted view of what was going on that allowed this mistake to happen. He will not fail in avenging his fallen friend.

When Billy's eyes finally focus in on Mysery's position, the dark Lord reveals his plan. "You see, the soul of little Scotty McAllister still lives, in a spiritual sort of way. The only difference is that the soul of your foster brother is now a servant of mine, and I have saved this one for last," Mysery admits with a demon's smile. "I had to test you, just to make sure you were truly what I wanted. If you weren't top quality, it wouldn't be worth my time. Do you know what I mean? Now, for the question of the day; can you, William, destroy your best friend before he destroys you?"

"I know one thing," Billy declares as he struggles to stand up. "I am going to kick your ass from here until Sunday, for thinking that you're funny."

"No," Mysery corrects, "that is not going to happen at all. You are a beaten man, William. But that is not good enough for me. You see, for me to be able to claim the power you possess, I must break your spirit completely. What better way to do this than have you beaten down by the very soul that you failed to protect?"

Billy stares at the event with total disbelief and wonders if this could really be possible. Billy Ray McBride has seen a lot of crazy stuff as of late. Hell, even his girl friend is super strong and damned near bullet proof. There's also JD with his force field and shit, Kaitlyn and her bunch of biological misfits are pretty crazy in their own right. But is it possible for a person's soul to be taken from their body and forced into an inanimate object? He has to deny this and fight on. Is there any room for moral judgment now that Scotty is dead?

Then, Billy comes to a realization. Scotty IS dead and there ain't no coming back from that. This has to be his direction of thought. If he thinks for one second that Scotty could somehow be in that statue, Billy might not be able to defend himself the way needed. "Say what you will, mad man! I don't believe in your shit!" He charges his hands with energy and points them both at Mysery.

The dark Lord simply snaps his fingers before Billy has a chance to launch his assault. The hard granite carving of the statue suddenly takes on a more malleable surface, as the abomination's eyes open and begins to glow blood red. As its mouth pries open for the first time, a moan of agony is released to state the suffering of the recreation. Mysery points at Billy as the granite monster turns its head to look at him. "There is the cause for your suffering. Destroy him, and I will release you from your torment."

Billy just stares at the granite goliath, unable to believe that this has really happened to his friend. As the unholy abomination steps towards Billy, he feels powerless against Mysery's creation. With no effort at all, the monster picks up the twisted frame of the globe it once supported on its shoulders, and hurls the iron wreckage directly at Billy.

At the last second, Billy comes to his senses and leaps clear of the metal weapon, ready to stand again to face off against his opponent. To his surprise, the stone goliath is already on top of Billy and slaps him across the chapel with tremendous force. Mysery just smiles as Billy's impact with the rows of pews causes the wooden benches to shatter into kindling. Again, the floor trembles and vibrates as the animated statue closes in on Billy. The way he stopped seemed to be enough to take Billy out for the count, but what the onlookers didn't see was Billy releasing enough energy to clear his path of travel and suffer less damage than expected.

With surprise on his side, Billy jumps to his feet and launches two massive blasts of energy that hit the stone carved opponent square in its chest. The stone statue is driven back where it releases an agonizing sound, as if the blast had caused it pain. This causes Billy to falter from his plan, wondering again if it were Scotty that was suffering Billy's offensive. This delay, this halted momentum falls back on Billy, as the granite opponent recovers and lashes out at him again. Its massive hands swing down on its prey, swatting Billy down to the floor where he barely escapes the crushing motive of his opponent.

"Ribs are broken," Billy, confesses, "Arm might be fractured too." Favoring his left arm, Billy uses his right to hit the goliath again with another blast of energy. "Can't keep this up much longer," he thinks, recognizing that his energy stores seem to be weakening. Seeing how the spot on the monster's back is glowing where Mysery touched his cane to the granite surface, Billy focuses on the target and fires a concentrated beam, saying, "I hope that ain't you, Scotty. If it is, then I'm sorry."

Billy's aim is true as the impact sends the granite statue flying back across the chapel, before being embedded in the marble clad walls. "He turns to face Mysery again, and says, "Like I said before, I hope that isn't the best you've got." The answer to his statement comes just as quick when Mysery hits Billy with a blast of energy, sending him flying into a group of minions that quickly take the offensive.

A rumbling roar comes from outside the mausoleum, echoing through the corridors and catacombs connected with the burial chapel. Suddenly, the wall explodes, not far from Billy, with the debris taking out quite a few of Billy's attackers. The granite monster knows only one thing, and that is to kill Billy to receive freedom. Now that the odds are evened up a little, the vigilante known as the Confederate Soldier can finally try to end this conflict without any more outside interference. With hands charged with energy, Billy stands ready for his opponent to step through the hole in the wall. "Well Scotty, if that is you, I guess this is your chance to find out if you really can take me." Billy fires another blast of energy, holding back a little trying to budget his batteries, so to speak. Unfortunately, the stone goliath simply brushes off the assault, and then continues its charge towards Billy.

As if there isn't enough for Billy to worry about, Mysery decides to intervene, blindsiding the rebel vigilante with a blast of energy from his cane that drives Billy right into the path of the granite juggernaut. This time, Billy is sent hard to the floor as his opponent comes to a stop with little effort at all, sliding on his feet but never leaving them. Reaching down, it grabs Billy in one hand, and swings him into the air to collide with the marble clad wall, like a test car dummy hitting a brick wall. Billy crumbles to the broken floor when gravity takes control, gasping for air and trying to clear the fog from his mind. Ignoring the pain is not an option, but at the moment, he really doesn't have time to worry about it. The stone warrior picks Billy up again and holds him up so that the two combatants could look at each other, eye to eye. "Scotty, if you are in there, I'm sorry," Billy admits, between coughs of blood.

The seven foot goliath looks into Billy's eyes, and holds him up real close to study Billy's features. In a last ditch effort, Billy reaches up and pulls his mask from his face, just in case it helps his situation. If not, then at least people will know who he is when they find his body.

There was one thing that the dark Lord never counted on, and that was the love that is part of the friendship between Billy and Scotty. Scotty admired Billy's zest for life. He appreciated everything that Billy ever did for him, and could never be forced to do anything to forsake that. Billy Ray McBride was a true friend of Scotty, and possibly the best example of what a friend should be. Billy loved Scotty like a brother, and Scotty felt the same way. It is this lingering emotion that gives Billy a chance at survival. "NO!!!" Roars the stone monster as it flings Billy away. The essence of Scotty contradicts the commands of Lord Mysery causing the animated warrior to stumble about not knowing which way it should turn.

Unknowing that he had somehow made contact with Scotty's spirit, Billy assumes that being thrown away again was simply another assault. As he flies through the air, Billy launches another blast of energy that sends the living statue flying through another wall. This time the penetration causes a small section of the ceiling to collapse, giving the first sign of the weakened condition of the battlefield, and trapping the stone combatant on the other side. More debris caves in, pinning the fallen statue on the other side, and sealing the opening as well.

Overwhelming guilt falls upon Billy's weary heart, being unsure about what he has just done. He drops to one knee, and briefly considers a short prayer while he was in his current position. Before he can take the time to mourn the loss of his friend, Billy has to finish this. Standing up to face his opponent once more, he finds it an unbearable chore to accomplish. Mysery said that Billy was a beaten man. At the moment, Billy has to wonder how far that is from the truth.

Chapter XXII

Billy's strength is waning, and he knows it. He can't shake the nagging question of whether or not Scotty still lived inside the granite opponent Billy just defeated. At least, he hopes that he has defeated the battling monster. Beaten, bloody, and growing very weak, he knows that he has to find a way to finish this Mysery character off before anyone else gets hurt, or before the opportunity is lost for good. Even though he has dealt his own amount of pain and injury to his opponent, Billy can't seem to land the final blow, because of the constant interference of Mysery's minions, and Jezebel with her life sucking zombie, and rock monsters doing Mysery's bidding.

Somehow he has to find a way to bring this to an end, but Billy just isn't quite sure how to do this in his weakened state. Weakened state; it's more than the physical exertion and damage he's taken. Where is that monster that resides in him? For the first time in his life, at this moment that monster is subdued. Billy is suffering inside far worse than that over the sense of failure that he is feeling. Could this be the end? He never thought that he would die alone. Sure, he's always worked off the premise that he would pursue this quest for vengeance alone, but the funny thing about that is he has never had to, until now. "Well McBride, if ya gotta go, go with a bang!" With a couple of quick deep breaths, he's ready to go again.

Outside interference, that's what he needs, Billy thinks as he back flips one dark warrior into two others, while clothes lining another across the throat with Billy's arm. Three fast punches to another minion, finally gives Billy a chance to catch his breath and look around. It only lasts a second as Mysery continues his assault on Billy, hitting him again with another blast of dark energy. The dark Lord is weakening too. Jezana was right about how Mysery has taxed his abilities, trying to keep so many pieces of his grand scheme in check. Billy doesn't know this, but if he did the battle would surely swing in his favor. Since this is the case, he simply continues to do what he has to do, to keep the dark Lord from gaining the upper hand. First, he uses distraction. "Let me ask you somethin, spooky man. Do you know an evil villain known as Doomsayer? A friend of mine took the spook out and sent him back to hell where he belongs. I'm hoping to keep pace with Nick and do you the same way, pal."

"You are wrong, warrior. My true master has waited for eight hundred years for this time to come. At his side, we together shall cast this world into darkness and rule the masses," Mysery explains. "There is no mortal powerful enough to destroy Lord Doomsayer."

"Oh yeah?" Billy taunts. "Well JD was there to witness the whole thing, so if you need a reference, why don't you just ask him?" Billy lets his arrogance show with a smile.

JD is right on cue, boasting, "That's right, spooky man. The Guardian vaporized Doomsayer's spirit and I saw the whole thing! Looks like you chose the wrong players to side with in this 'take over the world' scenario."

Mysery asks in a condescending tone, "and, who might you be?"

Trying to be as intimidating as possible, JD replies, "I'm the student of the Guardian, his top student!"

"You're wrong," Mysery suggests. "My master will soon rule this world in darkness, and there is nothing any of you could do to stop this from transpiring." Mysery raises the crystal head of his cane up and stares at it while brandishing a devious grin. "In fact, the only being powerful enough to stop Doomsayer shall never have the chance. It is my duty to Lord Doomsayer to make sure."

"Dude, haven't you been paying attention? This Doomsayer character is toast," Billy explains. "Just so we keep the record straight; I'm here to do the same thing to you."

Enough!" Mysery points the cane at Billy and launches yet another blast of energy at the rebel vigilante, hitting him square in the chest. No one else picks up on it, but JD swears that it looked like Billy's body absorbed that blast, more than it exploding against him. "It is your thirst for the ego that is your undoing, young warrior." Perhaps I will simply take Lord Doomsayer's place, and claim this world for my own, just to honor him." Mysery launches a blast of dark energy at JD, in a futile attempt to quiet the young upstart.

"Billy, look out!" Kaitlyn warns, from behind JD's force field. Suddenly a sharp pain stabs into Billy's shoulder. He turns his head and tries to pull away, but Billy is already feeling the life force draining out of him. It is the undead vessel known only as Sepulcher that somehow managed to slip in behind Billy during all of the chaos of the battle. How does he save everyone, when at the moment he's the one in peril? That one is easy. Billy releases his energy at point blank range, blowing Sepulcher in pieces around the mausoleum. Unfortunately, this is the first time that he suffers the effects of his defense mechanism, as Billy is sent flying back into the crowd of Mysery's minions who were regrouping for their next assault.

This puts him in a bad way, weakened by battle, weakened even more by Sepulcher's touch, and now in the grasp of his enemy's lackeys. To keep him down, several blows are delivered with awesome force that injuries are produced to weaken Billy even more. None of them is life threatening. In fact, Billy's healing ability would have him back to normal in no time at all, if he gets the chance to catch his breath. As Mysery hurries over to take advantage of the situation, his new targets are JD and the others, "Your friends will suffer your fate, McBride," the dark Lord declares, looking back at Billy. "Or, is it that you who will suffer theirs? It appears that you have failed everyone. Concede to me now, and I will make their suffering as brief as possible." Mysery will have his victory and gain the power he requires to complete his goal for ultimate domination, just as it has been foreseen. Conceding to the dark Lord's demand, Billy simply collapses down onto his knees, and then half heartedly raises his hands. The fight in him is almost gone, and Billy has no idea how much more he can take.

Arrogance flows from the dark Lord, seeing his adversary surrendering in such a way. He looks to JD and the others and boasts, "fear not student of the Guardian. Your turn will come soon enough for your transgressions against my master." Walking over to Billy, Mysery surprises him kicking Billy to the ground. Billy drops down on all fours, and then collapses over to his side. As Mysery moves in again, he steps hard on Billy's side, as if claiming the kill. Billy suddenly surprises everyone, including the dark Lord, when he calls on his knowledge of wrestling, when he would use his opponents' weight against them, as he fought to break free. Caught off guard, Mysery is no different, losing his balance and stumbling away from Billy. Fighting through the pain of it all, Billy takes a defensive stance and tries to concentrate enough to focus on the head honcho. What's the old saying, "cut the head off and the snake dies?"

Mysery feels the momentum swinging in his favor. Now that Billy is down, Mysery means to keep it that way, saying, "Don't you see? There is nothing you can do to stop this. You are just a pawn in a very intricate game, and your purpose has been fulfilled.

"I will stop you!" Billy exclaims, as he struggles to keep himself upright.

For what, them?" Mysery asks, pointing at Billy's friends. "You cannot save them."

"Then I'll die trying!" For whatever reason, Billy blows Mysery a kiss, and then follows it up with an energy blast that the dark Lord simply swats away.

"Why won't you just die!?!" Lord Mysery swings his cane around, and unloads a massive blast of energy that sends Billy flying out into the middle of the floor. This time, Billy doesn't move, he doesn't offer any wit, or sarcasm to hide his pain. This time Billy Ray appears to be the one who is down for the count.

Mysery strolls over, and reaches into the chest of Sepulcher and plucks the black heart right out of the decayed torso. Immediately the dark servant is turned to dust, without the source of the dark power that animated it. Then, without care or worry, Mysery shoves the cursed organ into the chest of one of the nearby minions. The follower begins to convulse hysterically, as his limbs wither and his skin decays. Now this former follower is Sepulcher reborn, and he is ready to take the awesome power from Billy's body. Then, this dark creature will claim Billy's friends as well, simply because they are here for Lord Mysery to have.

As the dark Lord looks down upon Billy, and says, "The time has come for you to fall, young warrior. Perhaps, in another place and time, you could have claimed victory. I'm afraid that this day, it is not yours to have."

"Come on, Billy, snap out of it." JD watches intensely as Mysery forces the new version of Sepulcher down at Billy's face. He can't just stand around here and watch this happen any longer. His captors are unaware that JD has deployed his force field around himself and the girls. Of course, this means that some of the minions are within the energy bubble due to their proximity. It sucks to be them. JD lashes out surprising the girls and the minions inside his force field as well.

Billy knows that he has to find a way to end this. He knows that he is the only one who can. It's not for him, but for all of those who would suffer at the hands of this madman. Be careful Billy Ray. You might become the hero you don't want to be. If he is going out, then Billy is going to make sure that he takes this son of a bitch with him, and he's going to do it in style.

Using the toe of his boot, Mysery rolls Billy over to allow the transference to begin. To Mysery's surprise, Sepulcher is ripped away and sent flying across the room. The dark Lord looks over at JD, who flips Mysery the bird, as if admitting to the act. Billy's eyes open, charged with energy, and ready for his final play at this mad game. He looks over at JD and gives him a nod of appreciation. Staring up at Mysery, Billy says with confidence, "You obviously don't know who you are dealing with! We're the Confederate Soldiers, and I'm gonna send you back to hell!"

Mysery stares at the upstart with hatred in his black heart for William Raymond McBride. He raises his hand and launches a blast of dark energy that explodes against Billy, driving his opponent across the floor. Once his body slides to a stop, Billy just lies there playing possum. He can hear the dark Lord's minions moving in around him. He can smell Sepulcher's putrid odor getting closer. When he is sure that he can wait no longer, Billy rolls over to find that sepulcher is standing over him, and now bending over. Of course, Billy's act of movement also reveals that he has charged both of his hands with energy. Releasing that energy, Billy sends Sepulcher up into the air where the dark Lord's tool explodes against the stone slabs of the arched ceiling. Billy rolls his legs up over his head, flipping himself clear, as the ceiling and part of the graveyard, come crashing down onto the dark Lord. With his hold broken over Margaret, she falls to the ground, and scurries over into the shadows unsure how this outcome could ever swing in her favor again.

"Aye-yeee!!!" Jezebel comes to life leaping through the air with her claws pointed right at Billy. Her Lord, and master, has fallen and it is her duty to see to his safety. With the minions falling away because of the fear and apparent demise of their leader, JD seizes the opportunity to give his aid when it is needed most. Picking up the broken curtain rod at his feet, he flips it around aiming the broken end like a spear and hurls it into the air. Jezebel is hit with such force, when the makeshift spear penetrates her side, that her trajectory is changed, sending her flying away from Billy.

Could this be over? With Mysery down and Jezebel out of the picture, the minions start to fall back with no one to lead them. Billy looks over at JD and sees Taylor starting to come around. With Jezebel injured, her hold over Billy's woman was now broken. Kaitlyn and Saphyre are there too. Billy stumbles as he tries to stand, but with his strength fading fast. With no say so in the matter, he is forced to fall back down to the ground. "I'm sorry, Scotty." At least the others still have a fighting chance to get out of this alive. Billy might not, but JD should be able to make it happen again for the girls, protecting them with his force field. "I'm sorry, Taylor."

To his surprise, the mound of debris in the center of the floor erupts with an explosion of dark energy. JD is lucky to be able to get his force field up in time to protect him and the girls, but Billy takes the full brunt of the flying debris, ripping and tearing at his flesh with the impact. Agony envelopes his soul, as Billy rolls around on the floor again, writhing in pain. If he wasn't before, every part of his body now is bleeding from inflicted wounds. Already the voices in his head have thrown in the towel on him. How is this Mysery character still going? Billy rolls over to see that his assumptions are a bit premature, and that the dark Lord isn't hanging onto this side of life with ease. Like Billy, Mysery appears to be at the end of his line, broken and bloodied, and barely able to pull himself over the dirt and rubble. He is still able to move, which is more than Billy can do at the moment. This new sign of hope for darkness returns the spines of the minions, so to speak, bringing them back down on JD and the girls again.

This time, there is no hiding for them behind JD's force field. Taylor looks around and sees the remains of Scotty McAllister lying in a heap in the middle of the floor. Seeing Billy in his current condition, she knows that the loss has taken its toll on him, and probably caused him to act out without thinking. Billy has suffered enough loss this time. This time, Taylor is going to turn the rolls around and she is ready to be the giver of pain, the rescuer of the down trodden. As JD lowers his force field, she starts to fight and kick her way towards Billy, as JD uses his force field as a weapon, taking care of the ones Taylor missed. All the while, he must maintain his stand over Kaitlyn and Saphyre, unable to offer Billy or Taylor the assistance they need.

This is where the girls inform JD that they don't need to hide behind his protection any longer. Drawing on Taylor's strength to deny the dark warriors victory, Kaitlyn, and then Saphyre, venture out from behind JD's defenses to take the battle to their opponents. They have reached that point in their lives knowing what their part in this is. This isn't about selfish or petty feelings. This is bigger than they are, and both girls know that there are a lot more people out there who could suffer this same fate at the hands of this madman and his followers. There is a reason why they have been brought together, and neither Kaitlyn nor Saphyre is going to ignore the call any longer. If they are gonna go down, then they are gonna go down fighting.

The dark Lord claws at the floor, pulling his broken and dying body along, with one intention in mind. He now must find a new host body, and the perfect candidate is now in reach. Mysery knows of Billy's healing ability, and that his body would survive this conflict. Now that his adversary is weakened to the point of submission, Mysery can use his power to invade Billy's body, and cast out the vigilante's dying spirit. Victory is his, and he has accomplished his goal, regardless of how it took place.

Time is growing short for Billy. Blackness is trying to take over his conscious mind, making it hard for him to focus. Each movement adds excruciating pain to his already injured body. This time he isn't going to get away at the last moment. He feels Mysery's hands tugging on him as the dark Lord pulls himself alongside Billy. Then, he sees his angel of mercy closing in. Just as Mysery is almost eye to eye with her man, Taylor buries a jagged iron rod through Mysery's back, sinking it deep into the floor. The dark Lord howls out in agony, and then sends Taylor flying off through the air. She slams into the stone wall of the mausoleum, ending the threat she posed to the dark Lord for the moment.

Is this the ray of hope he needed, or did she delay the inevitable for Billy just a little longer. Taking everything he's got, Billy tries to pull away from his adversary, but Mysery refuses to let go. The strain of the opposing wills begins to show itself, as Mysery's body begins to rip and tear apart at the joints until the flesh of the vessel that housed the dark Lord's spirit falls away. For the first time, Billy can't deny the impossible, finding himself in the grips of an ethereal spirit.

Mysery is invading Billy's mind, trying to find an opening. There is no physical way of fighting this. Yes there is. He looks over at JD, and gives him a painful nod, hoping JD understands the meaning. Then he mumbles, "Want some, come get some." And with that, Billy releases the whole of his energy stores at point blank range.

In a brilliant flash of light, the result of the release vaporizes Mysery's demon spirit, ending the dark Lord's existence once and for all. Many of the minions who are in range of the devastating blast could not escape in time, and they too are eliminated as well. The rest simply scurried off into the darkness, mostly for self preservation. JD's force field kept him and the girls intact, but none of them was able to witness the result of their friend's action. Taylor is the first to look back to the center of the floor and is heartbroken over what she sees. There, where Billy was lying, is nothing but a charred mark burned into the soft marble tiles, in the shape of Billy's body.

JD can hear the emergency sirens outside, and they are closing in on the cemetery, but there is no way he can stop Taylor from running over to where she last saw her lover. So, to do the next best thing, JD follows her over to convince her that they had to leave. "Come on, Taylor, we can come back and look for Billy's, uh, we can look for him after everything calms down, and we can find our right frame of minds."

She jumps up in JD's face looking like she was ready to crush his skull in. "He's not dead!" She growls, "And don't you ever insinuate that he is again, Got it?"

"Okay Taylor, but we gotta go, now!" JD looks around and motions for Saphyre and Kaitlyn to come over and join him, as Taylor collapses into JD's arms. All around the room, he can see the red glowing eyes of the surviving minions, but JD has no idea why they continue to linger around. At the moment, he could really care less. Looking up into the night sky, through the enlarged hole in the roof, JD sees where the spiral staircase leads. It's the quickest and closest way out. He looks around again and has to wonder what did happen to Billy. Where do they all go, without him? "Come on, we really have to go," he reminds, hearing the sound of police radios coming into range. After several more tugs of her arm, Taylor concedes to JD's harassment, and leaves this place of doom with the rest of them.

Once they reach the top of the spiral staircase, JD pushes on the door hoping that somehow it would simply fall open against his weight and freedom would be theirs. Instead, the door doesn't even budge. He looks down and notices how some of Mysery's dark warriors were becoming a little more and more brave, starting to exit the shadows and move towards the staircase. "Come on now, I really don't have time for this."

Suddenly, the door swings open, revealing Nick standing on the other side. "Come on, JD, I don't know how much longer I can keep the cops away." Nick offers a surprised and grateful JD his hand, and then continues to pull the girls out of danger's presence once his student is out of the way.

It is only then, that Taylor becomes as stubborn as a mule about leaving. "No, I'm not leaving without Billy. You three head on back to the ranch. I'll find Billy and bring him home as soon as possible."

"I'm sorry Miss, but I don't think that's appropriate at the moment," Nick advises, pointing at the beams of light from the police officers' flashlights, moving through the cemetery.

Taylor stands up straight and gives Nick a twisted look. "I don't remember asking you what you think!"

JD quickly steps in, recognizing Nick's concern. "Easy, Taylor, Nick is here to help. That's the only reason why he's here." JD looks to his teacher, as if asking if that was true. If so, then that means JD and the others are in a lot more danger than he thought.

"Miss Taylor," Nick replies with a calming tone, "Go with JD and take these young ladies with you. I will find William and bring him to you. We will meet you at Billy's home; now please go, for your own safety."

Taylor wants to believe this, truly she does. But it still takes JD, Saphyre, and Kaitlyn to pull her away from Nick. "Take care of them, JD. I'll see you again, as soon as possible." He watches as the distraught and defeated trio disappears into the ground fog, and then he departs on his mission to save this unlikely ally.

Chapter XXIII

She has hid away now, all the while wondering what could happen next. With the remains of the mausoleum silenced, Margaret slinks out from behind a pile of rubble, and looks around wondering what she had to do, when everything seems to have fallen apart. What should she do? There is no one left to advise her. Has all of this ended in failure? She watched as Mysery's demon spirit burned away in Billy's energy blast. Therefore, her mother should be free, right? Why hasn't she contacted Margaret? Then, a voice calls out to Margaret from across the room.

Frantically searching for whoever was reaching out to her, Margaret scurries about like a rat, trying to find the sound of the voice. Behind a pile of broken pews lies Mysery's woman, Jezebel, with the curtain rod still skewered through her abdomen. The life is running out of this one, and she means to make amends. "I know why you came here, Cheri. You came here looking for power, but I honestly never thought you would succeed. You came here for power. I can tell you how to get it, but that comes with a price."

"Tell me where to find it, and I will give you anything," Margaret declares, wanting all of this to be over.

Jezebel smiles and says, "Find Mysery's cane, shatter the large jewel on top of the cane, and you will receive everything you have coming to you." Jezebel slumps over and waits for this body to die and release her.

Margaret takes the first clue she has and runs with it. She too can hear the police and emergency crews up in the cemetery and knows that time is running out. Where was Mysery the last time she saw him with the cane? It was during the conflict with McBride. Mysery still had it in his hand when Billy dropped the ceiling on him. Racing over to the center of the room, She frantically searches through the rubble and debris. Then, as if the dark side of luck is with her, Margaret uncovers the cane, in all its broken glory.

Grabbing the top section, she stares at it, not knowing if it was truly the key she seeks. With nothing but blind faith, Margaret sits the piece of the cane down on the floor, and then picks up a chunk of marble to smash the crystal orb. The pommel of the dark Lord's cane explodes with a flash of energy, sending Margaret flying back sliding across the floor.

Nothing. She doesn't feel any different. Teetering on the edge of a complete mental breakdown, Margaret collapses back beside a puddle of rain water. "I see no reward, and feel no different. Have I been duped? Have you forsaken me, mother?"

"Nae child, I have not left you. I am right here beside you." Jezana's voice answers. Margaret looks over at the puddle of water and sees Jezana's reflection on the surface. "Welcome me into your heart and receive the reward that was offered."

"I do!" Margaret answers hastily moving over in front of Jezana's image. "Give it to me now, mother!"

"And do you ask of it with your own free will?" The dark Priestess asks, as she rises up from the water.

"Yes," she answers. Before the word clears Margaret's lips, Jezana's spirit leaps at Margaret and forces its way into her body. In an instant, it is over, and the dark Priestess Jezana walks the world of the living once more. This time, she possesses the guise of the woman who just became the most powerful mobster in organized crime, Margaret Callistone.

"My Queen," Jezebel calls out, "I beg of you to forgive me and allow me to serve you again."

Jezana casually walks over and raises Jezebel from the floor with a simple gesture of Jezana's hand. "And why would I want the services of a traitor? You were once my favorite of them all, Jezebel. But when the time came and sides were chosen, you were not on mine." A flick of Jezana's wrist causes the spear to rip Jezebel in half, allowing Jezana to get at her demon spirit. With her hand clenched around the spirit's throat, Jezana ends Jezebel's existence much the way Billy did with Lord Mysery. "Come to me, children, your queen has returned." The minions all slip from the shadows and bow to their new leader. Looking around for her prize, she notices that the lower end of Mysery's cane is missing. "Quickly, children search the area and let no one stop you. I must have the scepter's base. It was attached to Mysery's cane."

While HER minions search the mausoleum, Jezana motions for Carlton to come to her. "Yes, my Queen?" He asks, walking up to her with no fear of her power.

"Lord Rayne," she says, referring to the demon possession within Carlton's form. "I have a need to reach out to my armies."

Carlton pulls a cell phone from his coat pocket and dials a number for her. "Lord Mayhem is on the line, my Queen."

Portraying Margaret, Jezana sets the next phase of her plan into motion. "It is done. Release the packet to the media as planned." Jezana knows that there is no way for her to allow Billy the possibility of making a recovery. She was imprisoned at the time, but she already knows that Billy is the center of the prophecy, and he possesses the power that could destroy even her. If he is alive, then every possible precaution must be taken, to ensure that Billy doesn't ever get that chance. This should, and will, ultimately send her unlikely ally to serve at her side. "Then, you must contact the hives around the world, and tell them that the time has arrived. The end of times is upon us, and the world must know us as the new leaders of the dark times to come. Rejoice, for your Queen has returned!"

"My queen," Carlton asks, as he receives the phone from her. "What of the unlikely ally?"

"I have already dispatched one of my faithful and his followers to collect our warrior friend," She explains.

"Then I must ask, why do you proceed to attack him with the information that will be released?"

"That is actually quite simple, faithful one. I simply aim to give him no other choice but to join my ranks, whether he wants to or not." Walking over to the massive hole in the wall, Jezana waves her hand causing the granite goliath to rise up out of the debris and float back through the hole, into the mausoleum. I did like what Lord Mysery used you for, my large stone warrior. Perhaps you can still have some amount of purpose."

Chapter XXIV

And the five will become many…

To the northeast of New Orleans, where the flood levels keep the low lying flood planes inundated with water, sits a lone house on a small mound of mud and saw grasses. If not for the thick and twisted roots of the pines scattered about, this small island might have given way to the seasonal floods long ago.

In this quaint, dilapidated shack,, on this small knoll surrounded by water, is an old Indian of the Chittiwachi tribe, who refuses to give up his family's heritage as a lifestyle. Almost a century ago, he was the last known shaman of his tribe. His name is Wind Dancer. In what serves as the living room of this meager abode, he sits on the floor in front of a blue flamed fire, healing his recently acquired wounds.

Survived only by his great grandchildren, Steven, and the twins, Michael and Allyson, the ancient grandfather has spent his spare time enlightening the teens about their people's history. Most of the time, it is for entertainment purposes, but there is always a message hidden within the tale.

Two of these great grandchildren arrive home with their only friend, Diego, to find their sanctuary in complete

214

disarray, and their grandfather sitting in the middle of the chaos. "Grandfather," Allyson asks, while looking around the room. Furniture was turned over and the dining table was reduced to splinters. Seeing the condition of her great grandfather only worries her more. "What happened here?"

Dropping down to her knees beside him, Allyson disturbs the flames of the fire. This causes the old man to open his eyes and say to her in a hushed tone, "Daughter, you must not extinguish the flames. I am not finished yet." After closing his eyes again for a few seconds more, the old man opens them again, and then climbs up his walking stick to stand.

When he raises his head to look at them again, Allison, Michael, and their best friend, marvel at the fact that he appeared to be in good health, or at least as good as a man his age. Allyson steps up in front of her Great grandfather, and pleads, "Grandfather, will you please tell us what happened here?"

Michael takes his place beside his older sister, but his attempt to be serious and concerned only causes him and Diego to snicker between each other. "Jon Michael, Diego," Wind Dancer calls out, "you must be rid of this childish attitude at once! I have a task for the three of you that must be met with success." Immediately, the two male teens snap to attention, mostly for what the old man had to offer.

After righting the sofa made of cut logs and stretched leather, Wind Dancer sits down and motions for the teens to take their places on the floor in front of him. They are not adults yet, ready to face what he has to propose, but they are no longer children, and destiny does not wait for a right time to reveal itself. "My children, I have sorrowful news to give you this night. Your brother, Steven, was tempted this day, and it was his dark nature that succumbed to the temptation." The old man sits back and places his hands on his knees as if he is about to deliver one of his tales. His face doesn't reveal the pain and suffering he still endures. To the teens, it's as if nothing has happened to him.

"Grandfather, I do hope that this won't be one of your long winded stories. After what we walked into here, I think we deserve the condensed version." She looks over at Michael and Diego and sees that they have joined her with their looks of concern.

Allow me to speak, Granddaughter, and I will tell you everything there is to know," he replies with a calming smile. "Your brother has been taken by a dark being from the spirit world, who seeks out a warrior of great strength. The three of you must go and see to it that this dark spirit does not succeed."

"I told you that Steven was evil in the way he treated me," Diego proclaims. "Y'all never saw him do it, but he always abused me like some kind of stray dog."

"Be quiet," the old man demands, as if infuriated by Diego's outburst. Then just as quickly, he returns to his tranquil nature before continuing. "I have been enlightened to an event that could seal the fate of all men. As the last of our people, you must represent the Chittiwachi to prevent the end of times."

This time, Diego is more humbled when speaking after raising his hand to do so. "But Grandfather, I'm not really a relative of you, Allyson, and Michael. What could I do to help?"

The old man stares at the young man for a moment, understanding the nature of his question. "You are more a part of this family than you think, Diego. Did we not hold a ceremony to give you a name? You are South Star, of the Chittiwachi people. You are a friend to my grandchildren, and loved by me as my son. That is enough qualifications for me.

Diego sits there dumbfounded by Wind Dancer's statements. He had always thought of Michael as more of the brother he never had, but this is the first time he ever heard Grandfather Wind Dancer referring to love or kinship regarding the Hispanic orphan. "Can I ask you something, Grandfather?"

"Certainly, Diego," the old man responds.

Uncomfortable at best, the young man asks, "If you really feel that way, why have I slept in the shed all these years?"

"This is simple, Diego. You never asked to come inside." Wind Dancer explains. "I was simply respecting your privacy."

"Grandfather," Michael asks, joining in the conversation, "what is it that we are supposed to do?"

"What you were meant to do, grandson. Go find this unlikely ally, and stop Steven and the spirit within him from accomplishing their goal. Then you must go with your new mentor to assure the survival of man."

"But Grandfather, you still haven't told us how we do this." Allyson's question comes across with doubt, both in their ability, and the validity of his request. After all, this seems a little far fetched even for her great grandfather.

The old man smiles at her as if he doesn't have a care in the world, and brushes her long black hair away from her face. "Child, you will soon know why this is happening, and what is truly at stake." He looks away and then retrieves three small carvings, each on a section of leather rope, from his shirt pocket. "This is how you will succeed." He hands Allyson a crude carving of a woman's form, one to Michael of a soaring hawk, and one to Diego of a great cat. "These totems will guide your thoughts and actions, and keep you safe in your time of need. Now go, before your opportunity is lost."

Apprehensive, the teens accept their gifts, and just look at each other before starting for the front door. Michael and Diego are intrigued, and excited about this new adventure, but Allyson, always the level headed one of the trio, stops to question her great grandfather one more time. "Grandfather, why do I feel like this is the last time I will see you? What is it that you aren't telling us?"

"My time on this plane of reality is coming to an end, my daughter. That is why I instructed you to go to this savior of humanity. He will be the one who guides your destiny from now on." He does his best to hide his failing health, but his strength appears to be dropping by the second.

"But Grandfather, I thought your ritual with the fire healed your wounds?"

"Again he offers her a reassuring smile, before saying, "No child, it was not to heal me, only to heal me long enough. Now you need to quit worrying about me and get going. Where I go is a far better place than what you will face in the near future." He stands up and walks away from her, moving even slower than usual. "I have my own journey that I must prepare for, at the moment. You have yours to begin as well."

He nods to Allyson, as if saying that everything will be alright. This causes her to run back to him one more time, saying, "I love you Grandfather." She grabs him one last time and gives him a big hug not wanting to let go.

"And, I love you too, Granddaughter." Wind Dancer separates himself from his great granddaughter's embrace so he can look into her eyes. "Your totem is Mother Earth, who first gave corn to our people. You must go now and let her spirit guide you through this trial."

"How do I do that?" She asks, wiping the tears from her cheeks.

"Like anything else, daughter, you must ask for the totem to guide you, and welcome its wisdom into your heart." He tries to turn away, but remembers one more thing that he needs to tell her. "Oh, and don't lose your totem, Wind Dancer, for it is your connection with the spirit. It would be bad for you to relinquish its power to your enemies, bad for you."

Outside the less than quaint home, Michael and Diego wait impatiently for Allyson to join them. When she exits the front door, Michael jumps at the chance to give her a ration of crap for making them wait. "Allyson, what were you doing in there? I don't think that this adventure of Grandfather's has any time allowed for you to be dragging your feet."

"Taking her role as the mature responsible one of the trio, Allyson stops her brother right there, and declares, "This adventure will be like no other, Jon Michael. We will see things that we have never known, and be tested time and again; with dire consequences should we fail."

To honor her great grandfather, Allyson holds her totem in her hands, lifting it slightly above her head. "Spirit of Mother Earth, give to me the guidance to follow my destiny, so that I can welcome it into my heart."

Michael and Diego watch in amazement as Allyson's entire body is bathed in a warm glow. Wanting to experience the same thing, both boys repeat Allyson's actions, holding their totems up in the air. "Oh great spirit," they begin, "give to me…"

"Wait," Allyson commands. "You must be serious for once, and truly welcome the spirit into your heart."

Diego, slowly lowers his arms, and then motions at Michael, saying, "You go first, amigo." He's not afraid. Diego just wants to be sure it's safe, that's all.

Obliging his friend, Michael raises his arms again, and says, "Great spirit of the hawk, give to me the guidance to follow my destiny, so that I can welcome it into my heart." Immediately, Michael is washed over with the same warm glow as Allyson, and when it fades, he feels a little more mature and a lot more invincible. Displaying a more serious attitude, Michael motions for Diego to complete the circle and join them for their new purpose. Once Diego has said his piece and is bathed in the warmth of the glow, Michael asks, "Well, how do you feel?"

"Incredible, Diego answers. "It's like I feel changed inside, stronger, ya know? But then it's more than that. I feel like my senses are better now. It's like I can see things and smell things better than I did before." He raises his nose to the air and sniffs. He becomes alarmed when he smells a scent coming from Grandfather's home. Somehow, he knows what it is and it troubles him. "Allyson, I sense death in the house. Is it?"

"Yes Diego, and now we must move on to meet our destinies and fulfill our grandfather's last request." Before she can say another word, Michael leaps into the air and takes flight, embracing the spirit of his totem. "Michael, what can you see from up there?" She asks, as he circles above her and Diego.

Marveling at his new found attribute, Michael climbs higher into the air, and then swoops back down to give his sister a report. I could see the entire delta from up there, but couldn't locate Steven, if that is what you're asking."

"That's okay," Diego says, "I've got his scent, and believe me he really smells worse than usual," he adds, using the hunter traits of his totem to locate Steven's trail. Without waiting for the request to be asked, he takes of into the saw grasses, following the scent of Allyson and Michael's missing sibling.

"Michael," Allyson says, using her newfound psychic abilities to communicate to her brother. "You follow Diego from above, and I will stay in contact with you and see what you see."

He nods to his sister, acknowledging her request, and then rises into the air once again. Catching up to Diego, Michael lets his friend take the lead. Allyson looks back at the house, and notices how it appears to be a lifeless structure succumbing to the swamp's assault of weather and decay. She knows that this is a sign that her great grandfather is gone, and there is only one thing left for her to do. She must honor the man, who has raised her for the past five years, by carrying out his last wishes. There is no way for the three of them to know what they are getting into, and if there was, they probably would decline out of self preservation. Focusing on her brother's thoughts, Allyson makes contact with Michael to follow his path with Diego.

A few miles away, lying in a large collection of water and mud, in the middle of the flood plane swamp, is a young man dressed in a tattered and torn black and blue jumpsuit. Unconscious for some time now, he awakens, choking, coughing, and spitting the foul water from his mouth and lungs. He has no idea where he is, or how he got there, much less why he is here. There is no explanation to the nature of the costume he is wearing, or how it became so damaged. The worst part of it all is that he has no idea who he is.

His mind is a blank; unable to call on any memories as clues to his identity, and this is a very unsettling for him. Questions race through his mind, like why is he out here in the wilderness, and how did he get here? He bangs his fist against the side of his head, as if hoping it would set something right and unlock his memory. Why was he dumped here? He doesn't know the answer, but he's sure that this is a logical line of thought to concentrate on. The problem is that without some basis to build from, his theories can't begin to form.

Still, there is an investigative nature trapped inside of him that forces this lost young man to stand up and look around. Maybe if he can determine where he is, he might be able to figure out how he got here. Again another problem arises in that he isn't sure where he came from, so this swamp could really be anywhere. The night sky offers him no clues, but he probably wouldn't recognize them any way. Again he smacks himself in the side of his head, hoping to jar his memory. All the act does is add to the measure of pain he is already feeling. What could he have been involved with that would leave him in this condition.

A sound of movement in the underbrush nearby causes him to strike a defensive stance, as he scans the vines and bushes for any signs of danger. This is a good thing, or at least somewhere to start, because he remembers how to defend himself. Then again, maybe it's not a memory, but more like instinct that he is calling upon. This might be some kind of explanation for the condition of his clothing, if he was recently on the downside of a losing battle.

Again there is a scruffling in the bushes, closer to him this time, giving the confused young man a better chance of zeroing in on the sound. To his surprise, a large wild hog breaks into the clearing and is now running for its life directly at him. It isn't hard for him to recognize the apparent danger of this situation. The four hundred pound beast is charging right at him, and offers no sign of changing its path. He raises his hands as if he thought it could stop the hog, and then opts to dive out of the way just before the collision could take place. Something must have spooked the beast, to send it fleeing like that, and he is sure that he doesn't want any part of whatever that is.

Suddenly, while his attention is on the wild hog, the young man is tackled from behind and driven back down to the ground. "I knew that I could find you, our unlikely ally," the attacker declares, in a growling voice. Billy rolls over to see that it is Steven, jumping up to his feet. The demon within creates long sharp claws to extend from the tips of Steven's fingers, as pointed teeth fill his mouth.

"I don't know why you were looking for me, but I'm pretty sure that I didn't want to be found by you." Again Billy raises his hands with his palms pointed at his attacker, even though he doesn't quite understand the nature of the act. Taking the next best option, he rolls his hands into fists, and then brings them in closer to his body for better protection. "Are you sure that you want to mess with me?"

"Yes I am," Steven admits, ready to take the fight to Billy. "It doesn't matter if you remember or not, unlikely ally. It is my duty to seek you out, and return you to my master, the dark Queen. You will go with us one way or another."

Before Steven can take one step towards his prey, Diego drives Steven to the ground, much the way Steven did to Billy. Only in this case, Diego doesn't give his opponent the opportunity to take a stand against him. With years of abuse pent up inside of him, Diego uses this opportunity to exact his revenge. "It's a shame that you're possessed by some kind of spirit, because I would enjoy this so much more if it were just me and you, Steven."

"You are right," Steven admits, looking up at Diego with red glowing eyes. "If you were just facing your friend Steven, you might stand a chance against him." With no effort at all, Steven launches Diego into the air, sending him flying off into the nearby trees.

"Maybe two against one makes for better odds in our favor," Michael implies, swooping down out of the air and lifting Steven high into the air. Pretty sure that Steven would suffer battle ending wounds from a drop at this height, Michael simply lets go of his half brother without any remorse. Like Diego, Michael has suffered an intolerable life of abuse from Steven since their mother passed away.

There in the night sky, Michael hovers above Steven as he falls away, smiling back at Michael. For a brief instant, Michael looks around and can see the spirit of the hawk flapping its wings to keep him aloft. Looking back down, Michael sees another pair of wings, and these cause him to panic a little. Before Steven hits the ground, the demon possession creates a pair of reptilian looking wings to sprout right out of Steven's back, saving the brother from certain doom. That is just weird, but the troubling part is that Steven is now flying back up towards Michael.

As usual, Allyson is Michael's saving grace. Only this time, she doesn't physically intervene. It's more like she is simply seen by Steven as he spots her moving in to aid his prey. Believing Michael is more of a nuisance than a threat, Steven abandons his pursuit to take his attack to the younger sister.

"Mister, are you alright?" She asks, making her presence known to the mystery man of the swamp. When Billy raises his hands in defense, she quickly takes a step back and offers an explanation. "Hold on now, I'm not here to hurt you. I've been sent here to help."

"Little lady," Billy explains, "I don't know who you are, or where this is, so I hope that you're not offended if I don't relax, okay?"

"You're in Louisiana, about five miles from the Mississippi River," she explains. "What's your name?"

"I don't know that either," Billy answers in a disappointed tone. Who is he really, and why did that other guy attack him? There are too many questions unanswered, and that causes a soul burning anger to ignite inside of him. "Who are you to be offering me help?"

Before Allyson can offer an explanation for her presence, Steven drops in and knocks her to the ground before returning his attention back to Billy. "Did you miss me?" He asks, leaping at Billy with blinding speed, to take him back down to the ground again. The ominous sight of his full transformation seems to give Steven the upper hand as he asks, "Are you ready to surrender to me now?" Billy breaks free from Steven's grasp, latches onto Steven, and flips the possessed opponent away. Forgetting about his pain for the moment, Billy stands, ready to take the fight to his opponent. "Not even on my worst day," he answers, taking notice to Allyson standing up behind Steven. When she nods to him, Billy takes a leap of faith and rushes Steven. At the same time, Allyson uses her newfound psychic ability to trap Steven and hold him in place, while Billy delivers his offensive assault.

There is no hesitation from Billy, as he delivers a crushing punch to Steven's jaw, and then following it up with a knee to Steven's stomach, as Billy rolls to the side. Steven may not be able to move his arms and legs, but he is far from defenseless. Staring at Billy with eyes glowing brighter and brighter, Steven releases two beams of energy that hit Billy with explosive force. In turn, Billy is sent backwards, head over heels, across the ground. With Billy's attack halted, and Allyson's concentration broken, Steven turns to her and says, "You are the one responsible for my temporary apprehension, aren't you?" Using the same mind trick that she used on him, Steven lifts Allyson from the ground and sends her flying off through the thick tangled limbs of the nearby trees.

With her interference eliminated, Steven starts for his prey once more, only to be interrupted by Michael again. Diving in on Steven, Michael points his legs forward to kick Steven in the back of his head with both feet. As soon as Michael soars back up into the sky, Steven jumps up and wipes the mud from his face, infuriated by the futile attempts made by these children. He sees that his prey is still down for the moment, and believes that he must finish his siblings off if he is going to complete his task. Enraged by the constant barrage, Steven takes chase after Michael ready to end this for good.

Higher and higher he climbs, gaining on Michael by the second. Before Michael is even aware of the approaching danger, the possessed brother latches onto him and pulls Michael in close. With a mouth full of sharp teeth smiling, Steven says, "Grandfather gave you a gift, didn't he?" Grabbing the glowing totem hanging around Michael's neck, Steven asks, "I bet you can't fly without this, can you?"

Down below, Diego leaps through the air and tackles Allyson, trying to end her painful flight through the trees. With her safely tucked away in his arms, Diego shields her from their impact with the ground with his own body. Uninjured by the act, he looks in her eyes and says, "I think grandfather might have underestimated us for this."

Suddenly, Michael's body hits the ground with a muffled thud right in front of the two teens, horrifying both Diego and Allyson with the sight. "If it's any consolation, I think you're right about that," Steven agrees, dropping in to stand on Michael's body. "Would you like your end to be painless, or do you want to end up like this?" Steven uses his clawed foot to lift Michael's lifeless head as an example of what's to come for them.

Once more, Steven is stopped from exacting his threats, when Billy rushes in to stand in front of the frightened pair of teens. "Why don't you back off, pal. If your fight is with me, then leave them out of this!"

"Oh, I would, savior of humanity, but they are the ones who joined in with their interference. For that, they must pay the price." Steven slings his hands out to his sides, extending his claws to the full length of six inches.

"Steven," Allyson asks, with tears in her eyes, "why are you doing this? If you are still in there, then you have to find a way to fight the control held over you, and stop this."

"I'm sorry, young female, but your brother is no longer in here. I am Sytaine, second priest to the dark queen, Jezana." Looking at Billy, he asks, "You remember me, don't you rebel?"

"Sorry pal, but the name doesn't ring a bell," Billy responds. In a way, he wishes it did register in his void of a memory, and that it would somehow unlock the rest.

"I know who you are," Nick responds, appearing out of nowhere from the trees closest to Billy. "I've been looking for you," he explains to his friend, without looking in Billy's direction.

"Guardian," Sytaine growls, aggravated by Nick's arrival. "You may have stopped me for now, but you cannot prevent the inevitable." With that, Sytaine takes to the air and disappears into the night.

Nick starts to take chase, only to be stopped by Billy. There is something that seems familiar about this newcomer that forces Billy to take another leap of faith. "Hold on, pal," Billy suggests, and then asks, "How much do you know about me?"

"McBride, I know enough about you now to know that I need to get you home as soon as possible." Nick turns to face Billy and sees the doubt and concern showing all over the young man's face. "You really don't remember anything, do you?"

"Mister, I remember waking up in the middle of a giant mud puddle, in the middle of nowhere. These three came to my aid, but I can't tell you why," Billy adds, pointing at

Allyson and Diego rushing over to Michael's body. "Before any of that, my mind is a blank chalk board freshly erased."

Acknowledging Billy's dilemma, Nick turns to face Billy and holds the talisman out in front of him. "Hold this in your hands for a moment, and everything will be returned to you." Nick jiggles the chain a little, causing the talisman to dance slightly in the air. "Now, William, we don't have time to waste."

Faith is a heavy burden in times like this. But, it is something that Billy needs right now more than ever. For now the apparent danger seems to be over. The three teens are no threat to him. Hell, one of them gave his life defending Billy and the others. Nick is an easy one. What's the old saying, "The enemy of my enemy is my friend?" Logic dictates his actions based on faith, forcing him to reach out and take hold of the golden artifact. Instantly, the locks on his memory are thrown off, overwhelming Billy's mind with memories both good and painful.

Everything returns to him, from the feelings of a neglected childhood, to the heart wrenching visions of his father's murder. Mixed in with that is a menagerie of joyful times, and his love for Taylor. He remembers his first encounter with Nick in Miami, and when he was introduced to Sytaine in New York. The dreams, the suffering, Margaret, and his battle with the dark Lord Mysery, all come back to Billy, reigniting the flame of anger and rage inside of him.

The young man lying over to the side will be added to the list of fallen, and they will be avenged by him. "Nick, we need to check on that kid over there, and then get them and us outta here."

"Billy, I don't think we have time to waste here," Nick suggests.

"I don't think you understand, Nick. That wasn't a suggestion. He was hurt, probably killed while trying to help me. I won't turn my back on them." Doing the best he can, Billy hurries over to the trio of teens.

"Diego," Michael calls out, surprising his sister and best friend. He is dying, and yet Michael is not fearful. For a brief moment in time, he served as a hero defending someone who could not defend themselves. Because of this, he will join his forefathers in the halls of honor. It is a strange concept for a young man of his age, but Michael is proud of his actions all the same. "Diego, you love my sister. I know you have all along. Now it is time for you to take the role as her protector."

"I won't let you down, Michael," Diego promises. With that, Michael closes his eyes for the last time.

Fearing the thought of being alone, Allyson hides her face against Diego's shoulder, as she seeks comfort in his arms. Her brother's revelation about his best friend's feelings towards her gives Allyson reason to open up about her feelings towards Diego. "Oh God, don't let go of me, Diego. I don't ever want to be alone."

"I've got ya love," he vows, feeling the same way about loneliness.

"Are the two of you alright?" Billy asks, as he walks up to Allyson and Diego. Taking it upon himself to carry out the duty of tending to Michael, Billy scoops the dead teen up into his arms, and says to Diego, "We'll take you wherever you need to go."

Diego looks at Billy with pain in his eyes and replies, "Ya know I bet that if you were that self confident a little while ago, you wouldn't be holding him in your arms right now."

"Stop it, Diego," Allyson demands, pulling away from her friend. "Now is not the time to cast false blame." Looking at Billy, she tries to refrain from showing her emotions for the loss of her brother. "Mr. McBride, we were instructed to go with you."

Surprised by her statement, Billy has to ask, "How do you know my name?"

"Besides being psychic, I also have a keen sense of hearing." Allyson points at Nick, and adds, "I heard your friend say your name when he first appeared."

"And, why must you go with him, little lady?" Nick asks, curious about her statement.

"Because my grandfather said that it was our destiny to help you prevent the end of times," Allyson answers.

Billy was shown a lot when he touched the talisman. The truth about what has happened cannot be denied any longer. With this as his frame of mind, Billy has no other choice but to embrace what will happen, and fight like he never has before, to prevent the doom of the world. "Well, there you have it, ninja man. They're going with us. I've got a feeling that we're going to need all the help that we can get."

Without offering Nick any warning, Billy Drops Michael's legs free, to launch an energy blast that sends two of Jezana's minions flying off through the air. "Thanks," Nick replies. "There are more of them out there in the night. I can sense them moving in on our location. Do you think we can go now?"

"Why are you here, Nick?" Billy asks, scoops Michael up into his arms again.

"Let's just say that someone told me that you needed my help," Nick explains, while scanning the darkness for movement.

"Really? And you felt that coming back, risking being locked up for the rest of your life was worth having the bragging rights of bailing my ass out again?"

Nick takes Michael's body from Billy's arms, recognizing that the rebel vigilante was in no shape to carry the fallen young man. "Maybe I'm doing this because one day I may need your help. Just because I live by a certain code, don't take my efforts for more or less than what they are. Trust me, William, I have been shown the truth of what's to come, and I have accepted the fact that everything happens for a reason. Perhaps that is a mindset that you should explore as well."

"Really?" Diego asks, with sarcasm.

"Yeah, karate man," Billy responds, aching from head to toe, and needing his former ally's assistance. "I have a certain red head that I need to find."

"She is with JD and the other two girls," Nick informs. "They're headed back to your home."

Billy has to ask, "What about Scotty?"

Chapter XXV

Once back at Billy's ranch, Taylor seems lost to the world as she walks aimlessly around the master bedroom, still holding the tarot card she received in New Orleans. After everything that has happened to her, to them, she is alone again without the man she loves. Part of her believes that somehow, somewhere, Billy is still alive. She wants to be connected to him, thus the wearing of his shirt, but it isn't enough. That's why she has continued to walk around the room, looking and holding each and every item in the room that belongs to him. There is but one question that keeps running through her mind. How many times will she go through this before Billy is with her for good? She wants the opportunity to find out who he is and what it takes to be part of his life.

Then, she sees something that could give her more of what she needs. Beside Billy's computer keyboard, on the small desk beside the bedroom balcony doors, is the computer disk that Commander Ryker gave to Billy. Supposedly, this holds the answers about the mysterious Billy Ray McBride.

Sitting down at the computer desk, Taylor starts up the computer and then inserts the disk. After a few seconds, the prompts are displayed, and the disk begins to run. The information is nothing fancy, just the basic personal report file from almost two decades ago that Commander Ryker had paraphrased for Billy's sake. The fact that the original file was listed as DSC classified top secret is found to be intriguing.

Ryker starts off his story as if he has known Billy most of his life. Although, no one would have guessed that, by the way Ryker and his team conducted themselves in New York when the others first met the Task Force Zebra team. It was probably because until now, this was all "hush hush" and hidden away, top secret.

> Almost eighteen years ago, your father, my friend and colleague, was partners with Special Agent Jonathan Justice, during his early years with the Federal Bureau of Investigation.

"That verifies his ties with Kaitlyn, and her involvement in New York," Taylor mumbles.

> You must admit that it really is a small world, and if you didn't recognize that fact before, I am sure that you can see the truth of it now, after your destined encounters in New York.
>
> The ties between your father and his partner, to Darkside Command were through Jonathan's wife, Julie. Her special "gift" made her the perfect candidate for the recruitment to my team. Like her daughter Karen, who is following in her mother's footsteps, Julie was my Medical officer in

the original covert ops team, Task Force Zebra.

Julie was on maternity leave from DSC operations, expecting their second child on that fateful day of your life. Her career and talents meshed with your mother's similar traits, striking up a strong friendship between the two women, to match their husbands' friendship and careers. It is all of these ties between family and friends that lead to the ultimate change in your life.

The chain of events that lead to who you are today, started at the very ranch where you now reside. You were three years old, at the time, and the Justice family had traveled to Alabama for their yearly reunion with the McBride household. Jonathan, Julie, and little Karen, were with you and your family that summer day, when little Billy Ray decided to go exploring, while the families were preparing for a cookout.

I guess some things never change in a person, and like now, you were always into something. On this day I speak of, you had wandered into the corrals amongst the horses. While little Karen played on a blanket in the yard, and the parents talked about old times and caught up on current affairs, little Billy Ray wanted to introduce himself to the biggest thoroughbred on the ranch. The odds were against you, and there was no one around to stop the inevitable.

The old stud horse was sickly, and beyond his years in age, and your sudden appearance spooked the old animal. Your parents, along with the Justices, were already searching the ranch grounds for you, but they entered the stables a second too late. Your poor mother could only watch in horror, as the old horse stomped around your body, already delivering a lethal blow to your head.

The one saving grace at the moment was Julie being there and able to use her gift to hold you together, while your mother and the paramedics struggled to keep you alive. Needless to say, Sarah and Julie rode with you to the hospital where they were met by a staff of doctors and specialists, who worked on you for fourteen hours. Still, after doing all that they could, there was little they could do to save you, because of the damage inflicted. Your mother was devastated and your father pushed to his emotional limits, over the thought of losing you.

If credit is due, my Medical Officer is the one who saved your life, and ultimately changed it forever, creating the person that you are today. You see, a couple of years before this, our team was sent in to Syria, where our mission was to take out an arms dealer who was supplying weapons to several terrorist factions. The mission was a success, in many ways, because one of the items confiscated was from the Russian side of the cold war.

Before the Soviet Union was dissolved, several military and political leaders set out to develop certain contingencies that could give the balance of power to the Russians. One such project was a biological experiment where the Russian soldiers would be genetically enhanced to make them more durable on the battle field. This experiment was headed up by their top scientist in genetic research, Dr. Sergei Volokov. Included on this disk is a copy of Dr. Volokov's journal, but the nuts and bolts of it goes like this.

Dr. Volokov developed a serum that would enhance the subject's healing abilities, cutting down on the loss of men at the frontlines, and allow their bodies to heal quicker, so that the soldiers could return to duty faster. As in all things, there was deception taking place, where the government leaders in charge wanted to take the project further, adding biological weapons to the formula.

Unknown to Dr. Volokov, samples were tampered with, and a formula was derived to complete what was expected. When the deceit and corruption fell apart, one sample was spared simply by chance. One of the saboteurs took it upon herself to confiscate the vial and hid it away to be used as proof of her involvement, and what the government was trying to do, in case something were to happen to her.

Unfortunately, this assistant was killed, just like the rest of the scientists involved and the entire project was buried. However, the person that this assistant gave the serum sample decided he would make whatever profit he could. Finding a buyer for the sample and file, the traitor became rich, and then dead, as the result of a double-cross. From then on, the sample, research files, and even Dr. Volokov's journal sat in a cold unit, until it was discovered by my team. With no hard evidence to prove its authenticity, it was quarantined and put in cold storage. Supposedly, Sergei had a daughter, and the rumor was that she was the living proof that the serum was a success. Since she has never been located, there is no way to corroborate Dr. Volokov's journal. The ace was that Julie had read the good doctor's journal, ran her own experiments during off time, and had a computer simulation that proved the serum worked. Her efforts were dismissed, but she still knew the truth.

Any way, this is where Julie, several of my team members, and even me, put our careers on the line, all to save your hide. Julie knew of the serum's possible attributes, and being a mother of one, with another on the way, her maternal instincts kicked in knowing that if she was in Sarah's situation, Julie would want someone to do the same for her.

With Walter completely supporting the decision, and Jonathan slightly reluctant, Julie contacted a member of our team, who is a teleporter. I know, I know, but by now you have seen enough abnormalities in the world of man that you can wrap your head around this one as well. His name is James Nordike, and his soul purpose with our team was his unique talent to deploy and extract our team via his ability of teleportation. Julie saved his life several times while we were in the field, and she didn't hesitate to play that card to coerce him into helping them.

In a matter of seconds, Jimmy was at Julie's side. A few minutes later, and the small group was outside the main headquarters of Darkside Command. Both of my soldiers knew that if they teleported inside, the arrival would set off every alarm in the facility. So, they simply used their security clearances to walk right in without conflict while your father and Justice waited outside. A few minutes later, Julie was walking out of the cryogenics storage with the vial of serum, and right into the presence of me and several DSC security guards. Believe it or not, your father and Jonathan were willing to give up their lives and careers, to hold us back and allow Julie and Jimmy to escape. Minutes later, your mother was injecting you with the serum. The rest is history, more or less. Maybe one day, you and your sister, Natalya, will run into each other and be able to compare notes.

Taylor looks across the room at the mirror as tears stream down her face. "Oh Billy, please come home to me."

To my good friend Paul. Even though two thousand miles separate us now, your honesty and insight for my stories will always be valuable to me.

Be sure to check out my website for updates on an all new series of books, with the first featuring the Neighborhood Watch. This book starts off what I call The Dime Store Series, a selection of shorter stories that supplement The End of Times saga. The first story picks up with the heroes of this story returning home to Billy's ranch in Alabama. Along the way Kaitlyn tells Saphyre about her exploits in New York, with her friends who called themselves the Neighborhood Watch.

This is a way for me to fill in the blanks about supporting characters in the End of Times saga, without drifting too far out of the scope of the main story. Hope you enjoy it. Until then, be sure to check out the preview of the next book in the End of Times series titled, The Crimson Tempest.

Welcome to the frontline.

www.frontlinefiction.com

"Making the headlines, tonight; a small mining town in western Virginia was the setting for the latest in what can only be described as a horrific scene of slaughter." Gail passes the story on to her co-anchor, as the number two camera lights up, pointed at Dana.

"That's right, Gail," she agrees, taking the cue from her coworker. "Though, the reports are a mix of chaos and far fetched fantasy, the best way to describe what you are about to see, is horrific. What we are about to show you is quite disturbing, and not for the weak of heart."

A news feed begins to run showing an affiliate's news reporter and camera crew following the National Guard into what looks like a gruesome war zone. "We are here in Lucifer's Gap," the reporter explains, as the camera man pans the visual across the blood stained landscape. Bodies lie all around mutilated and hacked up as if some team of madmen had cut their way through the small sleepy town. There is no reason or explanation why this has happened, and possibly no one would have found out, if not for a very lucky family who somehow managed to escape with their lives."

"Hey you, get that camera out of here," one high ranking Guard official demands, covering the lens of the camera as he rushes up to the news crew. With that, the feed goes dead, bringing the cameras back on in front of Dana and Gail.

"We will keep you updated on this tragic story as soon as more information is brought to light," Dana explains, trying to hold back her emotions...